THE SINKING MAN

Book 1 of The Sinking Man Series

Justin S. Leslie

J.S.L

eBook ISBN: 979-8-9862914-9-9
Paperback ISBN: 979-8-9918422-0-4

Contact Information email: Abaddonbooks@hotmail.com

Facebook: @Maxabaddonbooks

Website: www.JustinLeslie.com

"Even if I knew that tomorrow the world would go to pieces, I would still plant my apple tree."

MARTIN LUTHER KING JR.

NOTE FROM THE AUTHOR

Greetings, fellow ZOMBIE survivors!!

Welcome to the first full-length novel of *The Sinking Man* series! Until now, you've journeyed through the world of Ben and his crew via the five gripping novellas: *Sheltered*, *Awakened*, *Released*, *Fractured*, and *Swarmed*. If you're new to the saga, I encourage you to read or listen to these first to understand how this unlikely band of survivors came together, especially how Ben and Sarah found each other at the end of the world.

The series centers on Ben, a man spiraling into a reality far darker than he ever imagined. Now, the group must face the consequences of their choices in Tallahassee, with even higher stakes looming on the horizon. Ben, fueled by his need to protect those he loves, must fight harder than ever before. But as the battle intensifies, one question remains: how long can he keep himself from sinking too deep... or is it already too late?

PROLOGUE

The calming rhythm of dripping water perked Dustin's ears as he slowly awoke. Sandpaper greeted his mouth as what felt like several days' worth of not drinking grated his tongue.

Taking a deep breath, he flexed his wrists and legs only to find them bound by what he suspected were zip ties. Not wanting to bring attention to his now awake state, the once-upon-a-time operator calmed his nerves as a light whimper hooked his breath. It was a familiar voice he knew in the deepest pits of his heart. His wife Tina was also in the same condition close by.

As the sound of water lightly echoed in the silence, Dustin strained his ears for any other signs of life. The lack of any footsteps or breathing unnerved him. It was entirely possible that their captors were watching them through a live video feed, scrutinizing their every move.

Before succumbing to the drug's effects, Tina had uttered a single name: Amanda. She had shared stories of their adventures in Tallahassee, never delving into the specifics of this person, not out of indifference but out of a deep-rooted fear. Tina knew Amanda all too well, and that knowledge was enough to send a chill down her spine.

At one point, Ben came to Tallahassee to save his wife Sarah, who had been in a relatively decent situation, only to find a group of zealots trying to make the world a better place after the actual zombie apocalypse.

Sarah and Ben had been welcomed into the group. Tina, due to her rough demeanor, had been less fortunate. Initially, Amanda, head of the city's onboarding and security team, thought she was an asset that could be used on her team. After Tina disagreed with her treatment and subsequent expulsion of a family outside the protective wall of Tallahassee, Amanda not only forced Tina out of the city, but she did so with the intent of her never coming back.

Dustin whispered without moving, doing his best ventriloquist act by not moving his lips. "Don't move. Don't let them know we are awake if they are watching. Shuffle around if you need to, but don't act like you're struggling."

Tina let out a more formal grunt in response. Dustin swallowed in desperate need of a drink, thinking back to his days in training before joining a team. His mouth was a desert, completely dry. It was a virtual desert of discomfort on his tongue. If he were to eat, which he could tell he was also hungry, it wouldn't make it past his throat, likely getting lodged in place.

Focusing on this fact, he quickly realized they had been out for days. "I know you're thirsty," Dustin whispered. "I need you to stay still. Act like you're asleep. I'm going to see who's watching us."

On those words, Dustin flexed his wrists, finding only two zip ties from his measure around his wrists. This was something on which he had trained. Quickly shifting his wrists as if playing a turbo-charged set of maracas, the heat from the two zip ties rubbing together started warming to the point of a light burn on his wrist.

While not trying to smile, he knew the outcome. Within two minutes, Dustin, in one final showing of brute strength, flung his shoulders forward, using his body mass instead of his arm strength, snapping the zip ties.

Rather than freeing Tina immediately, he quickly threw off the thick towel wrapped in plastic from his head, now able to see the odd relaxing vibe of an upscale hotel room. Swiveling his head to take in as much detail as he could, a sink dripped from an open bathroom door.

The sound of a radio being keyed in the hallway put the man in motion as he ran to Tina, making quick work of her bindings. While he wanted to wait, the fact that they were in a hotel room and not a prison cell meant they had a chance to escape.

Static from the radio on the other side of the door crackled as the sounds of a key being put in the door clicked. Dustin, seeing their chance, ran to the back of the room, only to make the mistake of looking out the window. They were stories high on a flat-surfaced glass building.

Instead of jumping, he would charge whoever came through that door. "You good?" he mouthed to Tina as she gave a quick thumbs up, also rolling her tongue around her cemented mouth. They needed water.

Just as Dustin was set to rush the door, the phone in the room rang. A man's voice from outside leaned against the door, talking. "Answer it. It's for you. Oh, and I have food and water. No chance of you two getting out of here. You're in the suite. I sat the food in the entrance hall. The main doors are sealed shut."

The two glanced at each other in confusion as the sounds of another set of doors slammed shut from outside their room. Dustin scanned the room, looking for anything he could use as a weapon, only to find it had been sterilized.

A nerve-echoing ring started grating at their already frayed nerves. "To hell with it," Dustin said, picking up the receiver.

"I see you two are awake," Amanda said calmly over the crackling line.

CHAPTER 1

The Idle Days of Summer

The oppressive summer humidity hung thick as the crackle of an electrified bug zapper snapped like popcorn. The sounds of water being disturbed were followed by the rapid patter of bare feet, ending in a resounding slash as Ian curled into a ball, shouting "Cannonball!" while doing so.

Water speckled onto Sarah's romance novel as Ben leaned forward, covering his cocktail glass. Now that the unseasonal winter in North Florida was in the rearview mirror, the inhabitants of the Sanctuary had decided to clean Ben's pool and take some much-needed time to themselves away from the dying world outside the protective walls of the upscale neighborhood off the shores of the mighty Saint Johns River just south of Jacksonville Florida.

Since fighting off the remnants of a rogue group attempting to take over the Sanctuary and all its comforts, things had been relatively calm. With the new solar power system now fully up and running to support the other houses, Tina and Dustin were the only ones missing from the small functioning group.

The two had decided to return to Tallahassee to find more information on the FEMA bunkers around the North East Florida Jacksonville area, despite the protests from the others.

Dan, Shelly, John, Nicole, Ian, and Samantha, also known as Sam, the other inhabitants of the Sanctuary, were set to have a radio check-in with the adventurous couple.

Ben and Sarah, the original inhabitants of the Sanctuary, had spent hours, if not days, toiling over any other reasons they would have to head back West to a now burned-out Tallahassee. The city was now in ruins, all thanks to their own escape.

Eve, the AI system, chimed in the background, fully operational after her recent update. The artificial intelligence system was still in working condition, only noting a handful of satellite communication losses due to likely failures, with them no longer being tracked or staffed.

"Five minutes until communications check. Might I suggest turning the radio down?" Eve hummed. Yacht Rock's greatest hits playlist served up by Eve, the house's AI system blared Jimmy Buffett as the mood shifted.

Splashes from Ian and Sam in the pool stopped as Ben stood up, pulling on his button-up shirt, declaring he had at one point been to Margaritaville. While tacky, Ben liked the flowery shirt, reminding him of better days long since gone. Days that an actual zombie apocalypse had abruptly cut off, something he often joked about before it genuinely happened.

As an actor, Ben had even opted for a role in a few shows, taking on the end of the world as they knew it. Sarah snapped her book shut, the damp pages wrinkling.

"Well, today we see if they make it this time," Sarah breathed out. Tina and Dustin had been gone for three months unexpectedly missing their last check-in. With Eve no longer able to use satellites to communicate over long distances, they had been hamstrung up to about fifty miles through their radios.

Dan walked out of Ben's house with a straight face. The man had a heart as big as his personality, often wearing his emotions on his face for everyone to see. "The radios set up. Let's get to it." Having a background in Ham radio, Dan had found the hobby his wife Shelly often made fun of a new commodity in the crumbling world around them.

"You two stay out here. If we hear something, I'll let you know," Ben said, referring to the younger Ian and Sam. After losing Kelly, it had been a breath of fresh air to see new love slowly blooming. John had still been silent on the entire situation, but if given a chance while on the run into the now wilderness, Ben would follow up. Ian, being with Kelly before meeting the group, had been rocked to his core after losing her.

The kitchen served as both the group's central space and Dan's radio station, as well as Eve's main computer hub. John fist-bumped Ben as Shelly handed Sarah a glass of lemonade.

The prepper package Ben and Sarah had ordered was initially deemed a late-night mistake. Thankfully, the return policy did not include drunken late-night purchases. It was as if they'd known what was about to happen.

Being well off from not only Sarah being a doctor but also Ben, a disgraced actor at the time, the package had cost them tens of thousands of dollars, which was now considered well-spent money. This included a top-of-the-line solar energy system.

Since also meeting another group consisting of Adam and Alison near a Costco, they had filled their stores to the brim, able to sustain them for years if not decades with the offset of a now growing garden and the clucking group of chickens they had acquired during their travels only a couple of miles from the Sanctuary.

With four still uninhabited houses, they had taken the furthest house next to the water and turned it into an indoor-outdoor upscale chicken coop for only the most refined roosters and chickens alike.

"Key it up," Ben noted as Dan tuned in the main agreed-upon channels, as well as the backup frequencies in case of emergency.

Static crackled from two speakers while the group stood resolute, waiting to hear the voices of their friends. Before setting off, they had put together a set of guidelines, and this radio check was what they called a red flag. In the event they missed more than two radio checks, they were to assume the worst. This included a plan to go after them if needed, but it ended in them no longer being either within range or alive.

Due to the distance, Dustin and Tina had set up a signal repeater in the old house they stayed in before meeting Ben.

This was the new reality of the world they now lived in. Every time you stepped outside the walls of the Sanctuary, there was a chance you would never come back. On the bright side, they were fully armed, stocked with provisions, to include power from two massive solar power systems, and after the past year, enough experience to handle most threats.

While Adam and Allison didn't stay at the Sanctuary, they were in constant radio contact fifteen miles away. They had even left one of their high-end RVs in case needed. When stepping back, Ben felt a sense of accomplishment for pulling this motley crew together.

Another five minutes passed, as a snap and pause caught the group's attention, followed by more static. "What was that?" Ben asked, getting closer to the radio.

Dan chewed the inside of his lip. While he was still smoking, he had drastically cut back due to a dwindling supply.

"Someone keyed up a radio on one of the frequencies. Remember how I found you guys?" Dan reminisced, making Ben's lips droop. The man had used a search and rescue signal tracker.

"Shit," Ben sighed. "Does that mean someone is trying to find us?"

"Perhaps. Or they could be just out of range," Dan started. Maybe someone could hear us and was scared to talk. I don't think it was them."

Eve cut in. "The signal is encrypted. Might I recommend some easy listening to calm everyone's nerves? I detect elevated heart rates."

Yacht rock started seeping into the background as Sarah pressed the mute button on the wall-mounted entertainment system Eve was designed to manage. "Somethings not right. Eve is right. No one should have those channels programmed."

Just as the words skimmed her lips, Ian and Sam walked into the kitchen, rubbing towels through their wet hair. "What's up?" Ian asked, only to stop after seeing the concerned faces in the room.

"They didn't make the radio check," Ben grumped.

John spoke up. "Someone's on the net. Not sure what that means."

Ian, being the youngest of the group, walked to the radio, dripping water on the kitchen floor. This was something Sarah would usually scold anyone, including the lord himself for doing.

"Doesn't that mean they missed two? We're supposed to go get them?" Ian asked no one in particular.

"Something like that," Ben replied. "No, that was if we had some idea of where they were or what was going on. Last time we talked to them, they had just entered the city."

Nicole walked into the kitchen, having come from their watch on the roof, as John walked up to her with a light hug. This was now a full-time job. The group took turns standing lookout on Ben's roof, able to oversee the large wall surrounding the gated community leading to the water's edge.

"They miss check-in?" Nicole asked as Ben handed John a

glass of whiskey from a bottle he had just opened.

"Yeah. Someone also keyed up the radio. Not sure what that means yet," Ben followed as Dan continued to work on the radio's digital screen.

Nicole set her lips flat. "Aren't we supposed to make a run in two days?"

"Yeah," Ian said, finally throwing on a T-shirt. We're supposed to go back to the northern section of Fleming Island. We never really made it that far. We always stopped at the High School."

Ben continued chewing on the inside of his cheek in thought. "They could be anywhere or, like Dan said, just out of range. Someone keyed that radio, and as Eve stated, it's encrypted. They are more than capable people."

Shelly turned to the group. She and Dan, in reality, had been long-time friends with the pair. "You can say that again. So you're saying we hang out a few days and see what happens?"

"Something like that," Ben replied. A phrase he found himself using more often than not. "I think we need to stay by the radio. We needed today to unwind. It's been a long couple of months, and this is the first day I can remember that I almost forgot where we were."

Sarah smiled, sliding her arm around his waist and facing the group. "We have plans and a reason to go out. I agree. We should keep people here and still make the trip. The updated images Eve sent us of Fleming Island show most of the buildings intact. It seems they used the area as a FEMA evacuation center before moving to NAS Jax."

Naval Air Station Jacksonville was once home to the Navy's sub-hunters and the central evacuation hub for North East Florida. Unfortunately for its inhabitants, it had been destroyed after being overrun, Something Ian and Kelly were well aware of before her passing.

John spoke up, knowing the area as well as the others. "Not trying to change the subject, but those images," He pointed at the screen on the kitchen wall as Eve brought up several pictures. "show a FEMA camp, and the stores don't look looted. We could find everything we need to get and keep this garden going, not to mention medicines."

"Priorities," Ben huffed. I'm not happy with the situation, but we have to keep focused on getting ready for the long haul. We don't know if the winter will be worse next year."

They were also working under the assumption that they would be able to find much-needed medicine when their stores ran out before anything exposed to nature went bad. Sarah had even put together a list of what they needed to look out for and the average shelf life when not stored properly. The chilly weather had bought them a gift: time.

The trip to Fleming Island was just one of many targets they had looked at. With its access to the river as an easy escape route in case of trouble, as well as the road being mostly clear, it was a no-brainer not to risk going to unfamiliar locations. Locations they hadn't been to after the chaos of the world stopped and started all at the same time. When it came to planning these trips, they had come to the conclusion that they would only take one such risk that far away from the Sanctuary a year. The rest of their scavenging trips for needed items would be closer locations.

"Want me to call Adam and Allison?" Dan asked, raising his eyebrows.

"Let's get them here," Ben said, taking one final swig of his glass. "Well, nothing is going to change for now. I say we enjoy the rest of this day."

Dan motioned for the group to leave. He would sit by the radio while he took his turn on overwatch. Before the words left his mouth, Ian had grabbed Sam by the arm and was already running back toward the pool.

CHAPTER 2

Morning Glory

The morning sun kissed the tree line as Ben walked up to the roof, handing Sarah a cup of coffee. After three more days of no word from their friends, the Sanctuary inhabitants had kept occupied making plans for their trip to Fleming Island and the FEMA camp it contained.

Ben dropped into the chair beside Sarah as she smiled. "You know I need to get some sleep?"

"About that. I've been thinking." She cut him off.

"Ah, growing up, I see."

Ben stuck his tongue out as the two grinned at the interaction. The morning sun always put them in a good mood. While it was mostly the sunset they had focused on when building their house, the sunrises were just as spectacular, reflecting off the river.

"I'm serious. We have plenty of security cameras. I was thinking about moving one up here. That way, we can monitor over the wall without always having someone up here," he paused, sipping his coffee. The fact that he made it to the roof without spilling either cup was a small victory. "I was talking with Eve, and we can likely set up motion sensors on the wall to work with the camera."

"What's the catch?" Sarah asked as Ben nodded his head.

"We have to get the sensors. We need the ones we already have for the house. There's a Home Depot on the island that carries them. I remember seeing them there. It's not like people were looting motion detectors."

"You sure about that?" Sarah followed in thought. The images clearly show the place was left alone for the most part. That's another thing. I hate it when they call it an Island. It sounds so fancy. It's just a chunk of land off the river connected by bridges."

Ben contemplated the statement. "Technically, you're right. My only thing is we need to be careful. Adam and Allison said we could take the MRAP. The bridge is still crossable."

The MRAP was an up-armored military truck with a roof-mounted minigun capable of mowing down large areas of the undead. It had also proven effective in playing bowling for zombies.

Sarah took a deep breath as the dew glistened off the spider webs and on the trees. "The river is safer. We know the route. Why the sudden change of heart?"

"We're limited on what we can bring back across the river. I know we can stage stuff and ferry it across, but I want to check out the Buckman Bridge. It's been a while since we went up that way. The roads were mostly clear," Ben noted as if trying to sell his wife on the idea.

"Okay. I take it Adam will want to go. That's fine with me. Allison and a few others can stay here. We were planning on that either way."

Ben smiled as he stood up just as Ian arrived for his shift. "Hey guys. Any fun up here last night?"

Sarah cleared her throat. "We had a straggler in the woods, but that was it." She was referring to a zombie.

Roughly once a week, a few random zombies would pass through the area. Nothing close to the numbers they had once encountered.

"Fair enough," Ian joked, using Ben's catchphrase. His youthful smile made the others join him. "Oh, I almost forgot. John and Nicole cooked breakfast. Bacon and fresh eggs. They figured if we were getting set to head out, it's a wonderful time to break out the fine china."

The aroma of rehydrated bacon made Ben's mouth water. While it was part of Ben and Sarah's original stores, Costco had proven to be a gold mine of frozen meats, including several ration kits, including bacon. Pigs and a cow were also on the list of things to get that were, in reality, attainable in the surrounding area.

When it came to turning the Sanctuary into a small farm, sustaining the animals was a topic up for debate. Ben recommended going to the library while on the island and stocking up on any information not available through Eve. Luckily, the AI had a vast hard drive full of farming details, as did the computer that came with the prepper package. There were still some gaps that they needed to fill about sustainably feeding livestock.

"John, sometimes you just get it right," Ben joked as John smiled, handing him a glass of freshly squeezed orange juice. On the outskirts of the neighborhood, orange trees had proven a plentiful bounty. It's almost like you have good news....., or bad."

John set his lips flat. "Well. I want everyone to be good before we head out. I have also been thinking."

"That's never good," Nicole followed with the snap of a towel on the man's posterior.

Ben nodded for him to proceed. "When we get this run completed, I want to head West. See if we can find any clues on what happened to Tina and Dustin."

"What happened? Hopefully nothing. We have a map of their planned targets. They were going to the processing center where you two used to work as a starting point in the city." Ben pointed at Sarah and Nicole, who were seemingly forced to work in the city.

After traveling all the way across the country from Denver, Sarah found herself stuck in Tallahassee, being kept there because she was a Doctor—a much-needed commodity in a dying world. In reality, she had been in Denver working with the Department of Defense regarding the virus that was ravaging not only the country but the world.

Sarah looked pensively at Nicole as she dropped a scoop of eggs on her plate. "I don't think I would go much further than that. I know you worked in the surrounding area, but we don't need to lose any more people."

She was making a good point. While they had a decent-sized group, it wasn't enough to stress their provisions, but in the same breath, it was enough to keep things moving and secure.

John nodded as Adam walked in, stretched, and pulled his long beard down. They had stayed since receiving the call.

"You guys heading out West?" he asked.

"Maybe," John replied. "It's a group decision."

Everyone agreed with a round of grunts from mouthfuls of food. Allison was sleeping in, having covered the graveyard shift in the middle of the night. Dan was on the radio drinking coffee, having already helped himself before the others arrived. He had been glued to the station since the missed radio check. Ben quickly scanned the radio, seeing greasy finger smudges on the touchscreen.

Ben stood up after wiping his fingers off. "All right. I have a few tweaks to the trip tomorrow. I want to take the MRAP and go via the road, skipping the river. We can also take my truck, which will let us load up more provisions if we find them. Plus, we need to check on the route and the bridge."

The logic of the statement furthered the approval of the group he was looking for. With that, they finished breakfast charting out timelines.

**

Tomorrow came before they felt the prior day was over. As with all trips outside the safe embrace of the Sanctuary, it was hard to sleep before going out. With John and Nicole wanting to go West, they opted to stay behind and prep for their trip.

Ben, Sarah, Dan, Shelly, Ian, and Adam would make the trip to Fleming Island. Sam and Allison would monitor the radio, talking to the group while also keeping an eye on the other channels Tina and Dustin were on. As for John and Nicole, they would spend the time planning for their trip. They would also be on standby to head out in case anything went wrong, which it usually did.

Dan walked up to Ben as he put on his vest with several magazines and two grenades snuggly tucked away in his rig, ready for use at a moment's notice. The rest of his gear was full-on military fatigues from a mix of one of his prized prior movie roles and the retired admiral who used to be his neighbor.

"What's up, man?" Ben asked as Dan blew out a lungful of smoke.

"Someone keyed up the radio again last night. I didn't want to say anything and get everyone worked up, but someone's out there on our net. Our secured net," Dan emphasized.

Ben agreed, clipping on a flashlight. "Any ideas?"

"I'm taking the rescue transponder with us. I want to see how close, if at all, that signal is or where it's coming from."

"Does it matter?" Ben asked, not fully knowing how to

work the device.

"Yeah, it matters. The only reason we can't do much here is all the interference with our station being on the same channels. We get far enough away from here I should be able to tell what direction the radio is. Maybe even get a ping how far off."

Ben threw a bag of food in the back of his truck, which had a solar-panel roof over the bed. "Sounds like a plan. It might help with John and Nicole. Give John a heads-up before we go. I don't want him taking off blindly."

Dan turned and jogged toward the house, leaving behind him a puff of smoke from his cigarette. Sarah jumped in the truck and leaned over. "What was that all about?"

"Dan thinks he can get some idea of where the radio is being used. Or not used. It's a good idea. I asked him to tell John. He seems dead set on leaving. You know him. He does his own thing sometimes."

Sarah smiled. "He just cares. We all do. We're all worried. He was on the road out there for a long time, and out of anyone, I would think he would be the person to go."

Ben took in the exterior of his battle-hardened Toyota Tacoma one last time glancing around the open area in front of his house used for staging. Scars and burns from his own trip out West displayed themselves like proud trophies of a hard-won fight on the truck's front end.

With its hybrid engine and several months of work, the truck was once again back in full working condition, including its external cameras. Adam had taken the time to find the additional parts needed at the lot they now called home away from the Sanctuary. This included a heavy-duty front grill that would more than allow the vehicle to plow through the undead.

As was the norm for Ben, the interior was now back to as pristine a condition as he could manage after all its abuse since first leaving to find Sarah. He took pride in his truck and swore that he would one day be buried in it.

Eve cut in. "Hello everyone. I've loaded a playlist for our trip. Also, note that I have a limited GPS signal, but I have updated the maps to reflect any choke points from our last trip."

"Thanks, Eve," Ben said, turning to the MRAP and getting a thumbs-up from Adam. Running out of the house, Dan also gave a thumbs-up, heading toward the gunner's turret while the others stayed tucked safely away in the belly of the armored beast of war.

CHAPTER 3

On the Road Again

Not much had changed other than a few more buildings being burnt out for some unforeseen reason on the way to Highway 295. Mother Nature, as was the new norm, had continued her march on civilization, embracing the road and its surroundings. Grass and various weeds lined the road like parade goers waiting for the main float to pass by.

"Think we should stop anywhere? You know, stretch our legs and get back in the game?" Ben asked Sarah as they crossed the Julington Creek bridge, part of the road still washed out.

"Not much of a game if you ask me," she replied smiling, while at the same time turning down the Beach Boys song Eve had selected for their playlist. They had learned not to argue with the AI's pick of tunes.   "Sure," Sarah finally conceded. "What about the battery store? We can just pull in and take a quick break."

"That works," Ben shifted to the radio. "Adam, you copy?"

"Loud and clear," the man quickly replied.

"We're going to make a quick stop at the battery store before we get to the bridge. Get out, make sure everything's ready to go and get our game faces on," Ben affirmed.

Dan cut in. "Can't hurt. I haven't seen a damn thing since

we left."

With Adam leading the small convoy, Ben and Sarah followed as they continued to weave between cars that once meant something to someone. It was unnerving not seeing any zombies since they left the Sanctuary. In Ben's mind, he was convinced the undead knew they were coming and were plotting a massive ambush. The intrusive thought left Ben's mind as Adam finally pulled over after going a staggering ten miles per hour for the last hour.

Following their training, the group, except Dan in the turret and Adam in the MRAP, slowly exited their vehicles and scanned the area before moving.

The wind rustled nearby trees, accompanied by the occasional clank of a loose building sign. Being summer, the weather was oppressively humid and sunny.

No clouds dotted the skies as the familiar stench of a decaying world greeted Ben and the others. A few mangled corpses from their last visit littered the parking lot as Ben checked the action on his rifle.

"All clear," Ben said, relaxing his posture. The others walked a few steps to the front of his truck still on edge. While they talked in the open, in the wild, as they were now calling it, they kept their voices down to a low conversational tone. If needed, they would switch to the radios and earpieces each of them had.

"I don't remember it being this quiet," Ian spoke up as the others agreed in a chorus of grunts and nods.

"Maybe they're all gone," Shelly suggested as Ben shook his head. Often, on late nights, everyone had suggested they would eventually die out or rot. John, on the other hand, having first-hand knowledge, stated that Chris, back in Tallahassee before going underground in their bunker, had tested the theory. They concluded that as long as the undead had something to fuel them, they'd remain 'alive' or 'dead,' depending on how you looked at it.

"No, they're still here. The sun has them all hiding in the shade somewhere. The fact that we still see a random one near us is enough to tell me we don't want to be in the open at night."

A light bird call came from the gunner's turret as Dan pointed at his eyes with his ring and index finger followed by pointing between two buildings across the street. There, tucked between two buildings, was a zombie leaning against a wall, looking directly at them with hollow sockets where eyes once sat.

Ben pulled up his rifle, looking through his scope. While the zombie was moving slowly, it looked to be stuck to the exterior wall of the building. Not just any building but one of those twenty-four-hour emergency rooms. It looked wilted from being out in the sun, lending to why they stayed in the shade during the day. It was an instinct of survival. The only thing to date they had concluded from watching them. At night, all bets were off as they would come out of whatever hole or spot they had lumbered into.

"What do you want to do?" Ian asked as Shelly glanced at Sarah, who was also checking her weapon.

Ben slowly clicked his weapon to single fire from full-on kiss my ass and have a lovely day fully automatic mode. Equipped with a silencer, this shot was nothing for the man. "One less problem."

He steadied his breath before taking the shot and lightly tapped the trigger. The whipping snap of his bullet hissed as the zombie's torso exploded in a splat of gore, dropping it instantly. While not a headshot, the trauma he had unleashed on the zombie was enough to ensure it never moved again.

"Well, now that we have that out of the way, we are on a schedule," Sarah reminded the group.

"Is everyone good?" Ben asked, seeing their faces morph from the smiles they had when getting out of the vehicles to an understanding that they were no longer safe and cozy poolside back at the Sanctuary. This was precisely what Ben wanted... a chance to get everyone focused.

"Yeah," Shelly slowly replied as the group headed back to their vehicles.

For this trip, the plan was to make it to Fleming Island by no later than one o'clock. Knowing the area was indeed full of zombies. They would make their way to their targeted location and take what they could before sundown. By five, they'd be back on the road. If they were delayed, they'd hunker down in one of the planned houses or return to the Buckman Bridge and stay in the dead center of it until morning, allowing them an area they could defend.

If things got too bad on the bridge, John and Nicole would take a boat up the river to retrieve them. Of course, that involved diving off the bridge and making it to whatever piece of river bank they could find.

While Ben had a limited supply of the high-octane ammunition left, he wanted to get a feel for his rifle again after not shooting at live targets in months—something the man wasn't complaining about.

Ben took one last look at the area as the convoy pulled onto the interstate toward the Buckman Bridg. Glancing to his right, he stopped momentarily to pay homage to the gas station that first introduced him to the world of the undead.

"Is that the gas station?" Sarah asked as Ben nodded.

"Yeah. Seems like it was so long ago," Ben recalled as Sarah's smile didn't reach past her cheeks.

"I feel like I was on the road for years heading toward Florida," she said while Ben pulled onto the interstate. Due to the peppering of cars, they would be lucky to get over ten miles per hour.

"I still can't believe you went through that."

In reality, there were several parts of the trip that Sarah had and would keep to herself. Some of this was to keep Ben from feeling bad about her struggles to get home while he lived in luxury. This was a sore spot with Ben, and she knew it.

"We had a plan. See what happens when you stick to the plan?" Sarah genuinely smiled this time.

"Stick to the plan," Ben echoed, calling Dan, knowing he had a bird's eye view of the road. The Buckman Bridge was only a short mile from the turnoff. "How's it looking up there?"

"Well, it looks like a traffic jam this morning," Dan joked before correcting course. "It seems clear. There's a few turns ahead but no signs of zombies. Just what's left of them."

Ben nodded, liking the good news so far. Signs of a significant battle made itself known the closer they got to the bridge as several burnt-out cars, once set up as a barricade, now lay in ruins, pushed out of the way.

"Do you think this is the smartest thing to be doing with Dustin and Tina out there?" Ben asked out of nowhere, despite the group already having a conversation.

"As I keep saying, the world doesn't stop others from making a personal choice. They're still out there. Hey, look." She motioned with her hand.

In front of them, Adam had stopped the MRAP dead center of the bridge. The sun was making its way through the sky as Ben looked at the clock proclaiming it to be ten thirty.

"What's going on up there?" Ben asked as Dan replied.

"Boats by the base. Don't remember anyone mentioning those or them being on the imagery Eve pulled."

Ben quickly grabbed his phone, pulled up the picture, and zoomed in on the transferred image. There, on the shores of the

Naval Air Station, was a clear shoreline leading up to the end of the bridge just south of the base. They were close to the small area that was once used for a small secure base on the bridge and one of the small convoys safe areas in case they got stuck out at night.

"Just checked. You're right. What type of boats?" Ben asked as Dan chewed through the question. Pulling close, he could see Dan scanning the shoreline with a pair of binoculars.

"It looks like three mid-sized cabin boats. Enough to carry a group of people if you're sailing," Dan replied as the hairs on Ben's neck perked. Eve cut in.

"Your heart rate is elevated. Might I recommend a break and a light snack?"

"No. Eve, it looks like we may have company," Ben replied.

After returning to the battery shop, they found a Wi-Fi signal present and decided after several days to update Eve. This update included every AI and government protocol that the manufacturer had to offer, which was generally locked to the public. This gave Eve the ability to think and, at times, suggest courses of action.

"I scanned the images and see no other items have been moved. These boats have been there no more than two months."

Ben thought through the statement. He didn't like things he couldn't explain, and to date, after their last run-in with what they called bandits, he wasn't taking any chances.

"Sanctuary, you copy?"

"Loud and clear. We heard the radio traffic. What's the plan?" John replied, also monitoring the radio. Truth be told, the remaining group at the Sanctuary was all in the kitchen listening in.

"We keep moving," Ben started. The rest of the bridge is clear. If we get bogged down, we can stay here overnight. I know we prepped the boats, but be ready."

"That's a good copy," John quickly replied.

Hearing the conversation, Adam started pulling forward. The rest of the journey to Roosevelt Boulevard was uneventful as they turned south on Highway 17. Both vehicles scanned the area around the turnoff in case they were being watched.

Ben hadn't spoken since turning off the main interstate, knowing that if he were there, he would be watching that very intersection. Every member of the convey held their collective breaths as they continued south, finally reaching the Doctor's Inlet bridge.

Again, Adam came to a halt on the rest of the damaged structure. On the Northbound lane, multiple chunks of concrete were gone, leading to a massive hole in the road. They knew this already as Ben pulled his truck beside the MRAP.

The noon sun had taken hold by now, beaming down on the small convoy. Luckily for the group, the rest of the trip South would only take twenty minutes as the road had been cleared even prior to their last trip on the road to boat back over to the sanctuary in what felt like an eternity ago.

Bridges, according to Dustin, prior to leaving, were safe spots on the road where it would be hard to surprise anyone. They had taken this advice to heart and all dismounted, now standing in a circle with the driver's side of the MRAP open.

Dan lit a smoke, looking over the now green algae-covered inlet. Boast floated at odd intervals that were likely graves for their once-upon-a-time owners. A hurricane had passed by the prior year, also lending to the chaos often seen randomly floating on the water.

Shelly leaned against Ben's truck, pulling out a snack bar they had acquired from Costco. "I know those things are just hiding in the shadows. I can feel them."

"Yeah, me too," Ben added as Sarah motioned for Dan's

binoculars. "What are you looking for?"

"Are there any other boats that look out of place? We haven't seen or heard any on our part of the river, but that doesn't mean they aren't here," Sarah observed while climbing on top of the massive military vehicle.

In the distance, a flock of birds shot from a tree. This was a sign that they weren't happy with the company below meaning there were likely zombies in the area. "There," she pointed.

Ben and the others took turns looking at the two small paddle boats tied to a distant dock. Signs of recent use were evident. Ben pursed his lips.

"We know we're not the only ones who made it. It looks like one or two people are using those. Let's keep moving before we draw too much attention to ourselves."

The others nodded, piling back into their respective vehicles. Ben took a deep breath as the refreshing air conditioning stilled his nerves. That was the thing about spending so much time behind the protective walls of the Sanctuary. It made not only him but the others feel as if things hadn't gone to shit as badly as they truly had.

The radio crackled to life as John's voice interrupted the final leg of their journey. "Hey, guys. Someone keyed the radio up. I swore I could hear someone breathing."

"Shit," Ben huffed as he picked up the handheld receiver mounted in his truck. "We'll check the signal after we get to Fleming Island. I want to get there before we burn any time on it."

Dan cut in. "I'll turn it on once you guys dismount. The roads clear the rest of the way."

With that, Adam pushed the vehicle faster than it had gone in weeks, moving the convoy forward.

CHAPTER 4

Fleming Island Daydream

A massive Walmart sat to the left as the small yet determined convoy pulled onto County Road 220. To their right, a Target sat waiting for its shoppers to choose between the two once-upon-a-time icons of middle-class shopping.

Shipping containers sat on both sides of the road, creating a choke point leading to a makeshift gate. According to the images and their own experience just south of the area, the main hub of what was called an island was contained from East to West.

Once a local iconic establishment, Whitey's Fish Camp was located at the westernmost bridge, now a fortification leading onto the island. To their South, the island had only been secured by roads just past the library. Everything else was contained by another local landmark called Black Creek due to its deep, dark water.

Ben and the others, while obtaining their second solar power system, ran into a horde of the undead, which led them to believe the surrounding water and swamp areas trapped them— a fact they were all well aware of.

Adam came over the radio. "What do you want me to do?

Drive through it?"

Ben contemplated the makeshift gate, seeing a wheel and a chain still looking to be operational. He also took note of the piles of bones scattered around the outside of the shipping container.

"No. Get Ian and Shelly to jump out and help open the gate. We may need it," Ben said, pulling up the image Eve provided, confirming that the other roads were also blocked last time for his own self-assurance.

Dan scanned the area, giving the thumbs up as the small team dismounted. Ian waved his hand in front of his face. The smell of rotting zombies still lingered in the humid noontime sun.

"Man, it stinks," he guffawed as Ben shrugged.

"We're just not used to it after not being out. Grab the chain," Ben instructed as the gate was quickly moved enough for the vehicles to pass.

Ben turned back to Sarah after she had shifted into the driver's seat. "We'll walk us in."

Shelly and Ian both turned, understanding the direction. The snap of tires on loose rocks and the crackle of debris echoed in the quiet breeze.

Ben caught up with Shelly and Ian as they stared at the familiar shopping area. Restaurants and gas stations looked mostly untouched, aside from the two years of overgrowth.

"You notice something?" Shelly asked, pointing her rifle at the parking lots.

"No cars. They must have cleared the place out. Look at that," Ben motioned toward the first of two gas stations.

Under the fading awning was a machine gun nest with two larger caliber weapons rusting in the shade. Shell casings glinted in the light as they slowly passed the military equipment.

"If we have time, we need to check it out. There may be some ammo lying around," Ben said over the radio. He had switched to his earpiece with the automatic talk function.

The oddity of the scene was the lack of the undead in the immediate area. As they had learned, when the night fell, there were times when certain unseen animals would dispose of the undead. They had multiple ideas, but even John and the others from Tallahassee had not witnessed such an event out West.

"Should be right ahead in the Home Depot parking lot. I can see the white clam shells," Dan said, interrupting the moment.

A clamshell was the military term for a tent built with metal bracing, giving it a semi-permanent footprint. While easily destroyed, clam shells were also built for longevity. They could last for decades if not damaged and secured properly.

Signs of the undead started making themselves known as fresh tracks and smudge marks started streaking the buildings dotting the surrounding area. While likely not the entire mass of zombies they had encountered prior, it was enough to keep them focused.

As two o'clock approached, the vast set-up in the parking lot started taking shape. While images always gave one a good idea of the size of the scene, standing in front of the large group of tents solidified the operation running out of them was large enough to handle the entire inhabitants of the island community.

Two massive tents stood next to the Home Depot, and two smaller, makeshift buildings sat in front of them, with windows and secure entrances. Several rows of razor wire surrounded them, all leading to two entrance points with turnstile gates. The area was more secure than the images provided.

Ian turned to Ben as they pulled the convoy to a halt directly beside the main entrance to the tented area. "Notice there are no leftovers on the wire?"

Leftovers these days were remnants of zombies, meaning guts, tattered clothing, or anything else the undead would shed while in motion. Ben side-eyed the young man. "I'm thinking the mass we ran into hasn't made it here yet, or something is keeping them away."

"Or someone," Ian added. "Don't forget about whatever is eating them at night," he finished, mirroring Ben's thoughts.

The plan was simple. Shelly, Ian, Ben, and Sarah would explore the tents while Dan and Adam pulled overwatch. If needed, they could all pile into the MRAP.

Sarah pulled the truck next to the opening, backing in beside Adam. Eve had already synced with their watches as the timer flashed. A countdown indicating the amount of time they had left on-site to be back on the road and close enough to the Sanctuary to be safe, glowed ominously.

If they didn't leave by five, five thirty at the latest, they would go to plan B and stay on the Buckman Bridge.

Sarah smiled, checking the action on her sleek MP5. "Ready to do this?" she asked as the others nodded.

Ben made quick work of the gate with two quick hushed shots on the locking mechanism on the other side. While he and Ian had silenced weapons, Shelly and Sarah didn't. It only took one shot to attract attention. Attention they were certain they had already drawn.

"Want us to split up? Shelly and I can check out the Home Depot and get those sensors. On the way back, we can clear the large clam shell on the left. You and Ian can get the two smaller ones and then the other large tent?"

Sarah nodded her approval, trusting Ben and Shelly to do their best. While she didn't like splitting up, she also knew they each had a focused reason and the knowledge of what they were looking for. At this rate, they would not make it to the library.

"All right, constant radio contact. If it takes longer than an hour to get into and through the Home Depot, we move to the tents. " Ben pointed at the red cross sign on the closest small tent. They had assumed correctly that there were likely medical supplies present. This was furthered by the solar generator sitting beside the building, out of sight under a makeshift lean-to.

CHAPTER 5

For all your home and gardening needs

S helly and Ben made their way through the massive tents, finally arriving at the closed doors of the old homage to home improvement. Pollen and grime kept the inside of the building a mystery. Taking a deep breath, Ben turned to Shelly and lightly tapped on the door.

"Hear anything?" Shelly asked as Ben placed his ear to the large sliding doors.

Ben held up a finger, the sound of a random sign hanging off a cage of propane tanks lightly clanking. "No. Here," Ben handed her his rifle and pulled a small crowbar from his assault pack, which was also filled with ammo.

After a few light pulls, it was clear the doors were locked. Ben reached back into his pack, pulling out a small rag and wrapping it around the crowbar. With a few hushed smacks, the safety glass cracked into hundreds of small pellets, landing on the soft mat inside the entrance.

Ben looked back at Shelly. "Just in case we need to make a fast exit." They had learned their lesson at the ever-infamous Costco. A smaller exit could easily become a choke point for the undead.

Shelly handed his rifle back, clicking on the small flashlight mounted on her rifle. "I'll scan left."

No other words were needed as the two slowly entered the open space, lighting up the entrance area. A sign proclaiming low-interest rates for home air conditioning systems greeted them with a man in a worker's outfit smiling as if he had won the lottery.

Pallets of random building materials sat on large skids, ready to be rolled out into the makeshift camp. "We're in," Ben noted over the comms as Dan responded. "Nothing out here. I'm activating the transponder." He was referring to the radio tracker.

Ben glanced at Shelly, who pointed at her nose as he took a breath of the stale, musty air. He quickly regretted his decision as the smell of rotting flesh smacked him in the face. They were not alone, or at the least, there were dead bodies tucked away in the building.

Activating his radio's whisper mode, Ben activated the small mic on his helmet. "It smells fresh," Shelly nodded, rolling her shoulders.

Doing the same, she responded. The two had not taken more than two steps inside the dark cavern of unknown home goods. "Where are we going?"

"Down the main entranceway toward the lighting. It's a straight shot. In and out."

Just as the words left his mouth, the sounds of something dropping on the floor echoed as if it was a literal bomb going off, even though it was likely just a small box.

Taking a deep breath, Ben walked forward. With a wall of lightbulbs to their right, both Ben and Shelly were now focused on the open aisles to their left. Grills, garden tools, and the start of someone putting out Christmas decorations created a jumble of things that had, as suspected, not been disturbed.

"Clear," Shelly whispered as they passed the first two Isles. They would take their time.

"You hear that?" Ben asked, holding up his hand to stop.

Shelly strained as the sounds of shuffling and stench started growing louder. "I think we know where they crammed the stinkers."

Ben nodded. While they were clearly secured somewhere in the building, there were zombies in the building. "We haven't seen them yet. They're likely secured." While he didn't understand why, he just wanted to get the sensors and leave; they could figure the rest out later.

"Clear," Shelly again whispered as they passed the main entrance section. Two more isles and the main back isle stretching the distance of the store remained.

Ben took several quick steps forward, making his way to the main corridor, motioning for Shelly to press against the massive shelf behind them. He pointed at a shelf directly across, beaming his flashlight on a section labeled home security.

As soon as his light cut through the isles stretching the length of the store, the sounds of a riot breaking out started growling and huffing. Turning the corner would reveal what was keeping the undead back.

Sweat trickled down Ben's back, neatly pooling in his crack as he reflected on their next move. "I'll go for the sensors. You cover me. Don't move from here."

Shelly nodded. "I'm not liking this."

"When was the last time anyone liked anything or one that grunted."

Shelly snickered lightly, quickly pulling it in. "Phrasing there, actor boy." She grinned.

Ben held up three fingers, counting down to one, as he stepped forward. At the same time, Shelly beamed her flashlight down the aisle, seeing the wall of horror now pressing against a loosely secured chain metal fence.

"Hurry." This time, she didn't hold back. They already knew they were there and were getting worked into a frenzy in search of a meal. She took in the mess, seeing exposed ribs and gore now being pressed into, and threw the gaps in small patterned gaps in the fence.

"Hey guys," Shelly called over the radio, seeing Ben smacking the lock. Behind them, the sensors sat like prizes that would not be easy to get.

"Go ahead," Dan replied, sounding preoccupied.

"This place is packed with stinkers," she replied, using her name for the undead. She despised their stench more than anything.

"That's a good copy. We can't maneuver to the front of the store without ripping through the wire. You need us to come in there?" Dan asked, knowing his wife was in possible danger. He also trusted her and her ability to handle herself.

"No..., I don't know," She replied as Ben got a case of the F-its and ripped two rounds into the lock with his also silenced pistol.

"Bingo," he huffed, untying the sack on his waist, shoving no less than a dozen of the sensors into his bag as well as a control panel. "It's going to..... shit." He finished as the fence started buckling under the weight of the undead.

Not having any more patience, Shelly gritted her teeth, ripping several dozen rounds into the mass of moving bodies. The tink of bullets on the fence and the whap of direct hits echoed as Ben set himself in the middle of the aisle, following her lead.

Heads and bodies exploded under the impact of the special ammunition as Ben, in a moment of to hell with it, pulled a grenade from his vest.

The woman didn't need any further guidance as Ben pulled the pin, throwing as far as his mass allowed. By the time Ben reached the main entrance, Shelly was already shuffling through the small opening.

Turning, Ben Paused just as the grenade activated. Still beaming his flashlight toward the back of the store, a zombie's leg flew through the air as if in slow motion. The active ear protection Ben was wearing muffling the sound.

Looking up, Ben noticed the aisle they had used for cover while moving to the back of the store started swaying. In usual Ben fashion, he had completely wrecked the store. Even better, if that aisle fell over, it would block the entire entrance.

"Come on, come on," he hesitated as Shelly took several steps back, dropping to a knee in preparation to fire into the building.

With another wave as if to say goodbye, the massive shelf started crashing to the floor. Ben took this as his cue to leave, running headfirst through the hole.

A loud crash caught everyone's attention, even being heard by Dan. "You guys good?" he asked as Shelly replied with a hesitant, "Maybe. Depends on who's asking."

"Always the star of the show," Dan murmured, grinning to himself, looking back at the transponder. She would have told him otherwise.

Shelly looked at Ben as he set himself beside her. "I think they're cut off—at least what's left."

"You know, throwing grenades in a confirmed space, while effective, is slightly dangerous?"

"Yeah, it is," he replied, noticing a stack of plywood by the entrance. "Help me stack this against the door."

Shelly nodded. "You sure it's safe?"

"Safe as it's going to be. Let's get this closed up and to the tent."

Five minutes later, they had stacked enough wood in front of the entrance to keep an elephant away. "That should do it," Ben said, getting back on the radio. "Sarah, what's going on?"

"I should be asking you," she paused. "Jackpot. They even had power to their refrigeration system. We're heading toward the big tents. This place had a lot going on. We can talk later."

On that, Shelly and Ben turned to the large tent in front of them just as Sarah and Ian walked into view.

CHAPTER 6

Not that guy again

Sweat glistened in the sun while the once illustrious beacon of home construction creaked. The sounds of things falling continued to seep out of the building as the group stood between the two large tents.

"What the hell happened?" Ian asked before Sarah could.

"Well, the way I see it, someone locked all the people working these tents in there and did something to them," Ben replied.

Shelly shook her head, not liking the side quest she had just partaken in. Sarah exhaled deeply before speaking.

"Gas, someone locked them inside and used gas," she pointed at several barrels labeled aerosol poison sitting beside a portable air conditioner piped into the building.

Ben recalled the appendage he witnessed take flight like a baseball bat slung by a pissed-off batter. "That was likely them. I saw a leg with fatigues on."

"A leg?" Ian asked.

"I sort of threw a grenade in there. Anyway, who would do something like that? I mean, this place looks fairly secure. From what I can tell, it would take more than just zombies to cause this," Ben suggested as lights started flickering in the back of his mind.

"I know that look. What is it?" Sarah asked as Ben turned to Ian.

"Didn't you say Jim was down here stirring all sorts of shit?" Ben asked.

Jim was once upon a time Ben's neighbor and stalker. He also just happened to be a serial killer and the person who framed Ben for an onset death before everything went to hell. On the first night, Ben had brought Ian and Kelly back to the Sanctuary as their first guests. Jim had appeared and then, thanks to Ben, disappeared into the void of death, shooting him several times in front of the two young adults.

After that, it had been a game of how much trouble a dead man could cause. They had run into a house that he had obviously set up as a honeypot and even found him to be the cause of the raiders that almost took over the Sanctuary by letting them know where it was. Topping it all off was the fact that Jim was likely responsible for the fall of the remaining military and civilian forces just north of the interstate.

According to Ian and Kelly, one night, after recognizing the man's name, they told a story about someone who looked just like him with the same name who had sabotaged the security barriers keeping most of the massive herds of the undead out of the fairly large area the remaining military and law enforcement had secured.

It didn't take long for the entire stabilized community to be wiped out, leaving people like Ian and Kelly to fend for themselves in the wilds of what was left of Jacksonville.

"You think this was him?" Ian asked wild-eyed. It was clear thoughts of Kelly were seeping into his memories as a frown dropped on his face.

"He's responsible for all the other shitstorms around here. I bet if we looked hard enough, we would find some trace of him," Ben turned to Shelly. "He used to enjoy cutting people open and posing them. There's more, but he was one sick puppy."

"That has to really bother you," Shelly hesitated before continuing, not wanting to overstep. "I know he was your neighbor. I remember the story, but he was there and here for you."

Ben had already come to terms with the fact, smiling. "The gun giveth, the gun taketh away." This was a line from one of his movies.

"I remember seeing you say that in a movie," Shelly followed. "Simply badass. No, I'm not saying what he did is your fault. People like that do these things anyway. I'm saying you stopped him. I can tell you there are others out there. That's the one thing that stupid Council in Tallahassee got right. They weeded those people right out."

Sarah cut in. "Yeah, and they sent weak lambs to the slaughter that weren't useful enough for the city."

Ben glanced down at his watch, seeing Eve show his heart rate and time left. "Enough of that. We have one more tent to get through."

"No need," Ian blurted out. It was only three o'clock. "We walked in there after going through the other. It's stacked ceiling high with weapons, ammunition, and.., get this, mortars."

That caught Ben's attention. "What about the other tent and the smaller ones?"

"The smaller tents were slapped full of medical supplies. Everything we need. Some of it is bad, but a good amount is usable. We could load both trucks and still have plenty left over. I suggest we make another run if things work out," Sarah added.

"Are there any vehicles around here?" Shelly asked, thinking one step ahead.

"Yes. There were two more MRAP-style vehicles on the other side of the tents. They were under some makeshift cover, so we couldn't see them from the satellite images. Not sure we have time to work on them," Sarah said, turning back to the entrance gate.

Ben stopped. "Hold up. What about rations and food?"

Ian smiled, chucking an honest-to-god Twinkie at the man—something they had also run into when first meeting Adam and Allison. "Oh yeah. The good stuff, too. Military rations and a pile of vacuum-sealed food. Some of it's bad, but man, it would double our food stores."

"Looks like you guys were busy. We might even get time to hit the library," Ben added as Sarah shook her head.

"The medicine we found is too important—insulin, penicillin, properly stored blood, you name it. It's too valuable to waste any time on not getting this stuff back. We can boat over and get the rest later. Maybe load up a few weapons."

On those words of finality, the group headed back to Adam and Dan. Adam sat with his leg propped up, talking with Allison. At the same time, Dan puffed feverishly on a cigarette, something Ben noticed right away.

"I'm guessing you heard the good news?" Ben asked as Adam nodded.

"Just waiting for you two to get things sorted. We loading up?" Adam asked as Dan continued to focus on the radio tracker.

"Dan. You all right up there?" Ben asked, pausing.

"Maybe. I just talked to John. We need them to be on the channel so Dustin and Tina can get whoever it is to key up the radio again. They did it about ten minutes ago."

Ben sucked in a breath. Not realizing it, he and Shelly had spent almost forty-five minutes in the Home Depot between getting in, grabbing their prize, and placing the plywood over the hole they had made. He also didn't like that Dan was now referring to someone other than Dustin and Tina on the encrypted channel.

Dan finally looked over, setting the tracker down. "Did something happen in there?"

Adam looked up. "You didn't hear all that commotion?"

"Yeah," Dan corrected himself, having been completely focused on the tracker.

Shelly took the chance to fill in the gaps. "Ben here was reliving his action movie days. Threw a grenade inside the store."

"Oh, yeah, cool. Is everything okay?" Dan followed, getting an entire round of concerned glances.

"Hey. Dan," Ben huffed louder. Shelly gave him the go-ahead nod to push him.

"I think this thing's either messed up or getting some type of weird signal. I don't know."

Shelly climbed onto the MRAP, finally reaching the gunner's turret. "Hey babe. What don't you know?"

Dan pulled out another cigarette, lighting it off the one he was feverishly puffing on. "This thing is telling me Tina and Dustin's radios are in the Jacksonville area."

Silence dropped like an unwanted bomb. Dan had been so focused on the device he was suffering from tunnel vision, blocking out everything else around him.

Ben spoke up next. "You said plural. Both their radios?"

"Yup. I mean," Dan corrected himself, starting to realize he was overly focused on the device now sitting on his lap. "It could be messed up. I want to check it again when we get to the bridge."

Not liking the notion, Ben refocused the group. "We will

check. Like you said. That thing could be off. There could be a radio signal booster around here. Hell, who knows? Maybe that's what keeps the zombies away from this small area."

While he was talking out of his third point of contact, Sarah screwed her face up at the statement. "Wait a minute. Wait a minute," she repeated. "That's right. Somethings keeping that horde to our south out of here. I mean, nothing's off the table. Why not?"

"Maybe we can look at that later, but for the here and now, we need to get this load back home," Ben wasn't distracting from his wife's statement but rather realized time, as always, was marching on. "If we load up all the meds, you think we have enough room to load up some of the heavy weapons you found?"

Sarah nodded, also glancing down at her smartwatch. Eve was synched with all the devices they had acquired for everyone in their circle. "Most of it can fit into the MRAP. We can put two other cases in the truck and should have plenty of room. What weapons are you thinking?"

"Ian, you said there were some mortars over there. What else?" Ben asked as Ian smiled.

CHAPTER 7

Changes

The sun slowly headed toward the horizon as Adam pulled the MRAP to a rolling stop. Eve chimed in with a reminder: it was five o'clock. The clouds started shifting to a hazy shade of reddish-orange, supporting the much-needed reminder that they weren't fighting zombies by this point but rather time.

Ben leaned forward. They had spent more time than planned loading up their bounty. Most of this was spent looking through the weapons and rations to take back. For Dan, the trip had been a gold mind. Sealed in a large trunk were hundreds of cartons of freshly kept cigarettes.

After some debate, Shelly agreed to let Dan bring as many as would fit in the remaining space. Ben glanced over his shoulder as several stacks of Marlboro lights sat tucked away before turning back to the slowing vehicle in front of them. Dan had even secured them with a seat belt.

Sitting beside the cancer-dealing sticks of yesteryear sat several cans of belted 7.62mm linked ammunition for the three 240 bravo fully automatic heavy machine guns they finally landed on grabbing. Ben had even found multiple cans of the much sought-after high-octane ammunition for his rifle.

"What's going on?" Ben asked over the radio as Dan replied.

"The onramp to the highway is blocked. It wasn't when we headed to the island."

Ben reflected on the term Island that he hated, pulling up beside the MRAP. "Nope. It wasn't," Ben replied. Sarah shifted in her seat, placing her gun on her lap, with a concerned look.

"Everyone stay in your vehicles," Ben instructed, pulling forward to the offramp they used to pull onto Highway Seventeen.

The clear road, while looking too much like a piece of cheese in a mouse trap, was their only option. On the other side, a retention pond was offset by a six-foot-tall concrete divider, which prevented them from going around the pile of cars now in the way.

Ben keyed the radio, still in the shaded underpass. "The other sides clear. I don't see anything." He looked at Sarah, who nodded.

"It looks clear," she whispered as if trying to stay quiet to help.

"Coming around. I'll take the lead," Adam proclaimed as the roar of the MRAP peeled by the Toyota, screaming up the offramp.

"Guess he ain't messing around," Ben said as Dan swiveled the gunner's turret around, scanning the left side of the road, landing back in front of the small convoy.

"I'm not stopping until we get to the halfway point of the bridge. I'm going to push some cars out of the way, but we aren't slowing down," Adam informed Ben. John cut in, having monitored the recent development.

"You need us to head that way?" he asked.

Sarah grabbed the radio as Ben focused on the road. While still only going a blistering twenty miles per hour, they were now bobbing and weaving abandoned burnt-out cars at a significantly faster rate than their initial trip.

"No," Sarah objected, scanning the road. The only thing keeping her nerves calm was the concrete barriers on either side of the highway. They would be on the bridge in a couple of minutes. "If someone's out here messing with us, we don't want to draw any more attention to where we're going or coming from."

Sam, Nicole, Allison, and John all stood in the kitchen staring at the radio. Allision spoke first as John worked through Sarah's statement.

"I think she's saying they need to stay out for the night. I don't know about that. It gives whoever blocked the road a chance to get closer or a better position to watch them."

"Perhaps," Nicole added, tapping her fingers on the marble counter. "Maybe they can stay on the bridge. Most of the houses we identified as safehouses are off Highway 17. They're past that."

John flexed his jaw. "If they stay on the bridge, they could likely see anyone moving. The MRAP has a thermal camera that works like a charm at night. They would see if anyone was around."

"Anyone close," Allison piled on.

"Hey guys," John keyed the radio. "You saying you're staying out for the night?"

Sarah leaned forward, looking at the quickly sinking sun. While still on schedule, time was moving on, and any deviation would have them on the road at night.

"Yeah, we stay on the bridge. It will be the safest bet. Plus, we can see if anyone is following us," Ben said to Sarah, also thinking about not only the thermal camera but also the machine guns now in their position.

"That's a good copy. We are holding at our middle-of-the-road safehouse." This was the code word for the location on the bridge. While they weren't talking on the channel to communicate with Dustin and Tina, both groups were still cautious.

"Good copy. We'll have the secondary pick-up method prepped and ready," John was referring to taking the boat to the Buckman bridge if needed. "Get set and call us. We'll continue to monitor the net."

The tone of the conversation had changed. Now on the bridge, Adam started the last few turns through junked cars to the center point they had identified. It had clearly been used as a secure location at some point and easily defended if needed.

Two cars sat at angles on both sides, with an opening just large enough to fit the massive MRAP through. Vehicles were stacked along the middle divider, giving another level of security, including two vans that the prior inhabitants of the small base had likely occupied.

Once upon a time, distracted commuters passed over the bridge, staring at their phones instead of the road, trying to find their favorite song. Husbands and wives all trying to escape the grind of their daily commute, stuck in soul-draining traffic.

"Pull in first," Adam instructed.

Ben pulled forward as his nerves started warning him something wasn't right. "You okay?" Sarah asked, leaning over.

"Yeah. Something's bothering me. The boats, the onramp. Fleming island. All of it. Every damn time we leave the Sanctuary." The growl of Adam turning around and facing outward stopped Ben's thought.

Ben pulled forward, filling the gap between the two stacked cars on the opposite side. Sarah took a deep breath. "You know. I often forget the worlds raging around us now that

I'm back home. Think about it. I saw the reality of everything heading East. We would be stupid to think there's not others."

Ben reflected on the comment. "The problem is what others are out here doing. They blocked that road for a reason. I'm not sure why they aren't here. Maybe they thought we would be out longer, or we were heading home. I have a feeling they weren't expecting us to be back through so quickly."

Sarah considered the statement: "It makes sense. Let's see what the others are doing."

"You are now past the return cutoff timeline," Eve chirped. "I have a recommendation."

This caught Ben's attention. Eve had, on occasion, shown an ability to think independently. The AI system that had been unlocked at the end of the world was the pun of several Skynet Terminator jokes. If the zombies didn't end things, all the systems held behind government secret programs now unlocked would.

It was ironic that it took one disgruntled Pentagon employee two minutes to release the floodgates. While Eve had access to a wealth of information the others would find interesting, it was all down to asking the right questions. But, as just happened, Eve had a moderate ability to think on her own.

"Okay," Ben said, picking up his rifle.

"I suggest you take the motion sensors retrieved and hook them up to the vehicles facing outward. That way, you can rest and not stare at the road all night."

Eve had a great point. They would need some rest, and Eve would be able to monitor the system. Ben and the others could explore the small encampment in the middle of the bridge and carefully lay out their next moves.

Ben and Sarah grabbed the sensors quickly, hooking two of them to the front of the truck before calling the other vehicle. After running a set of cables from the solar panel mounted on the roof of the truck topper, Eve confirmed on Ben's smartwatch that she had synced with the system.

"Hey guys, we're heading over. Eve suggested we hook up the motion sensors. It will give us some time to regroup," Ben stated, looking at the back end of the MRAP roughly five hundred feet away.

"You sure?" Dan replied, sounding unsure.

"Check your watches," Ben followed as Dan looked down, seeing a scanning signal on his watch.

They had secured a watch for everyone. "I'll be dammed." He followed. A small chart showing the area in front of the Toyota flashed. While the small image wasn't detailed, it clearly showed no movement.

"The sensitivity setting will require a creature larger than a cat to activate the alarm," Eve interjected. "How about some easy listening?"

"No, you've done enough Eve," Ben said, reaching the MRAP as Shelly opened the back door.

"I love a good change of plans," Shelly joked, taking one of the sensors from Sarah and quickly unwrapping it. "Which reminds me. What's our next move?"

Dan jumped down from the gunner's turret as Adam and Ian walked out of the massive truck. With everyone standing in a circle, Ben stepped in the middle.

"We don't want to lead whoever it is back home. We've had enough of that. With the infrared camera and these sensors on the truck, we can stand watch on the bridge. If someone's behind us, we'll see them. Even more, we can handle them if needed."

Dan reached up to light a cigarette and reconsidered now that the sun had crested the horizon. There would be no signs of them on the bridge if they could help it. The man leaned into the back of the vehicle, lighting his smoke before talking.

"I agree. The route West was clear. They likely didn't know what direction we were going. I don't think they expected us to come back through so quickly. Maybe some scouts that headed back home, or wherever."

The group nodded, agreeing with Dan. "I want to keep an eye on those boats. I'm thinking they didn't stray too far. Hook up the motion sensors, and we can look around. Looks like there's some leftover gear, not to mention those vans."

"Or the undead," Ian added, noting that they may simply have been resting when they passed through earlier.

"Good point. Silenced weapons only unless needed. I'm going to unload one of those machine guns. Dan, you know how to set it up?" Ben asked as the man grinned.

"Man, I need to get a raise," Dan followed. Shelly and Sarah walked out in front of the MRAP, setting up the sensors while Dan and Ben unloaded the machine gun.

After twenty minutes, the M240 was set up on Ben's truck as Dan and Adam loaded back aboard their vehicle. Ian and Shelly would watch to the East with the Toyota while Ben and Sarah inspected the vans.

Ben called the Sanctuary once the defenses were set up. "Anything on your end?"

John answered, talking over the sounds of the others in the background. No sleep would be had. "Nothing here. We checked the river for lights or boats but didn't see anything. We're ready to go if you make the call."

"Understood. We'll report back every thirty minutes. Same as usual. If we miss two check-ins, there's a problem. If all hell breaks loose, you'll likely be able to hear it."

Ben was right. Sound traveled on the river, especially at night on calm waters. While it might sound like nothing more than light snaps in the distance, they would be able to hear a change. "That's a good copy. We'll have someone in the crow's nest listening or watching."

"Good copy. We see anything, we'll let you know," Ben concluded, turning to Sarah.

"Take a little walk?" Sarah asked as Ian gave them a thumbs up.

The once star-crossed lovers headed toward the two vans in the center of the bridge, pulling out their silenced pistols. "You think there's any zombies on the bridge?" Sarah followed as Ben shrugged.

His armor plate carrier clicked in the quiet night. With the moon taking hold of the struggle over day and night, the deep, dark sky was reflected by the water below. If someone weren't looking, they would not think the bridge was now home to a small group of survivors.

"Yeah, there always is," Ben paused, looking North toward the city of Jacksonville. "Look." He pointed.

In one of the taller buildings, several tiny speckles of light looked like distant stars sitting just over the city.

"You think someone's there?" Sarah asked.

"Maybe. It could just be solar lights. I don't think I ever looked at the city from a distance at night. For all we know, those people may be here to check that out."

Sarah shook her head. "No. I don't think so. We would have heard the boats if they came up the river. I would think they came from the area around the city. Or picked up the boats somewhere close to the base. There was a dam fleet of them heading toward the base and the city from the reports I read."

"Another problem, for another time. I can tell you, that's one place we aren't going. It's like hell up there. Half the city is a wasteland. Pistols up," Ben reminded her, turning toward the closest van.

Ben moved forward, tapping his gun on the back door. He took several steps back, waiting for a response. Nothing, dead silence. Leaning forward, he pulled the handle to find it unlocked. Sarah stood back, locked onto the rear of the van.

"Clear," He whispered. Quickly cracking a small chem light, Ben chucked it into the van. Once a work vehicle, a bed, and a workbench sat covered in papers and maps. A small radio was tucked in between the front seats next to an open soda can. On the interior walls, random rock band posters were hung to give the small space a feeling of home.

Jumping in, Ben placed the chem light on the workbench. Anyone more than fifty meters away would not be able to see the glow. "Close the door," Ben said as Sarah joined him.

Spreading the maps out, it was clear they had been scouting and color-coding the Jacksonville area. South of the Buckman bridge, the area was marked in red. Several areas near San Marco were marked as secure locations, with Xs marking random buildings.

"Look at this one," Sarah pointed at a printed-out map of an area close to the Sanctuary.

"Wonder what that's all about," Ben said. The reality of Jim running around working with the group landed in his thoughts like a sledgehammer on ice.

Seeing the look on his face and the prior conversations about how the city fell, she also made the connection. "He had them looking for us."

"He was likely trying to get them to clear the area. When he showed up at the house, he looked rough. You can't predict the undead. He probably thought the city would hold," Ben huffed, getting frustrated at the mere thought of the man. Even if he was wrong about Jim causing the chaos on Fleming Island, he had thought about the man twice in one day.

"I'll grab the maps. We'll take them with us," Sarah said, pulling them into a pile.

Scanning the small vehicle, Ben wondered what happened on that bridge. He often thought of the old saying about what if the water could speak in situations such as this. Not only did the depths of the ocean and river hold many secrets, but they were also places of safety for those who knew how to respect them.

Sitting the pile of papers on the concrete, Ben and Sarah moved to the next van. Following the same methodology, Ben lightly tapped on the back door. Already letting their guard down, Ben moved to open the door just as the thump of flesh slapped the back interior of the van.

"Shit," Ben huffed, knowing he was about to open the door. "Alright. I open the door, we let it come out, then I'll handle it."

"Hey guys, bad news," Sarah whispered over the radio. There are zombies in the second van. Keep an eye on us." This was followed by Dan's immediate swivel of the gunner's turret.

Ben pulled out his knife, not wanting to draw any attention. While their pistols were silenced, they still made enough noise to carry over the water.

"You good?" Sarah asked as she took several steps back, covering Ben.

Leaning his back on the side of the van, Ben slowly tested the door also to find it unlocked. Twisting his arm, he slowly swung the door open as the door flung the rest of the way open. It wasn't a fast-moving crazy, but rather a rotted zombie leaning on the door.

Flash smacked the pavement as hollow, empty eye sockets scanned the area for a meal. Ben immediately noticed several missing chunks from gunfire had ripped holes in the slow-moving zombie.

"Jesus," Ben breathed out before he swung his arm around, slamming his famed Rambo knife through the creature's skull with a slopping shlunk. The once very much alive creature spasmed lightly before altogether dropping to the pavement.

The smell hit them first from not only the back of the van but the mutilated figure in front of them. Time and rot had taken its toll on the zombie.

"Someone opened the van, shot that thing up, then slammed the door closed," Sarah noted as Ben pulled a handkerchief over his face to ward off the smell.

Ben cracked another small chem light, dropping it inside the van. The horror of the scene made Ben freeze. The other bodies piled inside had been taken out in finality. Whoever the poor soul was they had just released had likely been playing dead while finally succumbing to their injuries.

Not wanting to disturb the grave, Ben pointed at the door, turning to the body on the ground and motioning for Sarah to help him move it back inside. Grabbing the undead's legs, the feel of flesh easily releasing from bone almost made Ben gag, as the same happened to the man's arms.

Quickly clicking the door shut, the two walked toward the MRAP to get some fresh air and report back, now holding the maps.

"What's up?" Dan asked under his breath. He was back in the focused mode he had been in earlier while working on the tracker.

"Someone killed them, or they had been injured. Who knows. Someone opened the back of that van and sprayed it down like a dam fireman putting out a fire," Ben replied as Adam popped out the back of the vehicle.

"That sucks," Adam said, pointing up at Dan. "More news on the tracker front. I'll let Dan fill you in on that. The cameras clear," he followed, pointing at the large screen hanging down from the ceiling in between the driver and passenger seat. This also included a secondary monitor in the rear of the truck.

Ben walked inside the vehicle as Sarah started looking at the stack of maps. "Dan, what's up?"

Dan unhooked his belt, sliding down inside the vehicle, handing Ben the tracker. "I don't know how to put this, but I checked twice since we got on this bridge. The radio was keyed up about two minutes ago and again while we were traveling. I had this thing on just in case."

"And?" Ben asked, seeing the concerned look on his face.

"They're in Jacksonville. There's no mistaking it. From what I can tell, they're somewhere On the West side of the bridge. It looks like the signal moved."

Sarah, hearing this, looked up. "How accurate is that thing?"

"I mean," Dan stammered. "ten miles, maybe fifteen. If they are broadcasting or using the radio, I can get a fairly accurate heading. The issue is they aren't using the radio much."

"You think they may be doing the same to us?" Ben asked, stilling the group.

"Yeah, I suppose. It would make sense," Dan said, lighting another cigarette next to Ben. The smoke wafted over Ben's face. If it weren't for the fact that it was washing the stench of the van out of his and Sarah's noses, Ben would have thrown the cancer stick onto the ground. Dan, seeing this, waved the smoke out of Ben's face.

"Sorry man. This just means..., I don't know what this means." Dan shrugged.

Ben had grabbed the cigarette out of Dan's mouth on more than one occasion, only to have Dan pull another out of some seemingly magical area and light another one. It was, in all actuality, an ongoing gag to mess with each other the way friends and family do.

The implications of knowing Dustin and Tina had been in Tallahassee and were now in the general area without calling was more than concerning. Ben finally landed on a sound response: "This is bad."

Dan frowned, also working through the implications. While not saying it out loud, this meant that either someone had taken their radios and were close to the sanctuary, or it was indeed Dustin and Tina, and they were up to something they didn't want the others to know about. Either way, it was not promising.

"It would take an army to get those two," Ben followed as the others nodded.

"So what's the plan?" Adam asked, now sitting in the driver's seat, watching the infrared camera feed. The camera was encased in a ball directly below the gunner's turret above the windshield. Its ability to not only zoom in but also see heat signatures at night was priceless.

Ben chewed on his words. "Plan. Get back without being followed for now," He shifted over to Dan. "How hard was it to truly track us down?"

"Whelp." He started, taking a draw from his smoke, mindful of blowing it to the back door out of the others' faces. They were all now tucked inside the back of the MRAP. "You guys were moving all over the place after the signal started. Once I got it nailed down and you weren't all over the place, it was easy. Time consuming, but easy."

"That's right," Ben recalled. "You said every time we keyed or got on the radio, you just set off in that direction. It's not precise, but if one kept going, you would eventually run into the signal."

After being reminded of the entire story, Sarah asked a

52

valid question: "Has the signal moved today?"

"Nope," Dan replied. The sound of something clanking on the other side of the stacked cars separating the interstate froze the conversation as Ian came over the radio from Ben's truck.

"You guys hear that?"

"Yeah," Ben quickly replied.

Dan climbed onto the gunner's turret to get a better view. While the camera worked in front of the vehicle, it wasn't as high as the turret. At the same time, the movement sensor pinged everyone's watches.

"Two signals are being detected," Eve advised as Dan slowly lowered himself back inside, raising his index finger in front of his lips in the universal sign to shut the hell up.

"Two slow movers. They're heading West. They just passed the barricade and aren't turning," Dan whispered, slowly sliding the well-oiled hatch of the turret shut.

Adam shifted to the camera. The familiar dying purple glow showed two zombies shuffling down the road. The concrete divider was tall enough to keep the unwanted guests from crawling over.

Ian, hearing the entire interaction, spoke up. "We have eyes on the other lanes. Those things are on the other side of the stacked cars."

Figuring they had made enough noise to garner the attention of two zombies that had likely been under a car, the group decided to stay the course and not draw any further attention to themselves. After five minutes of watching the slow, shuffling zombies, Adam shifted to the distance shoreline of Naval Air Station Jacksonville, also known as NAS Jax.

"Check it out," Adam almost barked, quickly pulling it back in like a loud burp on a first date.

The others, still in the back of the MRAP, turned to the

monitor as several heat sources lit up the area just north of the boats. Adam squinted as if it helped. "I think they're setting something up. Maybe camp for the night?"

"If memory serves, the base is still fenced off even after the bombing. It would take more than zombies to get in there, especially after they beefed up the gates and fencing before the bombing. They're in the open because it's safe," Ian recalled, chewing on his bottom lip.

Ben chimed in. "You would have to be stupid to stay out in the open at night."

Sarah grinned, seeing the humor in the statement. "We're the only ones out here not smart enough to find a safe place to stay."

"You have a way with words, babe," Ben gushed in jest, refocusing. "They for sure would know about the blocked-off intersection."

CHAPTER 8

Night Moves

N ight lay on the bridge like a thick blanket, covering the entire area in a thick layer of foggy, shower-like humidity. After watching the group of ten people on the shores of the naval base, Ben was starting to grow restless.

The group they were previously watching had been moving in and out of a building several feet away from the shoreline, taking out crates of supplies. After thirty minutes, a thick fog crept up the river, obscuring their view to just a few feet on either side of the bridge.

Working through the data on the tracker and a map, Dan concluded the signal was coming from their west and slightly north. While not a complete confirmation, the signal was strong enough for the man to conclude the radios were likely within ten miles of their current location.

"I would bet all the de-hydrated bacon back home those radios are on that base, with those people,' Ben concluded.

Ian and Shelly jogged to the MRAP to regroup before switching with Ben and Sarah. While the misty fog made it nearly impossible to see, it also called for a group re-evaluation of the situation.

"He's right," Sarah supported. "There are no such things as coincidences anymore like this. That shit went out the door when ninety-five percent of America's population was wiped out."

Ian, having a hopeful mind, frowned. "How do we know it's that many? I mean, maybe Washington state is clear, or Michigan, hell, even Maine."

Sarah shrugged. "I'm just going off what I heard before the base in Denver fell."

Ben, wanting to focus on the task at hand, scratched his stubbly beard. "Dan, you said earlier the signal was coming from the northwest. Does that mean the base for sure?"

"Let me..., let you...., take a guess," Dan drawled out, already laying out the general direction.

"Yeah," Ben replied. "I figured as much. Just making sure."

"Yup," Dan said, lighting a cigarette. This time around, no one complained as the smoke rolled around the cabin.

"Cameras washed out. Damn fog," Adam spoke up, still trying to adjust its contrast to get some type of image through the fog.

"Well, I guess that's it for the night. The way I see it, the fog might just be what helps us out in the morning. As soon as we get a hint of daylight, we can move without being seen," Ben spoke up, cutting through everyone's wondering minds. People had a tendency to do that when they were a combination of tired and nervous.

"I'm calling John," Dan informed the group, picking up the radio.

After ten more minutes of planning for the morning, Ban and Sarah headed back to the Tacoma, taking their time to listen to any other external threats. Luckily for the group, the sensors were easily calibrated to detect motion. While the range had been cut back significantly, they still had one hundred feet of room to scan.

Ben opened the door for his wife as she grinned, waiting to get inside to talk. "Such a gentleman," she joked as the stressed look on Ben's face pushed her to lean over grabbing his chin, pulling him into a light kiss.

"You think they're alive?" Ben asked out of nowhere.

"Those two. For sure. I know what you're thinking."

Ben smiled, his teeth showing. "You sure about that? Your clothes are still on."

"No time for love, Dr. Jones," she joked, leaning back in her seat.

Ben sighed, doing the same, letting his head bounce on the headrest. "That we have a problem, and we need to figure out what's going on?"

"Yeah. I know we agree. John got really quiet on the radio when Dan told him about the situation. It almost sounds like he wants to go back west."

Sarah shrugged. "You're thinking too much into it."

"Maybe you're right. It's just that thing with Kelly. That whole situation seemed off. He's a great guy. I just don't understand him sometimes."

"He took Kelly away when she was about to turn and handled the situation. That's not easy for anyone. You know, I understand you're stressed out. We all are. It's the end of the world, honey. We are the aliens now," Sarah waxed poetic.

Ben took a breath so deep his stomach almost touched the steering wheel. "We're going to go get those two. And..., I'm going to make sure this doesn't happen again."

"Sexy," Sarah gushed, picking on the man. "Let's not play like we know that something happened in Tallahassee. Those people....., You know they're the leftover, and they somehow got their hands on Dustin and Tina."

Ben stared at the foggy road in front of them. "Oh yeah. It's those assholes for sure. I just didn't want to say it out loud. Hey," Ben supposed, with an air of confidence. "You think that lady I left there without an ear has anything to do with this?"

"You mean Amanda? Probably. I told you not to underestimate her."

"Why is it everyone I meet at some point makes things go to shit? I mean, I gave her a chance. No one saw Jim coming. It's like we're in a fish bowl with only a handful of fish."

Sarah reflected on the statement, realizing Ben was carrying everything that had happened to them and the others on his shoulders as well. She looked at the man she was in love with, taking in how strong and massive he was. Muscles bulged from Ben's uniform, his hands able to tear a person apart if needed, gently rested on the bottom of the steering wheel.

"It's all of us know. We take care of our people," Sarah huffed. "Shit, I never thought I'd say something out of one of your movies."

"In the morning, we'll get home and figure out what to do. The more I think about it, the more I want to just stay home. But," Ben pursed his lips. "This time. This time," he repeated. "I'm going to take charge of things. No more group decisions. I'm going to call the shots."

Ben leaned over, opened the glove box, and grabbed a small flask. Unscrewing the lid, he took a swig of whiskey from it, the tangy smell catching Sarah's attention. He reached the flask over as Sarah took it, following suit.

The sharp bite of the high-proof whiskey made the woman shiver as she breathed out. "I don't see how you drink that stuff, but I understand. The burn is a," she took a breath. "it's the toll you pay for the reward. "

Ben smiled. "That's it babe. It's the end of the world, and

I feel fine. All those whiskey connoisseurs preaching about the taste. At the end of the world, it's Crown Royal...," Ben drawled out the royal. "that beat them all. All those people praising a fancy label. Total bullshit."

The conversation was one of reflection and also knowing the moment would soon be replaced with the chaos of the undead world quickly surrounding them.

CHAPTER 9

The Fog of War

A n alarm chimed, pulling Ben and the others back to reality. While Ian had pulled the last security shift, Eve was surgical with her wake-up calls.

Yawning, Ben stretched, almost pushing into Sarah. She rolled her shoulders, smacking her lips, pushing the pasty taste out of her mouth. Still covered under the veil of night, the fog had thickened over the past couple of hours due to the water being warmer than the cool air that had flowed up the river.

"Eve," Ben said as Dan's voice came over the radio.

"You guys up?" Dan asked as Ben keyed the handheld.

"Yup. We should be ready to move in five. Seeing if Eve has anything to say," Ben noted as Eve chirped to life.

"Good morning. The temperature is fifty-nine degrees. With the current density of moisture in the air, we should have sufficient cover to exit the bridge. This includes the sound-dampening effect of the fog. I suggest switching both vehicles to electrical operation until we reach San Jose. How about some light, easy listening?"

"No Eve. It's time to work. Any movement from the sensors?"

"No. I also calibrated the sound function embedded in the sensors, and there are no alerts," Eve replied as Sarah handed Ben a cup of water and his toothbrush. "Thanks, babe," Ben said, talking as he started brushing his teeth. "You...get...us ...a cup....of coffee..., and I'll cook dinner tonight."

Sarah grinned, pulling two water-activated heater bags out of the small pack between her legs. "On the way. Oh, and you're totally cooking dinner."

Within five minutes, both vehicles were primed and ready to go. Adam had slowly turned the MRAP around, now directly behind Ben's trusty Toyota.

"Do they think they heard us?" Adam asked over the radio while Ben shook his head, responding thoughtfully. "No. I would think we would have known by now. Do I think they're watching? Yes."

On those words, the dark black of the pre-dawn sky morphed into a deep purple. It was time to go. "Heading out," Ben said, giving Adam enough room to pull around him, taking the lead once again.

Not able to see more than ten feet in front of their vehicles, Adam was moving at a blistering five miles per hour. With no lights on and needing to keep as silent as possible, Ben's nerves were starting to electrify his body once again.

"Dan, can you see anything up there?" Ben asked, barely able to make the man's silhouette out in the gunner's turret.

"I sure as shit can't see through this soup, but I can hear things shuffling around. I have a feeling we drew a slow-moving crowd last night that, if I was a betting man, the rotters are stuck on the other side of the bridge.

"Great," Sarah huffed. "We have a good hour before the sun's fully up. They stay out for a few hours past sunrise. You think we should stop once we hit San Marco?"

"No, we keep moving unless we can't," Ben followed. Thoughts of Dustin and Tina starting to solidify in his mind.

"You plan on going back out once we get settled back home?" Sarah asked in the form of a statement.

"Yup. I want to get John and these weapons situated. Not sure from there, but something is not right. I think you said it last night."

"What? That it could be the leftovers from out west?"

"Precisely that. Think about it. They somehow got their hands on Dustin and Tina and are here trying to find us. Revenge is a fickle bitch, or something along those lines," Ben said, refocusing on the quickly thinning fog.

A metal clank signified they had finally passed over the bridge. Red lights hazed in front of them as Adam quickly hit the brakes, bringing the MRAP to a stop.

"What's up?" Ben asked as Dan replied. The sound of him lighting up a smoke before talking came through the truck's speakers.

"Zombies. A dam pile of them. Slow movers, all piled up by our exit. The Westbound lanes blocked as you know so....," Dan drawled.

Adam cut in before Ben could respond. "I think we can plow through them. You have that new grill. I can't see past the turnoff, but this thing will get us through a bunch of slow movers."

Slow movers, generally referred to as zombies, near the end of their undead life cycle. Slow, cumbersome, and, in most cases, already falling apart. They were significantly easier to push out of the way, or as Adam called them, *crunchy speed bumps.*

Ben keyed the mike. "I say we go slow. We plow through

them, and it could make all kinds of noise. If it gets too bad, we'll jamb it in reverse."

"Sounds like a plan," Adam replied. In the background, Ian spoke up. "It's the only plan."

Not needing any further fancy timelines or details, Adam started to veer into the eastbound lane, heading toward the exit ramp.

"You think…" Ben was cut off by the first slunk of something being pushed out of the way in front of them. Glancing to their right, a hand grasped through the fog as if grabbing for them just out of reach, only to disappear again. The still purple sky made the scene resemble a nightmarish trip.

Several more thumps and a pop snapped to their left as if in stereo as several more bodies faded into the mid-morning light. The next thud twirled like a drunken ballerina spinning and turning directly in front of Ben and Sarah as they bath leaned back in their seat.

With only one arm and a still angry set of eyes, the zombie Adam had just pushed out of the way turned and was now directly in front of their truck. Ben gently tapped the accelerator as the grill pushed the creature back, only to have it reset itself.

"Looks at its eyes. It's like it's staring at us," Sarah said, not taking her eyes off the several more figures rolling to their right and left.

"Was," Ben mumbled as he pressed forward, only for the momentum of the truck to catch the creature and pull it under the truck. Unlike the heavily armored military vehicle in front of them, the Toyota rocked like it had just run over a large speed bump.

The wet crack of the zombie's skull made Ben clinch his teeth while they continued to drive forward, pressing closer to the MRAP. Ben coughed lightly, clearing his throat.

"It reminds me of driving through the fire heading to Tallahassee. It was like they knew what was going to happen but didn't care," he sourly reminded.

"Just keep going," Sarah replied as Adam's voice came through the truck's speakers.

"They're getting thick. I'm turning right."

Ben hugged his truck so close to the massive beast of war in front of them that the bumpers almost touched. The sensation of the truck moving down the onramp finally eased his nerves.

No longer seeing the random zombies being pushed out of the way, things changed as Adam took a sharp right onto San Marco.

The fog lifted, revealing the undead shuffling along the roadside, resembling swaying branches. It wasn't that there were thousands or even hundreds, but it all went back to the fact that the creatures had a sort of sixth sense.

Something was pulling them out of the road and back into the cover of shade out of the sun. This was what they had deemed as shadowing. In some instances, they witnessed zombies doing odd things that were likely related to their past lives.

Actions such as trying to get into a car or checking their watches came to mind when having the conversation. On one occasion, Ben had been convinced some of them still remembered how to open doors.

"Looks like they're mostly in the fog," Adam said, picking up the pace.

"Any signs of the people we saw last night?" Ben asked, pulling back slightly, creating space between the two vehicles.

"Nothing from up here," Dan added.

John's voice added to the conversation. "Good to hear you

all made it off the bridge." They had, of course, been monitoring the conversation, leaving the radio clear in case the small convoy needed to talk while moving.

"Looks clear. A few stragglers, but their heading out of the open areas," Ben glanced up, seeing blue skies with no traces of clouds starting to push the clouds away from the coast line several miles away.

"Sounds good. We'll have the gate open. Sam and Nicole are by the water in case they hear any boats or noise from up North," John relayed.

Sarah stretched beside Ben. "I didn't sleep for shit last night."

"Same here," Ben echoed. "Once we get back, we'll see where things are. I'm betting John's already making plans to head out."

Sarah nodded as Eve put on light jazz. Ben took in a deep breath, seeing the smudge marks on not only his hood but the back sides of Adam's truck. He truly wanted to know how many of the undead had been on the bridge.

After an hour of uninterrupted driving, the unassuming turn-off to the Sanctuary was as bland and hidden as always. With the spring season now heading into full-on summer, leaves, and deep green foliage concealed the turnoff. If you didn't know it was there, you would simply drive by. They would come out later and cover any tire tracks visible from the road if needed. Since it hadn't rained in a week, it wasn't as much of a concern.

John and Allison stood by the gate as Sam and Nicole ran up, having been by the water. The look on their faces told Ben that the front of the MRAP was significantly gorier than the rear.

"Dam, I was only thinking you ran into a handful?" John asked as the group dismounted their vehicles.

Embedded in Ben's truck's newly installed brush grill was

a tattered shirt proclaiming Jaguar's playoff champions, ripped from the one straggler that danced its way in front of them.

"We couldn't see them all," Adam noted, also taking in the mess. "I can tell you they were thinning out pretty quick."

"They're going somewhere," Ben said, pulling out his knife and cutting off the remaining shirt before throwing it outside the main gate. "Let's get the trucks washed, then hit the house." Shifting gears, he turned to Dan. "Can you hook that tracker up to Eve and see if we can get the information you pulled on a map overlay?"

"Eve?" Dan asked as the AI chirped to life, still coming over Ben's truck speakers.

"Yes, we should be able to integrate the system."

"Sounds like a plan," Ben added, turning to John. While adrenaline was still coursing through his veins, the thought of people, not a group of people so close, was starting to become his main focus. "Anyone key the radio up since last night?"

"No. I also took a log of the times they have. It seems to be fairly consistent. Not on the minute, but close, give or take five minutes."

"That means it's likely not an automated signal," Dan stated, closing the main gate.

"It also sounds like they're trying to figure out our location. I know that transponder thingy helps, but I also know there's military equipment out there that is just as if not more effective."

"Yup," Dan said. Shelly and Sarah started unloading the secured medicine as Dan walked over, focusing on his prize. The pile of cigarettes secured in the back of Ben's truck was well worth the trip in the man's mind.

Sam walked from the side of Ben's house, pulling the several-foot-long hose behind her. Ian ran up, helping her as she saw his disheveled hair. "Save the day?"

"Maybe," the young man grinned. "We found some pretty heavy weapons at the camp. The place is like a gold mine."

"Yeah," John turned. "Let me see them?"

Ben opened the camper top as John let out a low whistle. "They had more?"

"Yeah. A lot more. If it weren't for those people, I'd say we go back out. Maybe take the boat and some golf carts."

Knowing the kind of firepower the two weapons held, John smiled. "You could cut an army of those dam things down with those."

"That's what Dan said," Ben added, helping to unload the several cases of ammunition.

CHAPTER 10

Blind

Dustin and Tina

Tina felt the throbbing start before the aches as she slowly refocused on reality. After talking with Amanda, it had become quickly evident their food had been laced with drugs to knock the two out once again.

"You awake?" Tina slapped her mouth, again the sandpaper feeling of not drinking water turning to paste on her tongue.

"Yeah. How you feeling?" Dustin asked, handing her a cup of water.

"Like I got hit by a truck. Where are we?" Her eyes started to focus on the slated metal walls and hard wooden floor.

"In a shipping container. Looks like there's AC, and they left us food and water."

"I'm not eating another dam thing they give us," Tina said before swishing the water around her mouth before spitting it out.

"It's okay. I drank some an hour ago. I wanted to let you sleep."

On those words, Tina downed the entire bottle without question. She trusted Dustin, and if he was okay, she knew he had likely tested the same water before handing it over.

"They moved us. I was out but started waking up a while ago. I believe we're on the back of a truck. Before I fully came to, I could tell we were moving along pretty fast. And it's been another two hours. We stopped about thirty minutes ago," Dustin explained, also handing her a chunk of bread. "I checked it also."

Tina ravaged the bread as if it was her last meal. The truth of the matter was that Amanda and the others had kept them drugged for the better part of five days. She looked down, seeing the pile of food Dustin had ingested.

"They want us alive. I mean, we didn't really tell them much," Tina noted as Dustin shook his head.

"They're looking for the others and what we told them about the FEMA bunkers. We gave them that much as to why we were out. I have a feeling that whoever was not let in the underground shelters isn't too happy about it."

"Yeah, and Ben shot her ear off, or whatever happened," Tina was starting to come around. The mix of food and water focusing her mind.

"Remember what Amanda said. They had a way of finding people and where they were from. I'm not sure that's the full truth, but I think they can likely narrow it down to the county. We were moving fast. If I was to guess, we were on Interstate 10 heading East to Jacksonville."

"Shit, and we missed the second radio check-in. You think the others are out looking for us?" Tina asked, grabbing the rest of the loaf of bread.

"No. Ben and the others are level-headed for the most part. If they don't know where we went missing, they'll hang tight. Worried, yes, but I don't think they'll just randomly go looking for us."

"They know we made it to Tallahassee. Oh shit. Are they listening to us?" Tina supposed, looking around the container."

"I don't think so. While this thing's hooked up to power, I looked around earlier. I know where to check. I just don't think we should talk in specifics, just in case. I already figure they have the radios and have been trying to use them. We didn't have time to delete the channels. They for sure have heard them on the radio."

Trying to stand up, Tina's legs felt as if she had been on a boat for weeks and just hit dry land. Finally, she stood fully up. The conex had, at one point, been used as a field construction office, even including a small bathroom. Walking toward it, Dustin grabbed Tina's hand.

"It's hooked up to a small tank, likely on the outside of the container. If you can, try to use the bucket I sat in there. If they don't open this thing, we'll need the water in it."

While disgusting, Tina had learned from Dustin that when in a survival situation, you need as many options as possible. If that included drinking old toilet water, as long as it was clean and able to keep them moving, then so be it. Tina wasn't as hardened or used to the austere conditions as her husband, who also happened to be a former operator in an Army Special Forces unit.

"What's the plan?" Tina asked, walking out of the small, walled-off bathroom, having used the bucket.

"We hang tight. Get our strength back. Find what we can use here as a weapon, then figure it out from there. I heard voices when I was waking up, so they're around."

Tina walked around the edges of the conex interior, finally seeing a ray of light dimly peeking through a corner of the door. The dull light inside the space did not tell what time it was. That was the thing Dustin knew how to handle. Being disoriented was precisely what their captures were trying to force upon the two.

"Put your hand on the walls and roof. You'll be able to tell where the suns at for the most part," Dustin recalled. "Also, listen for birds. They chirp in the morning at a much higher rate. If we're by water, which almost everything is in Florida, listen for things like the tide. Put all that together plus that little sliver of light, and we should be able to figure out what time it is, at least."

While seemingly pointless, these were the types of things an average person didn't consider. Dustin wasn't a normal person. His training was far beyond anything Amanda could comprehend.

"Got it. What time do you think it is?" Tina asked as Dustin pointed at the roof.

"Feel it. Noon, if I was a betting man."

Muffled voices came from outside as Dustin lowered his voice. "I don't want to make any moves till we figure out what's going on. Worst-case scenario, we rush them. I'm not sure they know what we are fully capable of."

"Did they take our or your clothes off?" Tina asked, making a good point. Dustin had some rather telling tattoos on his back and shoulders, including a Special Forces crest on his chest.

"When did you actually start listening to me?" Dustin asked, surprised by how critically his wife was thinking. He had discussed this with her during a late night about how operators needed to be careful about identifying tattoos, advice they mostly ignored.

Tina smiled lightly, taking another sip of water after touching the roof and picking up a small pack of stale crackers. "Ten minutes ago," she replied, the statement giving them a momentary break from the reality around them as they smiled at each other.

"No. They shook us down, but I can tell they didn't take my shirt off. You?"

"Same. No changes to the bra marks," she stated as the voices stopped in front of the door.

"Don't act to awake. They will see we ate the food, but don't let them know you are fully alert in case we need to fight," Dustin instructed as Tina nodded.

After the click and clack of a chain lock being opened, light poured into the small space like a death ray, forcing the two to shield their eyes.

Amanda's voice reached them first, followed by Bill, also known as Billy the Kid, who stepped in beside her. The younger man was a wall of mass beside Amanda. Muscle stacked on slabs of muscle, ready to spring into action at a moment's notice. Having played college football, he had been one of the first on the scene to help Amanda, not making it to the bunkers.

"Back up to the wall," Bill ordered, ensuring they saw the shotgun he was holding. In a space that small, it didn't matter how you moved. If he fired, they were sure to get a handful of pellets implanted in their bodies, if not an appendage unwantedly removed.

Dustin and Tina backed up, squinting against the sudden burst of light. Amanda took the final step into the conex beside Bill. "I hope you found the food acceptable. We will be feeding you once a day. I suggest you eat it as you did here."

Dustin held his tongue, not wanting to ask questions. The more she talked. The more they knew. She started back up. "Now that we have that out of the way, I want to discuss what I need from you in more detail. You see, I know you were traveling with Ben and the others. Yes, I know who he is. I asked you once. This time, I will need a more specific answer."

Dustin started picking her words apart. She had clearly

taken them East, knowing the general area and direction but not the precise location. The man could work with this piece of information.

Dustin put his hand down, letting the light wash over his face. The shadows standing in front of him as he finally focused. "They're in the Jacksonville area."

Tina's heart started racing., not knowing where Dustin was going with this. She also trusted the man in these types of situations more than anyone else she could think of.

"While that's a start to build trust, I need to know where," she followed, venom in her voice this time. She was riding the edges of revenge and obsession in her words. Dustin also supposed those around her could see this.

"That's going to be a little tricky. They move around," Dustin followed as Amanda clicked her tongue on the roof of her mouth.

"We have your radios. They are at a place called the Sanctuary. You have very concerned friends. Friends that are on the road as we speak looking for you." While Amanda was bluffing, she was indeed aware of the vehicles traveling south on Highway 17 heading south. The one thing Ben had gotten right was they had already left to report back before they passed back through, not being seen on the bridge.

Dustin took in a breath, giving him room to think. "I wouldn't know. Listen," Dustin again started. This time, making the conversation more personal. "I know you recognize Tina. We weren't around those people till the city burned. Even then, I would use the term around loosely." There was some truth to his statement as they left shortly after joining Ben and the others showing on his face.

"It doesn't sound like it to me. They've either called or keyed the radio every six hours or so. Why?" Amanda asked. Bill rolled his shoulders, waving the shotgun barrel in Tina's general direction. Dustin didn't like the way this was starting to go.

Dustin figured half-truths were better than lying. The woman in front of him was perceptive. "We did hang around them for a while but left. We set up times to check in every couple of weeks to keep in touch."

Amanda stared through Dustin's soul, not blinking, as she slowly nodded. "I see. So you missed the radio check, and they are concerned?"

"Yes," Dustin replied as she turned to Tina.

"You. I know you were expelled from the city. Is that everything we need to know?" Amanda asked. Dustin didn't look at his wife, keeping laser-focused on the shotgun.

"We were becoming friends with them. I know they didn't mean to hurt you," Tina stated. She had heard Ben's story on several occasions. What she wasn't saying was the fact that she had started the fires that burnt the city, drawing in the undead. "I don't want to get involved in this either way. They are people who helped us. I don't have any loyalty to them."

The truth was, she did. She had grown close to Shelly and even the others, regardless of her at times hardened exterior—a wall she had built since being on her own without Dustin.

"Which reminds me," Amanda cocked her head. "Why were you in the city when it was attacked? Yes, I don't believe all that happened by some ordained event."

This caught both Dustin and Tina off guard. While she had walked Dustin through most of what happened, there were still several pieces that she had yet to explain. She had not only started the fire but killed dozens of people, living people in the process. This was something she wasn't proud of.

Picking up on Dustin's half-truths, Tina opted to follow his lead. "I always stayed close to the city. I'm sure you already know that. Well, until I headed to Jacksonville. When the walls and gates started getting overran, I didn't have much of anywhere to go. The countryside was burning, and the zombies were everywhere. It was like someone had led them there."

"That's the way it appears to have happened. It happened just as Ben was there getting Sarah, his wife," she emphasized the word *wife*, referring to Sarah. "Who else was with Ben and the others?"

Dustin knew Amanda was fishing and had reached the limits of her information. This was to Dustin's point. He always explained to Tina about listening to the questions being asked to build walls around what the other party truly knew.

He spoke up, taking the conversation back over. "Ben, Sarah, a young kid named Ian, Shelly, and Dan, who I'm sure you already are aware of," Dustin paused, remembering she had heard voices on the radio. Voices that likely included John, someone whose voice she obviously knew all too well. This was his chance to build some level of trust. "And John. I believe he used to work on one of your teams."

Tina glanced at Dustin. Again, while she trusted him, she didn't like him giving up all the people they were with. "Oh," Dustin continued. "There were a bunch of other folks that they communicated with nearby. I, well, we don't know much about them. We left."

Tina picked up on Dustin, exaggerating the possible threat. Amanda tilted her head, flexing her jaw as the leather strap over her ear shifted. For thirty seconds, no words were spoken.

Amanda reached over, lowering the barrel of Bill's shotgun. "Thank you for the conversation. I'll have fresh water and food brought in as long as we can talk openly like this. You'll find your current situation improving. If not," she again cocked her head.

Dustin raised his head high. "I'd say thank you, but the longer we're in here, the longer I don't see it that way."

Amanda glanced at Bill, shifting her eyes back to Dustin. "If you've lied to us, then I don't see it matters either way. If you are locked in here, there's no getting out. I know you were prior military. Andrew, on our team, processed your wife. You understand that liabilities are no longer a risk worth taking. For now, we will talk as needed. Once we have completed what we are doing, we can discuss your future. If there is a future."

This wasn't a threat but rather a promise. They were there not only to find the FEMA bunkers but also to eliminate Ben and the others. Amanda was satisfied with the truthfulness and information received from the conversation.

A red-headed younger man walked in with a whole tray of fresh food and water. He spoke up while sitting the tray down, "The food is good."

Amanda scowled at the man's positive demeanor before talking one last time: "If we need you to rest, I'll let you know so there are no more surprises. See, we can be civil."

On those words, the three walked out of the trailer, followed by the clang and click of the lock being secured on the outside door.

Dustin held his hand up for several minutes before finally lowering it to talk. "Keep it low. Let's eat."

Tina scooted the tray closer to the far end of the container. "Why did you tell them all that?"

"They already knew most of it. What they don't know is how many people are around here and precisely where. I planted the seed that there may be a few more folks running around. I'm sure John was on the radio, and she knew it. I wanted to let her know we can be trusted," Dustin grinned, pointing at the food.

"So what's next?" Tina asked, satisfied with Dustin.

"We get the hell out of here and get to the others first. I'm not saying it's going to be easy, but I'm working through the how. Did you notice that kid Andrew? He didn't seem on board with the situation here."

"I noticed that. Like he was just here helping out, we both know there were a ton of good people in Tallahassee, just living. You think we should take him out?" Tina asked

"Maybe take him with us. It's a gamble. I can likely get us out of here either way, given enough time. The door may be locked up, but the hinges aren't," Dustin pointed at the large, bolted hinges with thick bolts holding the door up. "Just need to figure out the how. Eat up. Everything you can, even if you're full. We need our energy."

CHAPTER 11

Ways

The early morning sun glistened off the small inlet as birds chirped in the distance. Unlike the day prior, the dense early morning fog had quickly exited, leaving the still calm waters reflecting the sky.

Ben sipped his coffee, listening for any noise being carried down the river. He sighed, feeling the weight of his pistol hanging off his hip. Since others had joined him, his early morning walks on his dock to relieve himself in the inlet in nothing more than a robe were a thing of the past.

The majority of the prior day had been spent resting and unloading the vehicles after some much-needed cleaning. Today, they would make plans to address the current situation.

After briefing the group on the current state of affairs, John and Nicole had opted to stay put and join the local search. A search that Ben figures would likely become more of a fight by the time it was all said and done.

Glancing to the house to his left, Dan walked out, also enjoying a calming morning cup of go juice. "We still good for eight?" Dan asked, just loud enough to hear. Ben gave him a thumbs up, walking back into the kitchen.

Sarah sat at the table, eating a bowl of cereal with

rehydrated powdered milk while watching reruns of The Office on the wall-mounted TV from their extensive library.

"Anything?" she asked as milk lightly dribbled off her chin. Ben sat down, pushing the cereal away. He needed a stiff drink to get him going—something he found himself doing on days such as this.

"Nothing. The sensors are good as well. I checked them first thing. I didn't realize we picked up the ones with built-in cameras. Those things are going to save us a lot of hassle."

"Hassle until something shows up," Sarah reminded Ben.

Eve took the opportunity to speak up. "We had twenty-two minor events, including a cat and several small rodents outside the fence. The noise detection on the sensors picked up no unnatural noises. Might I recommend some classical music to stimulate your mind?"

Ben smiled. "Yeah, sure. Keep it low." Beethoven started playing lightly in the background as John and Nicole knocked on the back door, having walked over a few minutes prior to the meeting.

"Hey guys," Ben greeted John as he reached out to shake his hand.

"Morning," John replied, looking at the cereal and seeing his favorite, Golden Grahams. "Mind if I grab a bowl?"

"Help yourself," Sarah gestured.

"I saw Ian and Sam heading this way. Adam and Allison are also out front talking about something. It sounded heated," John cautioned, taking a seat.

Ian and Sam arrived next, followed by Dan and Shelly, all avoiding Adam and Allison's heated discussion out front. Ben switched the TV to the digital map. Eve had spent all day overlaying with the signal from the signal tracker.

"Think we should wait on Adam and Allison?" Ian asked.

His youth, not catching up to the fact that when grown adult couples argued, you gave them space.

"No," Ben huffed. "They'll be in. They know we're all here by now. Dan, tell us what we are looking at."

Dan stood up, walking to the large, flat wall-mounted screen. "Eve analyzed the signal readings from both Fleming Island and the bridge. Luckily, we did both, or we wouldn't have been able to get this close. I think we already figured this, but the radio is smack dab in the middle of NAS JAX."

Eve chimed in. "There is a ninety-nine percent probability. The data is accurate. The two readings gave us the ability to triangulate the signal."

"Got it," Ben said, refocusing on Dan. "I know they heard us. They had to. Any ideas from anyone on why they keep using the radio?"

John pointed at the counter where the tracker sat, plugged into Eve's laptop. "Maybe they're doing the same to us."

Ben and some of the others had discussed this yesterday before crashing for well over twelve hours.

"Yeah. That's a thought. I'm just not sure these things are lying around everywhere. The more I think about it, the more I'm convinced they have Dustin and Tina and are baiting us to slip up. Give something away," Ben pondered to the group.

Sam spoke up, popping the tab off a Coke. "I wouldn't trust anything you hear over that thing. They may use them as bait."

While a valid point, the group knew how tough Dustin and Tina were. "Maybe. We'll keep an eye on that."

"No, wait. She may be onto something," Nicole raised her hand as if asking for permission to go to the bathroom. "What if we do just that?"

"Do what?" John asked as Ben started to get her point.

Nicole continued. "Either tell them we are going to be somewhere and, well…, not be, but be watching, or call them out and let them know, we know, they know."

Ben grinned. "I think we need to look at that as an absolute option. If we can keep them in a certain area, we might be able to handle them. Control the situation."

"Or, if they're keeping Dustin and Tina on the base, we can go get them," Ian added to a round of head nods.

Just then, Adam and Allison walked into the kitchen. They both wore neutral expressions.

"What's up?" Ben asked as Adam side-eyed Allison.

Adam spoke up, looking down at his shoes. "I'm not sure we're ready for all this. We're going to set this one out."

Ben looked surprised by this, as did the others. "We'll need someone to stay here, of course."

Allison cut in this time. "No. I mean, we want to get back home in case these people head that way."

Not fully believing the statement, Ben nodded. "It's your choice. You've done so much for us already."

Relief lightly washed over the two's faces. It was clear one wanted to stay, and one wanted to leave for the lot.

"Maybe we can talk some more," Adam noted, identifying him as the one who wanted to stay and help.

"That's fine. Let us know. We could use the MRAP, but the new weapons we found will help out," Sarah added, not wanting to push them any further.

Ben sipped his refreshed cup of coffee. "We could always get another MRAP from Fleming Island. Take the boat over and get one working."

Adam looked at his feet, knowing they had just thrown a wrench in the plans. "We have a copy of the service booklet. I believe we have another one back home as well."

Allison nodded. "Least we can do."

"It's not a bad idea. They won't see us coming across the Buckman, so we can take that off the board. I would feel better hitting the river if needed either way," John added.

"We can pick up more weapons there," Ben said, remembering the stacks of crates. "They have a little of everything."

"Maybe we can get them toward the overpass., or the mall area?" Sarah added.

"Or in one of the neighborhoods surrounding the island. It would give us quick access to the river," Sarah said as the resemblance of a plan was forming.

For the next thirty minutes, they worked through the logistics of the plan. They also had a pontoon boat rigged to carry golf carts and other items if needed. The trick was to go across undetected, which would mean hitting the river while it was raining.

The radio was another point of contention they were struggling to agree on. Ben, Sarah, Dan, and Shelly suggested throwing them off while making the run for more equipment and heading toward the base, while John, Nicole, Ian, and Sam wanted to ambush the group.

While not wholly split on the suggestion, the group started forming a mix of the two plans. John and Nicole offered to scout the base, while the other would call in a meet-up area to either ambush or observe just how big the group they were up against was.

Ben leaned back after finishing his third cup of go juice, not wanting to caffeinate himself further into a crazed madman. "This plan has potential. I'd rather observe first, but if an opportunity presents itself, we take it." He turned to Dan. "They had small mortars and some rocket-propelled grenades. You know how to use all that stuff?"

"I mean…," Dan drawled out. "It can't be that hard. They also have Claymores. I sure as shit know how to use those."

"Yeah," Ben spoke up. "I learned how to set those up while filming Night Soldiers."

"That was a kick-ass movie," Ian said, speaking up for the first time in several minutes.

Ben smiled. "Sucked making it, but that is one of the places I learned how to use most of this military gear."

Dan smacked his pockets, looking for a smoke, as Sarah shot him a warning look. "Habit. Sorry. I say we can figure it out. It may take a day or so. We can grab the gear and then find a place away from the base to use it. If I were in the area, I would eventually find that place."

Dan was making a good point. "We can find a place a mile or two away off the main roads," Ben suggested.

"The railroad tracks. There's one close to the island. It's a perfect way to maneuver. We just need to be able to get back to the water. Think about it. If something happens and we disappear on the river, it will give them a good idea of where to start looking," Sarah added, pausing in thought. "Black Creek. We can go up Black Creek, then find one of those neighborhoods close to the railroad tracks.".

"Maybe we can get another boat to take to the base," John said, referring to the jet skis they had acquired.

"The more, the better. I never thought about Black Creek. Perfect idea. We just need cover and an easy way to get out of dodge. Eve," Ben shifted as the AI chimed to life.

"Yes?"

"Can you calculate the probability of it raining or figure out how to access a random weather satellite? It doesn't have to be a local one," Ben suggested, knowing that the satellites overhead were quickly losing functionality.

"While I have not been able to access weather tracking data, I may be able to tie into a weather imagery satellite. It will not give us much data, but may provide cloud data."

"So you're saying if we see the clouds, we can likely predict rain?" Ben asked.

"It's Florida," Eve replied, waiting for the punchline to land.

"Was that a joke?" Ben inquired.

"Yes. My probability computations suggest that it is a joke based on reality."

The group chuckled as Eve let a light beep loose. "I will start working on linking with various systems. I will be offline for several hours. All security protocol will still be functional."

"Jump on it, weatherman," Ben concluded.

"When are you two leaving?" Sarah followed.

"We'll stay until tomorrow. I'm guessing you are all doing this sooner rather than later," Adam said, still looking unhappy with the decision.

Ben scanned the room. "Any objections to making the call tomorrow and heading out that afternoon? We still need to figure out who will stay here."

CHAPTER 12

I'm just doing my job

Dustin and Tina

The cool night settled in as Tina shuffled closer to Dustin. While the air conditioner was on during the day, they left the system running at night. Moisture clung to the walls of the metal conex, creating a light sheen to the room.

"I guess they forgot dinner," Tina said as Dustin wrapped his arm around her.

"Maybe. They're likely eating first. We haven't heard much today."

Dustin leaned forward, inspecting the makeshift wedge he was crafting from the bathroom door handle. Dustin planned to test it on the main entrance hinges when the guards next opened the door, aiming to avoid getting caught.

Just as the words left his mouth, the sounds of the chains being unraveled clunked against the door.

"Back up in there," Andrew instructed. It was the young, indifferent man Dustin had been talking about earlier.

"We're back," Dustin replied as the door lightly swung open. The butt of a shotgun poked through as another guard trained his weapon on the far end of the container.

"Here you go. Stew," Andrew lightly grinned, confirming their prior thoughts on the young man.

"What's in the stew?" Dustin asked, working to build rapport.

"You know. Stew is in the stew." Andrew let a light joking huff out.

"Hurry up in there." The more serious guard ordered.

"One minute," Andrew called back. "I'll leave water by the door."

"Hey man," Dustin started. "You know where we are?"

"NAS Jax."

"No talking in there," The guard again reinforced, not entering the room, looking back to someone talking to him from the outside.

This was good. Too good, Dustin thought. While it may take some time, every word counted. "Thanks Andrew. That's your name, right?" Dustin replied. Tina was letting him do all the talking.

"Yeah. You guys get some food in you. The boss wants to have another word with you in a couple of hours."

"Hey," the guard again gruffed.

"Just telling them the boss needs to talk to them," Andrew called back. "All clear, leaving the room."

On those words, the young man was gone; as the sounds of the chains being put back in place, a lock clattered against the outside door after being dropped.

"Well. I think you were right," Tina beamed, only to change her mood after seeing the self-described stew.

"It smells good enough," Dustin remarked. "Smells like they dumped a bunch of MREs in a can." MREs stood for Meals

Ready to Eat, or as Dustin always thought of them as shit blockers.

Designed for maximum caloric intake, the meals were made to slog through one's system like a drunk sloth on vacation. It could take days for a bowl movement if enough were consumed.

"No, I mean about the kid."

"Yeah, he's just here doing a job. A job I don't think he gives two shits about. If you ask me, I don't think they treat him all that well. You notice his eyes?" Dustin asked as Tina recalled his blazing blue windows to the soul.

"He looks smart. And in shape. Like he is smart enough to know this is stupid."

"Bingo. Plus, we know where we are. I wouldn't doubt they're going to try and get us on the radio at some point." Dustin supposed, only to be right once again as they would soon find out.

"You think the others know where we are?" Tina inquired, grabbing the gallon jug of water.

"If they went on that run Dan was talking about, there's a good chance they saw something out of place. We don't know how many vehicles are with us, but this thing doesn't sit in the back of a Pinto."

Tina chugged out of the gallon as water splashed on the edges of her mouth, running down her neck and to her chest. Dustin took in the woman he loved. Catching his eyes, she sat the jug down.

"What does all your training tell you about that?" she asked, now in a playful mood after knowing they were close to the Sanctuary.

Dustin's face was neutral, also knowing this meant the others could be in trouble. He smiled, smacking a slop of the yuck brown stew in his bowl. "That if your clothes are wet, you're better off taking them completely off and drying them out."

They both grinned as the conversation was cut short. The chains rattled on the door again, but unlike last time, the door swung open. Amanda stood beside Billy the Kid. Bill pulled up his shotgun, motioning for the other guard outside to bring in a small table.

"I see you are enjoying the stew," Amanda started. Please continue eating." The sound of the table thumping on the floor was followed by another guard carrying in their radios, a small tablet, and two speaker boxes.

"Do you want us to call the others?" Dustin asked, getting to the point. He was also scanning to see if Andrew was around. Standing behind the three guards now in the room, the young man held several zip ties and two bags. Amanda was ensuring the call would be made.

"Yes. I'm glad we're on such open terms here. Let me explain what is going to happen. Your friends have been calling or keying up that radio every couple of hours. I am going to have you read from a script, and from there, we will talk about furthering your comfort and accommodations."

It was clear she didn't know the true resolve of the two she held captive. It was also clear, however, to Dustin and Tina that Amanda was not playing and would rather throw them into a hoard of zombies instead of asking twice. This was likely how she treated her foot soldiers.

Dustin focused on the tablet connected by a USB cord to one of the radios. He recognized it as a cell phone signal tracker. Thoughts of Dan's tracker started coming to mind. What they had rigged up was a generic version of the tracker. While likely not as effective, Dustin figured it had got them in the general area.

Dustin took a sip of water, clearing the overly salted stew from his mouth. "What are you asking us to say?"

CHAPTER 13

Ground control to Major Ben

Maps lay sprawled out on the kitchen table as Sarah used Eve's main screen on the wall to mark areas. Doctor's Inlet Reserve, a small neighborhood located a few miles south of Whitey's Fish Camp, served as the ideal entry point for their plan.

Located half a mile south of County Road 220, the neighborhood was tucked away beside the railroad tracks. While not completely backed up to Black Creek, one would have to know the area to understand its geography and that it led out into the main river. A small bridge crossed the creek, providing cover and an easy escape route.

"There's a few two-story houses we can stage in," Sarah pointed out. "I say we use Whitey's as the location. Tell them it's our emergency meet point in case they can't respond but hear us."

Ben squinted at the screen. "It's perfect, with the bridge to Fleming Island nearby. They can get to it by water, and we can set up on the other side of the tributary coming off Doctors Inlet."

The body of water was considered an inlet directly off the

Saint Johns River. Whitey's Fish camp was not only a popular place to bar hop while on a boat but also a homage to the birthplace of Southern Rock, which happened to be the very area they were going.

Southern Rock hits like Sweet Home Alabama, and several of Lynard Skynyrd's greatest hits were written in a small shack called the Hell House on Black Creek. The only remaining reminder of the historic area was a small sign and slab of concrete. The Fish camp was also part of this, being a local haunt for the once-remaining members.

"We should be able to get to the Island from there as well. We didn't go that far West, but the images show it clearly until you get just past the neighborhood. It was like they were using the train tracks for transport," Dan added.

With Adam and Alison gone, the core group comfortably fit into the kitchen as everyone watched the plan unfold. John walked up, marking several areas along the bridge and adjacent shore lined with houses.

"If we choose to get after it, you can set two of those machine guns here and here." He marked two houses. Nicole and I can set up in one of the houses close to the mouth of the Inlet. We'll know what they're bringing to the fight and if Dustin and Tina are with them. If not, and it looks inviting, we can head to the base."

"And if they do have them, we let them know they're surrounded and go from there. If not, we take the risk and address the situation," Ben stated, meaning they would attack.

"What about the zombies? You know, trying to get some in the area?" Ian asked, making a good point.

"Hmph," Ben grumped. "It would not allow us to move fast. It could create a bottleneck. They'll be around either way if we try to do this while it's raining. We can leave early and try to get one of those MRAPs working if time permits. We run into zombies. We leave it for later."

"Who's staying here?" Samanatha asked, making a good point.

Ben and Sarah had discussed this beforehand and figured the fewer people who went, the less risk there would be. With their newfound stock of weapons and the likely element of surprise, they were planning on Samantha and Ian staying behind to secure the Sanctuary.

Ben cleared his throat. "I know you haven't been out much, but we want you and Ian to stay behind. With Adam and Allison gone, we talked about two people staying behind."

John glanced at Ben, who had not been part of his and Sarah's conversation. While this did not bother him, he had noticed Ben often making decisions without him. The truth of the matter was he appreciated the home the man had given him and Nicole.

Sam smiled. In all reality, the young woman had been out in the wild much longer than the others and enjoyed the rest. Ben turned to John, seeing the glance. "We were going to talk it over with the group, but it makes sense. Eve projected weather is coming this weekend, so we have to get moving."

"All good. Just wish those two stayed," John followed up.

Everyone nodded as Ian walked over to Sam, putting his arm around her waist. "We got this."

"Good," Ben continued. "We will be spread thin. I'm still not sold on splitting up."

John glanced at Nicole. "I think we can hang out for a few, and if things go south, we can head your way."

Nicole backed him up. "We could be there in a few minutes. It would be good to see what's heading your way."

Ben huffed, knowing they were right. If too many people were coming, they would dissolve into the shadows. "Agreed,"

Sarah spoke for the both of them."

"Dan?" Ban asked, making sure the plan and general assignments were in place. They would figure out the on-the-ground setup once they were there.

Shelly and Dan looked at each other. "We're good," Dan confirmed.

On those words, everyone settled back into planning the timeline. Within four hours, the plan was set. Within forty-eight hours, they would be leaving the protective walls of the sanctuary once again.

The radio message would be simple. If they could hear it but did not respond due to radio issues, they would meet at Whitey's Fish camp a day after leaving. This would give the group enough time to prepare for the unknown and gather more weapons.

Ben swirled the ice in his glass as the group started turning to leave. As with all things during the end of times, the radio chirped to life as Dustin's voice crackled through the speaker.

"Sanctuary, you copy?" Dustin said flatly. Static fizzed over the radio, and everyone in the room scrambled for no real reason. Dan finally grabbed the mic.

"Loud and a little clear. What's your status?" Dan asked as the rest of the room held their breath.

"A little bogged down but getting close to you. We ran into some trouble."

Dustin turned to Amanda, seeing her write new responses as the conversation developed. While he was sticking to the general script, she was making adjustments as they talked.

Dan glanced at Ben, who shook his head to let it play out. "Do we need to come to you?"

Dustin hesitated. "Possibly. Where are you guys currently located?"

Ben cocked his head, knowing this wasn't a typical question. Taking a deep breath, Dan replied, "Out. We've been grabbing a few things. We can link up at one of our rendezvous locations."

Dustin, knowing this wasn't a thing, smiled internally. They knew something was up, and they were playing along. Turning to Amanda, Dustin scribbled a few notes, telling her they had set locations, but he didn't know which one they were near. Amanda quickly scribbled a note telling the man to ask them about the general area.

"Good copy. We're southwest of the City, heading toward the Orange Park, Fleming Island area."

Ben nodded, understanding that Dustin was leading them in the general direction without revealing their exact location. They were right. Dustin and Tina were on the base. "Good copy. We can't get there for four days, but we can connect at the fish camp off the Inlet. We're out on a run."

A guard in the room with Amanda and the others stepped forward. "Whitey's Fish Camp."

Amanda glanced at Tina and Dustin as the two nodded without hesitation. Tina was, at this point, understanding what Dustin was thinking. This time, Ben spoke up. His voice sliced through Amanda's nerves like a sharp knife.

"We've been south and are now heading back north. What happened?" Ben asked, knowing that if Amanda was indeed there, his voice would trigger her. He was right.

Dustin paused as Amanda scribbled several notes. "Our radios went out. We finally got them fixed but decided to head east as we were set to anyways," Dustin had added, knowing it was false. We didn't find what we were looking for."

"That's a good copy. Be safe, and when you get closer, give

us a call. We'll check in at our normal cadence," Ben said, now forcing whoever was keeping them to have them on the radio at least once a day.

Amanda glared at Dustin, knowing he added that part. "Why did you say that?"

Leaning back, Tina spoke up, having been silent. "If our radios are working again, they would expect us to check in daily. We were supposed to be heading back over the next couple of weeks either way."

Amanda chewed on the statement. "I've had you for three weeks. You just got to the city. You took the risk for three weeks?" Her voice dictated this wasn't the time to bullshit, as Dustin took back over.

"We may be downplaying how close we have become with this group. You can tell by the conversation. We were also checking out the city. I've already told you about the FEMA bunkers. They don't know the conditions we encountered," Dustin added.

Amanda let the statement marinate in the air before talking again, also writing on the pad in front of them. "It sounds to me like you have a base of operation. Where is it?"

The one thing the others didn't fully know about Dustin, but Tina now fully understood, was that Dustin had been around a good portion of North Florida on his own exploring. He also knew several areas that could be secured in the same way as the Sanctuary.

"There's a Costco close to the interstate. The group had stayed there for some time before it was overrun. From there, Palatka."

He was referring to the small yet once-functioning shipping dock and warehouse John and Ben had taken out several zombies while securing the jet skis and dealing with the last intrusion on the Sanctuary. If checked, this would give

Amanda a trail to follow that showed people surviving and living on their own. If this dragged out longer than four days before they supposably met back up with the others, Dustin would lead them to a small encampment he found toward the beaches once filled with people he considered dangerous and not to be trusted. The man had addressed that situation. If needed, he would lead them on a wild goose chase.

Amanda slapped a map in front of him as he pointed toward the radio. "Go ahead," she hissed, feeling as if she was making headway.

"We'll check in tomorrow morning. We're going to head to the fish camp. Be safe out there," Dustin said as Ben closed the conversation.

"You too. We're on the road for a couple of days and will let you know if anything changes."

With that, the conversation was over. Ben stood straight in thought. "Four days."

John spoke first. "We need to move in the morning." He looked at the clock. It was getting close to dinner time.

Ben nodded. "I don't like this without hearing back from Adam and Allison, but I agree. Everyone else?"

Grunts of agreement followed as everyone started talking at once. There was not only planning to do but also getting ready for the morning trip. Sarah walked up beside Ben, grabbed his arm, gave it a light squeeze, and whispered in his ears while the others started talking through the rest of the evening.

"They're in trouble, and we need to help. I know what's going through your mind. Everyone in this room is more than capable and would do the same thing for you."

"Yup," Ben replied, smiling at his wife.

CHAPTER 14

Stars

Adam and Allison

The deteriorating road crackled under the massive MRAP's heavy tires. Although they had planned to return before nightfall, they ended up leaving later in the evening after several uneventful trips between their home base and the Sanctuary.

This particular stretch of road was hugged by trees and random gravel drives leading off to random houses. Once on this four-mile stretch of road, there would be no open area other than a small farm.

With the gunner turret sealed, Alison lightly jostled in her seat as Adam hit a familiar, large, unavoidable dip in the now grass-covered road. A snap and pop jarred the vehicle to a stop, as not only the engine cut off but also all power, bringing the massive once-upon-a-time beast of war to a grinding halt.

"What the hell," Adam huffed, pressing the engine on button several times in rapid succession.

Instead of the usual dinging of the electrical system, nothing happened. No power reached even the smallest component of the truck, as the smell of burning electronics caught both of their attention.

"Powers out on everything," Allison followed, flipping every switch within reach.

"Shit," Adam huffed. "Call the others. We may need some help."

"Allison reached down, pulling one of their radios out of the charging cradle, plugged into the vehicle's front power pack.

"Dammit," Alison cursed, holding the radio to her nose, smelling the smokey remnants of a battery that had just been shorted out. "It's dead. Whatever happened fried it." She picked up the second radio, confirming its fate.

Adam started thinking while unbuckling and quickly opening the gunner's hatch. Within a few short seconds, the heat of the day was already taking hold of the vehicle. The man also realized, through reading the manual, which happened to be the same manual they left behind, that the MRAP, while all its doors and hatches were closed, was a sealed system. This prevented concussions from explosions and possible chemical agents from reaching its occupants.

"Maybe the battery just came loose. We have to keep the gunner hatch open, or it will become a stuffy oven in here," Adam noted, followed by a smack on the driver's seat as he sat back down.

"We left the manual with the others," she said, knowing what he had just realized. Do you know how to check the battery? I know there's a backup, but it might also be fried or dead if we didn't check it."

"The Battery is under the back seat. I'll check it out, but it's going to take some time to open the hatch. I have to remove the back seat."

This also presented another level of butt-puckering issues. All the tools necessary to do so were back at their home base. Adam slumped down in one of the back seats facing each other.

"If we don't have the radios, we aren't going to be able to use Eve either," Alison noted.

While Eve worked off GPS satellites, her ability to communicate with two separate groups in her full functioning capacity was limited. With no radio to boost the signal, even getting a simple text message to the others could take some time. They had grown accustomed to using Eve, even when outside of the Sanctuary. This was something they had neither planned for nor realized would ever be an issue.

They could send a signal, but as long as Eve was actively working on some other task or open at the Sanctuary, they would have little to no use of her systems. Knowing this, Alison immediately tapped a message out on her smartwatch.

"They may or may not get it in time," she said as Adam just glared at the inside roof of the truck.

"How long till it starts getting dark?" Adam asked as Alison looked at the time.

"About two hours. I know what you're thinking. We're five miles away from home. You think we should hoof it on foot?"

Adam leaned forward. "I don't think we have a choice, babe," he replied, sounding defeated. In his mind, he was fighting an internal war with how careless and complacent he had become. This wasn't Alison's fault, but his for not planning on a secondary mode of transportation like Ben's.

It was SOP, or standard operating procedure, for Ben always to have a bike mounted on the side of his trusty Toyota, something he had done on several occasions while traveling back and forth. In all the excitement of the trip to Fleming Island, they had forgotten to bring theirs along this one time.

Mother Nature and the general cycle of life had become a fickle bitch in such situations, not allowing for the slightest lack of thought. Right then and there, the two promised each other that they would never forget the small things.

"Pack it up. Radio, extra ammo. We can't carry the minigun. It will have to wait. I'll lock it inside," Adam instructed as the two got to work.

Within ten minutes, the two were ready to go, as they were now fighting time. The list of enemies was long. While zombies did come out during the day, the chances of survival after sundown were dramatically decreased.

Pausing outside the truck, nothing other than the sound of swaying trees greeted their ears as they stepped off. After a handful of reflective minutes, Adam started talking about the entire situation.

"It was bound to happen sooner or later," Adam started as Alison shook her head.

"If we had just stayed home, we wouldn't be in this mess."

Adam stopped for a short second as they turned. "You know as well as I do we were living on liquor and Twinkies. The food wouldn't have kept us going, not to mention we didn't have the firepower to take on the Costco."

Alison continued and finally nodded as they started walking again, pausing one more time to listen for signs of the undead. "Still, we would have figured something out."

"I don't think so," Adam followed. "That hoard we took out in the area had been milling around for months. We can still hear them toward the interstate."

"I guess you're right. It's just we need to focus."
Adam chuckled lightly. "Or move to the Sanctuary."

The truth of the matter was they had discussed the option on several occasions. There was no logic in not staying there other than the two being used to being on their own and safe for so long without all the drama, as they called it. Bet that was the thing eating Adam away. Drama is what made life a thing. To date, it had produced years upon years of food, power, and safety, minus all the hell Jim had left strewn across northern Florida.

"I guess you're right. Even if we live there, it doesn't mean we have to go out on every trip. Tell you what honey. We get back and get our stuff, and I'll support it."

Adam grinned just as several birds launched out of the tree line, freezing the two in place. "Shit," Adam huffed, glancing down at his watch. "We have company. Let's keep moving."

The two of them started mall walking as the main turn in the road curved into the main stretch of road back to the lot. More birds flickered across the sky in front of them as sweat started trickling out of every pore on their bodies. Something was around them. Something big and something they would have to deal with.

Alison elbowed a now huffing Adam. "Whatever it is, it's around the corner." Adam nodded as they slowed, pulling up their rifles. Both had AR-15s with several full magazines. They could fight, but with limited resources, it would be a strategic decision to stand and fight, attracting others, or to run like they never had before. It was times like these that they wished they had followed some of the other's advice to exercise daily.

Turning the corner, the worst possible scenario presented itself. Dozens, if not hundreds, of zombies lumbered across the main road, cutting through the area like a lazy buzzsaw. A horde was making its way through the area.

That was another point of contention for the group, wondering where they all went. Heading north, at some point, all they could do was crossroads and bridges. Since some of the larger groups in the area stayed close to, if not on, Highway ninety-five, they concluded most of them were either bunched up north of Jacksonville or simply dropped into the river, eventually being shot out into the ocean. Either way, there were plenty of candidates down south to keep replenishing their numbers, being that Florida was one of the most populated states in the country.

"What are we going to do? There's no way we can get around them," Alison insisted as Adam scanned the area, seeing a lone mailbox leading off to a gravel driveway.

"Maybe check that house out? We can't go back," he pointed to the additional birds fleeing the area behind them. This meant there were likely two large groups on either side of them. It wasn't worth the risk.

Alison agreed as Adam turned. The man hesitated, looking down the shadowed path. "We get to the house. Secure it as quietly as possible and get settled in for the night. Who knows. We might get lucky and find a radio."

CHAPTER 15

Revenge

NAS JAX

Palatable tension floated around the small shipping container. Amanda stood over the table as Dustin marked the map with multiple locations. While most were familiar, several were new to Tina.

"While I appreciate you helping, I don't trust you," Amanda finally said, seeing several areas now marked on the map.

"Look," Dustin said, still trying to build rapport. My main concern in life is sitting beside me—my wife. I'm not here to get in your way or whatever this is. If our helping you gets us out of here in one piece, so be it."

Amanda nodded. "You have the right mind to survive in this landscape of shit. One that will soon find we aren't as helpless against its challenges as it thinks." She was talking in absolutes.

"Can I ask you a question?" Dustin followed. He wanted to see how far he could push the conversation.

Amanda stared at the man, letting him speak. "What about the bunkers in Tallahassee? Is everyone okay?"

She blew out indignantly. "Chris and the others. Yes. They aren't coming out of their little hole for another two years. No. They believe this will all be over by then."

Dustin and Tina didn't like her using the term for their friend's home. In all reality, they considered it their best option as well and were looking for the FEMA bunkers to help set them up. The two had discussed the long-term option on their trip West, concluding they were going to lay roots down at the Sanctuary.

"They might be right. Either way, my statement stands. We are not looking for any trouble," Dustin concluded as Amanda scoffed lightly.

"I believe you are closer to those people than you care to mention. I also believe you are all hanging on by a thread as to why they are out running the roads. We will see soon enough. I give you this. If things work out, maybe you two will consider traveling with us instead of being locked up here. Yes, I am not going to be leaving any loose strings. If, and I mean if, things work out, us letting you go could be a risk. One we will have to weigh. Again, if everything is on the up and up, things look good for you two," She genuinely smiled, turning to leave as several of the guards followed her.

Andrew stood at the door as Tina talked with Bill before calling Andrew to get them some better food. Tina exhaled as the door clanged shut, again locked.

"That went well," she started. Dustin took another sip of water.

"Both parties know something's up. I think I got our point across to Amanda, however."

Tina pushed the now-cold stew aside. "What was that all about?"

"The others know. There..." Dustin hesitated, wondering if others may, in fact, be listening. He leaned in close. "There is no meeting point this close to town. The only others are Lake City and a couple of exits, plus random spots on the backroads."

"You think they know where we are?" Tina whispered, the conversation now barely audible.

"No. But what I am sure of is they are watching the water. They mentioned that spot for a reason. It's accessible by water, and easy to see anyone coming and going. You remember that place."

Tina looked up, remembering a date they had once gone on. "Yeah, that's right. I bet they head that way before the four days."

"Yup. I have a feeling they built some time into that to make it there faster. I'm not so sure they'll be taking us with them," Dustin replied as the sounds of the lock clanged.

Andrew walked in, this time carrying what appeared to be freshly made sandwiches and a couple of bags of chips. His red hair reflected off the dim light. While the two had eaten some of the stew, a fresh meal would improve their mood and fuel them.

A random guard stood out front, giving Andrew the side-eye as he closed the door behind them. Andrew also carried a pad of paper and a pen. It was telling that Bill wasn't standing outside their door. They were already making arrangements.

"All right. Seems like the boss is happy," Andrew started, sounding like he could care less about everything that had just happened. Dustin again picked up on this.

"How about you? Thanks for the fresh food, by the way," Dustin said as Tina took the tray and sat it on the small table.

"No worries. I'm good. I just got word that I'm going to be hanging out with you guys for a while. At least I'll be keeping an eye on things." Andrew gestured, pointing at his eyes and then at the two sitting in front of him as if it were a joke. "Oh, before I forget. Amanda and Bill want you to write down anything else that might be important. Weapons they have. All that good stuff."

"You don't seem to care much about all this?" Dustin asked.

Andrew shrugged. "I don't. Look guys, it's the end of the world. You know it. I know, they…., not so much. I'm here till I figure out a long-term plan."

"So you're not with them? Do they know that?"

"Phhht. Maybe. I get all the shit work. I don't mind it. I'm safe, and things have gone okay so far." His face changed as thoughts of Tallahassee swept through his mind. "Well, things have been better, you know."

"Yeah, we know. You seem like a nice guy. Just not like the others."

Andrew shuffled, now aware the conversation was not one he felt completely comfortable having. Hope also shown on his face as Dustin had hit the right nerve with the young man. He wasn't like the others.

"I'm not. Before this all went down, I was about to graduate college as a bioengineer. Then, I was going to head to med school. You guys seem nice, too. Are all the others the same as you, or what as bad as I hear? I thought I heard some familiar names."

Dustin shifted, now having a genuine conversation with Andrew. "Yeah, they are. Better than us if you ask me. You would like them." He chuckled, pulling a grin from Tina.

"Amanda and the others said they are the ones that started the fires in the city and drew the herd in."

Tina didn't like this, knowing what she had done. Dustin took the statement. "No. They didn't. Bad timing, maybe, but think about how many people came to the city every week, then, of course, left, like me. The council, or whatever they call themselves, made a lot of enemies. You know, the one thing people seem to forget is that it doesn't mean that this stuff doesn't happen everywhere all the time. One of the people in that group was on a military base, and it went to shit. Jacksonville was doing okay for a while, then it went to shit. Some things are just inevitable. If you think you're bulletproof out here, you'll get yourself killed."

Andrew reflected on the statement. "That's what I'm worried about. I do know your friends aren't to be taken lightly. That much I know. I was close by when that actor guy Ben started pushing back on Amanda and the others."

"What would you do? His wife was taken hostage. You might know her. Sarah, the doctor who was working in the processing center," Dustin added as Andrew's face clearly showed he didn't.

"No one ever told me that. She was the nicest lady. I used to talk to her all the time at the coffee shop. No way. I mean, Amanda and Bill keep stuff to themselves, but I would think she would tell all of us this. Most of us, if not all, know her."

Tina grinned this time. "Well, then you'll know Nicole, who worked with her, and John, one of the main processors, is also with that group."

Andrew let out a low whistle, pulling it back in. "John? That guy is hardcore. Nicole, I used to talk to her when she was with Sarah. That's crazy."

"Sounds like they are keeping that hush for a reason. Some of you know them," Dustin responded, being genuine. He was now talking openly, also planting a seed with not only Andrew but anyone else he had confidence in.

"Man. This changes a few things," Andrew blew out.

"Anything that might help us?" Dustin was lying on the

table.

"Look. I would not be telling anyone else any of this. I'm not looking for trouble. To be honest with you, there's been several days that I just about slipped away at night. You two need to be careful. She is serious, and I'm not here to get in the middle of it," Andrew's tone shifted as everything just discussed started processing in his brain.

"Can I ask you one more question? No worries, and we aren't here to start trouble. We just want to get out of here and back on our own." Dustin added, seeing Andrew's face shift back to normal.

"It's your dime."

"How many people are with you guys?"

Andrew chewed on whether or not to respond. On the one hand, the young man knew the people in front of him, and the others were good. On the other, he didn't want to cross Bill or Amanda. "Two dozen. I have to go. You two take care of yourselves, and I'll be back in the morning. You're going to have to put up with me till Amanda needs to talk with you again.

Tina and Dustin both smiled. Andrew saw the sincerity in their faces as they returned the favor. "Just stay out of trouble, and things should be fine."

Andrew turned, locking the door once again. Before Tina could speak, Dustin leaned over, picking up the pen and examining it. There, on the end, was a small pinhole. Unscrewing the lid, a small battery popped out. She had sent him in with a recording device. After a few short clicks, Dustin had effectively wiped out the entire conversation that had taken place. Andrew clearly didn't know he was also being recorded.

"We should be fine. Just keep it low. Later tonight, I'll put the batteries back in, and we can talk. This will make us seem none the wiser and hopefully more trusted. She did this as a final test to see if she was going to kill us. We need to use this before getting it back to her for our advantage."

Tina grabbed one of the sandwiches. "What do you think about him." She was referring to Andrew.

"He's going to get us out of here. I don't think we need to work on escaping. Yet," Dustin hesitated on the word. "We just need to be ready. I wish I had a way of asking Sarah, Nicole, or John about him. They would know. They both said there were some really good people in the city. That included the security forces. I'm not even sure that's what he was doing. I forgot to ask."

Tina started thinking through the radio call: "We need to figure out a way to let them know the numbers and that they are likely going to head that way in a day or two."

"Agreed. We just need to figure it out by morning," Dustin said, smiling.

Feeling better about their situation, as much as they could, Dustin and Tina continued to stuff their faces with the significantly better meal they had previously tried to choke down.

CHAPTER 16

Together

Adam and Alison

G reen moss and mildew clung to the shaded two-story house like the ground. The surrounding forest was reaching up from the ground, taking the structure back into the soil it was born from. While the inhabitants of the Sanctuary planned their trip back to Fleming Island, Adam and Alison stood in front of a seemingly abandoned house.

A still functioning fence surrounded the property, also succumbing to the green wrath of Mother Nature. Moss hung from trees, casting moving shadows in the quickly darkening evening breeze.

"This place looks like something out of a horror movie," Alison noted as Adam shrugged.

"We live in one, in all fairness. They're getting closer," Adam said while the groaning sounds and shuffling of the undead echoed through the trees. Since not being kept up, the woods were a thick soup of branches and bushes.

Alison grimaced. Despite their survival, they had rarely been in a situation this dire. In most cases, they either had the

MRAP or were tucked neatly away in the lot.

"I wonder what the others would do?" Adam asked, not directing the question to either of them.

"Tap on the door. If there's anything inside, we should know pretty quickly. I mean, we have these rifles," Alison pointed down at the AR-15s they were now using versus the familiar grip of their shotguns. After a few days of solid training with Dan and John, the two had become comfortable with the weapon.

Adam stepped forward, noticing the windows were covered in muck. Wrapping his knuckles on the door, the man backed up several steps, waiting for a response. "How long do we wait?" he whispered as Alison held up two fingers.

The following two minutes felt like an eternity as several growls echoed from the other side of the tree line. Not wanting to be in the open any longer, Adam twisted the handle, finding it locked. "That's good news," he said, reaching down with all the knowledge of a prior homeowner lifting the dirty welcome matt. "Bingo," he smiled, making quick work of the lock after shimmying it in the rusted lock.

Musty, dank air blew out of the house, smacking them in the face. The rotten smell of decay setting in. "We clear the first floor, then go from there," Alison suggested as Adam slung his rifle, pulling out a larger-than-average machete.

Following his lead, Alison pulled out the one silenced weapon they had. A twenty-two caliber pistol. While not having any true stopping power, with the hollow point ammunition they had, one shot to the head would be enough to stop a zombie.

"God, it sticks," Dan complained as he slowly closed the door, locking it behind them.

Alison pointed toward the kitchen, turning on her flashlight. Pictures sat smudged as the medium-sized house opened up into a sitting room that likely didn't see much use.

To their left, a living room opened up into a kitchen with a sitting bar overlooking the room. While a late eighties design, the house at one point had been updated. Newer furniture sat stained with mildew and rot. The humidity had ravaged most of the interior of the house.

Entering the kitchen, smooth surfaces allowed for less mold. Boxes of cereal sat on the counter as the refrigerator was to Adam and Alison, the likely source of the smell. Black sludge oozed from the bottom of its door, congealing in a pool in front of the sink.

Checking the back door, Adam turned, giving a thumbs up to Alison. Leaning close, he whispered in her ear. "Let's not go into the garage. I say we go upstairs and find a room in working condition."

While it was hot inside the house, the shade provided by the trees kept it reasonably cool. Looking out the kitchen window, the sun was starting to set at a fast rate, making it hard to see into the overgrown bushes.

Satisfied the first floor was relatively clear, they headed upstairs, in what they could only describe as a haunted house straight out of a movie. The stairs revolted at the first sign of pressure as the squeak of loose nails froze Adam in place.

Testing several more areas, he eventually landed on pressing against the wall, making the trek up the tight stairs sideways. Now beaming his flashlight on the small opening leading off to four separate doors, Adam projected either of the two closest doors on either side to be the master bedroom.

A smell punched both their noses as they both stood in the small hallway, looking at the closed door like a gameshow where no prize was waiting if they selected the correct one, just pain.

"Somethings dead in there. I want to check it out," Adam insisted as Alision shook her head disapproving.

Black mold clung to one door in particular as Adam leaned forward. "It's coming from in there."

Adam tapped the door with his machete waiting for a flurry of activity that never came. After another minute, Alison stepped back, pulling up her pistol. "Go ahead. I'm not going in there."

Reaching down, Adam turned the doorknob, finding it protesting his entrance. With a firm twist, the door cracked open, and the smell of death and decay wafted into the open hallway, forcing him to remember to pull his handkerchief over his nose.

The scene in front of Adam was one of horror and tranquil peace. Laying in the bed, a couple sat beside each other, now joined by whatever their bodies had rotted into. On the nightstand, a bottle of pills sat beside an empty bottle of wine.

That was the peaceful part of the scene. Black gore, now covered in mold, spattered the back wall, leading Adam's eyes to the pistol in the hands of one of the indistinguishable figures. They had taken their own lives instead of dealing with the world falling apart around them.

Looking on a dresser, several piles of medications and what appeared to be a ventilator sat. The more Adam took in the room. The more he realized one of the persons in the bed was already dying and at home being treated. He recognized one of the medications, having lost his father to cancer.

Still frozen in place, Adam digested the odd serenity the couple shared in death. Only one had to pull the trigger. Even if one of them were fine, the other would not go on without his partner.

His eyes watered, not from the smell but from the sadness on display. "Goddammit," He huffed under his breath.

"What's in there?" Alison asked from the top of the stairs.

Turning, Adam made the sign of the cross before closing

the door. "It's a grave. We don't need to go back in there. Whoever lived here had a decision to make. It's....," he swallowed. "It's sad."

Alison, having saved herself the image, pointed toward the other door. "Was that the master?"

"No. One of the people who lived here was being treated for cancer. Let's get in the other room and settle in for the night. I don't want to stay here a minute longer than needed."

They correctly assumed the door to their right was the master bedroom as the door clicked open. Unlike the rest of the house, the master bedroom was moderately in working condition. Hazy dust had settled on the room, covering everything in a grey layer of protection.

Alison walked to the main closet, slowly sliding the door open. Old clothes hung as if waiting for their owner to put them on. Rows of shoes and handbags topped the walk-in closet off as she gave Adam a thumbs-up to clear the master bath.

Like the rest of the room, the bathroom looked as if someone had just closed the door and walked out. The mirror was only clear as Adam looked at his reflection, and the dwindling sun made the house dark.

"Close the door. We should be good," Adam said, walking over to the closet and pulling out several clean blankets from under the dust. Alison, seeing this, pulled the top blanket off as fresh, clean sheets contrasted the rest of the room.

"If nothing changes, we should be good here. The house has made it this long," Alison said, working to convince herself they were safe.

"You're right. We can clean a spot on the window and keep an eye out. Take turns getting some rest," Adam added as the both of them took a much-needed breath. While the smell in the house was coming from the other room, the master suite had been spared most of the odor.

After further investigation of the room, Alison found an exhaust fan leading into the attic through the bathroom still circulating air. As with most houses, a small solar panel sat atop the attic ventilator to keep air flowing in the master bedroom.

Night fell on a quiet night as the growls of the undead faded into the distance. "I think we can get some rest. Take turns. I'll go first, then you can wake me up in two hours, and then I'll take the rest of the night," Adam asked, as Alison nodded.

"That's fine. It's getting late. I'll wake you up in two hours," Alison noted as Adam laid on his back, going to sleep within minutes.

Alison stared into the dark room, her night eyes holding her senses. Light shadows and the groans of an old house kept her mind at ease, and she started laughing under her breath.

It wasn't the situation, but rather she was still more afraid of ghosts in the house than the undead. Taking a sip of water, Alison quickly realized she hadn't gone to the bathroom since leaving the sanctuary.

"Shit," she whispered to herself, standing up. The bathroom sat like a throne to a once great civilization. Walking into the room, turning her flashlight on low, Adam's snore forced her to turn as she investigated the toilet.

The sound of crickets chirped outside as she lifted the lid to find a bowl full of foggy water. "Bingo," she whispered to herself as she quickly realized the lack of toilet paper on the skeletal roll.

Looking up at the ceiling, the hallway bathroom came into focus. There had to be the paper gold in the other bathroom. It was worth it. While she could grab a garment or even a towel from the closet, she truly wanted toilet paper.

With her nerves at ease and secure in knowing the only space she needed to avoid was the room the house's occupants were in, Alison slowly stepped out of the bedroom, opening the door, standing in the hallway at the top of the stairs listening for any noise only to find silence.

Taking one more glance at Adam, Alison stepped forward, walking toward the bathroom with her pistol in hand. In one hour, she would get her rest, and in the morning, they would go home. As a surprise for Adam, she would grab a roll of toilet paper for him when he awoke.

Not thinking clearly, they hadn't cleared the upstairs bathroom outside the master suite. Alison slowly opened the door. Much like the other bathroom, an exhaust fan lightly spun, allowing the stale air to move in the room. With her eyes adjusted to the dark, she didn't need to use her flashlight with the full moon shining ambient light around the house and through the windows.

Looking down, a smile swept across her face as not only a fresh roll sat on the holder, but several others were neatly stacked on the back of the toilet. Seeing this, Alison's body pushed her to move as she could feel herself needing to go now more than ever.

The light click of her pistol sitting on the sink counter beside her was the only sound other than her sitting on the toilet as she shuffled to a comfortable position after wiping off the seat.

Alison sat there, letting her body relax as she leaned back. With her business over and in her relaxed mood, as if muscle memory overrode common sense, she reached back and flushed the toilet.

The sucking woosh made her cringe as she didn't notice the shower curtain lightly ripple in front of her. In the other room, Adam rustled, heavily asleep after the day's events.

After a few seconds of silence, Alison grinned at the situation. The shower curtain again rippled as she looked up. Nothing happened, so she let out a light chuckle, knowing her nerves were on edge.

'So stupid," Alison whispered to herself as she stood up, situating herself.

Wanting to see how long the luxury would last, Alison turned on the water to wash her hands. She was pleasantly surprised by the flowing stream of cool, clear water. The house had a well that was still operational.

Picking up a small dusty rag off the counter, Alison wiped the mirror before splashing water on her face. Blinking, she felt and heard it before she knew what was happening. There, in the mirror, was a zombie lunging out from behind the shower curtain.

Unlike most of the zombies crawling around the countryside, this one moved fast. It was crazy, as the inhabitants of the sanctuary called them—a freshly turned zombie capable of moving at human-like speeds also not yet sending out a foul odor.

As with everything in the world of the undead, her body started to move just as the shower curtain exploded behind her. She looked at the nightmarish reflection as blood sprayed the mirror like a freshly tapped oil well.

Alison jerked as arms wrapped around her body, allowing the zombie to further sink its rotted teeth into her neck, resulting in a spray of blood on the wall in front of Alison as she watched the reflection of her own death in the mirror.

Her eyes started hazing over as Adam burst through the door, hammering his machete into the skull of the crazy bearing down on his wife's neck. More gore joined the chorus of death as Adam reared back, slamming his blade into the creature one final time as it dropped on the floor as if it was never alive.

The problem with this was its teeth were still lodged in Alison's neck as the entire short five-second encounter ripped what was left of her skin to shreds.

Panicking, Adam grabbed the dirty washcloth on the counter, cupping it around Alison's neck. The pressure of his hand made her spasm as her hazed eyes rolled back into her head. Her body became dead weight as he slowly slunk down on the floor with his wife's body in his arms. The now disfigured zombie leaning against the tub watched as if ensuring it had brought maximum pain and suffering to those who had just disturbed its slumber.

Rocking back and forth, Adam turned his wife toward him, pulling her into a hug as her arms slowly made their way around him. Tears welled as anger flared in the man's very soul. "Please God, no...," he prayed to any and every God willing to listen.

Rage filled the man. Anger for choosing to leave the Sanctuary, Anger for not bringing bikes, anger for not just staying in the MRAP. Anger for not checking the other bathrooms. The others would have cleared every room. For a brief second, he questioned why his wife was there, only to realize he had been sleeping. Everything they had done was for nothing.

Spittle flew from gritted teeth as Adam thought of the other room. He would not leave his wife to die alone. His body wouldn't allow it as he held her tighter. For a brief moment, he could feel her hands lightly rub his sides before going slack.

He didn't want to look at her face, wanting to remember it one last time as she smiled before he shut his eyes before resting.

***

Two hours passed before Adam felt the life in his wife come back. Her slow embrace started to shift under his body weight. He hadn't let up an inch since first holding her on the floor.

"It's okay baby," he whispered. "Everything's going to be okay." Adam rocked on the floor as if trying to put a newborn to sleep. "I'm here. We're both here. I got you."

The last thing Adam felt before fading to black was the subtle sinking of teeth into his neck.

CHAPTER 17

Go time

The Sanctuary

The early morning dawn yawned awake as the aroma of freshly brewed coffee filled Ben's kitchen. Luckily for the Sanctuary crew, the pitter-patter of rain on the windows opened to dark grey clouds that powdered the morning sky.

"Have you heard from Adam and Alison yet?" Sarah asked as Dan shook his head.

"Nope. I'm guessing they're just tied up with something. We will try again later. You good with that?" Dan asked Ian, who was soaked to the bone, having loaded the last few weapons on the boat.

Eve chirped to life, already having a droning soundtrack of the Rolling Stones lightly playing in the background. "Relative humidity and current temperature fluctuations suggest the rain will be present for twenty-four hours. There is no change to the projection of more weather setting in. The probability of light precipitation and windy conditions shall persist through the day, bros."

"That's good news, Eve," Ben chuckled as the music turned up one or two points. "I want you to try connecting with Adam and Alison once we head out before we get on the other side of the river. That should give you enough time to transition over to us. Oh, and bros?"

"Will do," Eve hummed as John dropped his vest on the kitchen island. While Eve could do many things, being in two places at once was no longer one of them, with a recent shift in several satellites. As long as she was focused on one primary unit and they were in close proximity to each other, they would all be linked.

"Everything is ready to go. Two golf carts, two pull-behind trailers, and the bikes. Ammo, weapons, everything." John said as Nicole walked up, pecking him on the cheek before handing him a cup of hot go-juice.

"Perfect," Ben replied, happy with the gloomy weather for once. "I've got the maps loaded on a tablet for each couple, and Eve can alert us if needed. It looks like a straight shot from Black Creek. Once we all eat, we can reach out to Dustin and Tina one last time."

The rain slowed as the group ate their last freshly prepared meal, which included eggs. In its place, the wind howled. If the rain was slow, the wind would make do.

Dan keyed the radio as Ben finished his last piece of jam-covered toast. The mix of butter, grapes, and slightly burnt bread reminded him of Saturday mornings spent watching cartoons with a pile of toast on the table to grab as needed. His mother often did this as a backdrop to hours of TV.

"Dustin, Tina, you copy?" Dan asked. The two didn't respond for ten minutes.

"Go ahead," Dustin replied as Amanda and Bill stood over the two, with Andrew watching the door.

It had taken several minutes to get the radio to the couple.

The more Amanda realized they needed to be closer to a radio, the more she was working to find a way to keep them closer.

"Checking in to see if everything is okay. We're still three days out. Ran into a little snag, but we're good. We should start moving again later today," Dan replied as Dustin looked down at the pad of paper Amanda was writing on.

After reading it, Dustin shook his head, indicating that the message Amanda wanted to send wouldn't work. Another tactic he was using to build trust. Amanda cocked her head, finally nodding at Dustin to go ahead. She wanted him to ask for their location.

Dustin scribbled on the paper, telling her they never ask that question over the radio and that talking about our meeting spot was pushing it.

"Be safe out there. We're still on schedule if we don't run into anything," Dustin noticed the rain as it danced off the metal roof of the shipping container. "How's the weather? It's getting cloudy."

Bill, this time, shot the man a laser stare. Dustin, seeing he was pushing his luck, pulled it back in. "It's been raining here. I figure it's heading your way."

"A little," Dan replied as Ben grabbed the radio.

"We'll give you a call when we get moving later. If everything works out, we plan on staying at the meeting point for a couple of days," Ben stated, letting them know they weren't planning on going to another secondary location for some time. He still wasn't sure what the people with Dustin and Tina knew.

"Good copy. Be safe," Dustin concluded, setting the radio down.

Amanda looked at him. "Why did you end the conversation?"

"They don't talk much about plans over the radio. If I kept

asking your questions, they would know something is up."

Satisfied, Bill glanced at Amanda. "Very well," she started. We will be back later today. Andrew will take care of you till then."

Ben sat the radio down, looking around the room. "We have to get to that neighborhood today and, if time permits, the FEMA camp. Either way, we have to be setting up no later than tomorrow morning. They'll be coming early as well."

John picked up his vest, pulling it over his head. "No time like the present."

Light rain dusted the group as the modified pontoon and jet skis finally made it to the middle of the river before splitting off. With the morning fog still hanging onto the water, the mix of rain, wind, and fog allowed the group to move as fast as the electric motors they had mounted on the boats would allow. If needed, they would fully turn the boats on using the gas motors if the rain picked up.

Manning the pontoon, Ben, Sarah, Shelly, and Dan stood on the front end of the boat, lightly swaying in the waves, watching as John and Nicole headed north up the river toward Doctor's Inlet.

"You think they're good?" Shelly asked as Dan turned, watching them troll up the river.

"Yeah, they'll be fine," Dan paused, seeing a hump floating in front of them in the water. A zombie was in the river taking the trip north, up one of the only north-flowing rivers in North America.

The group shut up, taking in its features. They saw that it had been in the water for a long time. Bloated, covered in green slime, and not moving, the body had come a long way, likely blindly shuffling into the river at some point.

Ben glanced at his watch, seeing the timer now set for one hour. This was the amount of time it would take them to reach

Black Creek at this speed. The rain continued to patter as John and Nicole faded into the remaining morning fog.

Sarah put her arm around Ben as the smell of smoke wafted from Dan. "You guys think this is going to work?" Ben asked, reflecting on the days ahead.

"Like we planned? Nope," Dan replied, grinning.

Minutes felt like hours as the opening to Black Creek opened its arm as if wanting to hug the slow-moving pontoon boat. What shocked the group more than being one step closer to their plan being put in motion were the piles of undead that had been caught and washed up on the docks and heavily wooded banks of the tributary.

"Jesus. It's a damn graveyard," Ben huffed as the smell matched the view. The mix of depressing grey skies and light rain brought the world's end into focus.

"Stay focused," Sarah spoke up, turning the boat toward the center of the quickly narrowing waterways.

Sharp turns and more dead and, in some instances, skeletal bodies adorned the shores of Black Creek as if they were being stored there. Movement ruffled the tree line that slowly faded as they moved further into the dense dark waters.

Not a word was spoken the further they traveled, noticing the moving zombies on the shores thinning out. To the surprise and happiness of the group, a bridge appeared, crossing over the water like a beacon of light in the gloomy morning hours.

"That's it," Ben whispered as everyone's nerves started pinging. "Dan, get on the radio. See where the others are and check in with home base. Hopefully, they've heard from Adam and Alison."

Dan quickly keyed the radio as Sarah steered the boat to a patch of shoreline under the bridge covered in rocks. To the left, a clear section of land, as shown in the images pulled from Eve, led to the tracks that would allow them to unload the golf carts.

"John, you copy?"

"Good copy. What's your status?" Dan asked as the front of the pontoon thunked into the shore.

"Getting ready to offload. You guys?" John followed.

"We're about another ten minutes out. We can see the bridge over the Inlet's entrance. No signs of anyone else. We've been hugging the shore. It's jammed with bodies."

"Same here," Dan replied. "It cleared out some. We're on schedule."

"We'll let you know when we are set," John said. Dan shifted to the Sanctuary. "Ian, Sam, copy?"

"Loud and clear," Sam's voice echoed as Ben started unlatching the golf carts. With the all-terrain tires they had installed, it would make quick work of the steep hill up to the tracks and eventual road.

"Did the others make it back?" Ben asked, concerned about Adam and Alison.

"We haven't heard from them yet. It may be the weather. Eve said their watches are still active, but no one is replying. For all we know, they could be taking a shower. We have the other radio set to monitor our set net for them. We will keep checking," Sam replied as Dan lit another smoke, not liking the update.

"Good copy. I know you heard. We are at checkpoint one," Dan replied, bustling the radio in his vest beside the main one, monitoring the channel with Dustin and Tina.

On those words, Ben turned, scanning the tree line. "It looks clear. Don't understand why, but I'll take it. We're ready to go."

The group knew that as soon as they left the pontoon boat, there was no turning back. They were back in the wild, and in many ways, this could be the last time they had a moment of peace.

After several cuss words that would make the devil himself blush, the golf carts, trailer, and equipment were offloaded. The soggy ground had quickly turned the ground into a mire of muck and mud.

The whirl of electric motors hummed as the carts strained to pull the trailers up the short hill climb to the railroad tracks. Unlike the usual cadence, the couples split up as Dan and Ben rode together, leaving Sarah and Shelly in the second, bringing up the rear.

"I don't understand why there aren't any zombies out here," Ben stated as Dan nodded.

"I was thinking the same thing. With the amount dumped at the mouth of the creek, I would think they would be everywhere."

The two sat in speculative silence as the ground leveled out as they pulled onto the train tracks. "You notice that. There's places where they are and aren't."

"What are you thinking?" Dan asked as Ben pushed the golf cart over the metal rails.

"Well, if we can look at areas where we know they aren't, we can see if there is something they have in common. I'm not saying places like close to the Sanctuary where it's all trees and not a lot of houses. I'm thinking it has to be something else."

Dan simply nodded as he looked behind them, seeing their wives also speculating about something. Ben glanced at his tablet, seeing the turnoff at the city dump half a mile ahead. With no zombies in their way, they were ahead of schedule.

A small gravel access point to the train tracks emptied onto a small open field. Ben leaned forward, seeing the main road. In front of them, a closed gate stood resolute with a small lock. As usual, several bodies leaned against the fence on either side of the opening.

"You notice none of those dam things coming from the other direction?" Ben asked, as Dan nodded.

"Yup," was all the man said as he jumped out, knocking off the lock.

Nothing was left other than bones and memories of the four bodies smashed against the fence. For all he knew, they could have been living people who died there rather than zombies.

Sarah pulled up beside Ben's golf cart. "Everything good?"

"Yeah, it just seems odd there's not a lot of zombies out running around. You guys notice that?" Ben replied.

Shelly leaned forward. "We were just saying the same thing. With the overcast skies, they should be everywhere."

"Ready to go," Dan called, jumping back in the cart.

A smooth, leafy, and branch-covered road stretched in front of the team, making them feel emboldened by the lack of zombies. While they knew they were around, they were not in the immediate area.

Ben started to believe that someone had cleared them out or that the same fencing surrounded the area. This was quickly dispelled as they pulled into the mouth of Doctor's Inlet Reserve.

As planned, the small neighborhood sat back off Highway 220 enough to be out of sight. If one didn't know it was there, it would stay out of the eyeshot of anyone passing by.

As they pulled into the mass of houses, overgrown yards and decaying houses guarded the entrance like a sign to turn back. The condition of the houses was shocking compared to what they had experienced before. While Fleming Island was slowly being taken over by Mother Nature, the houses here were undisturbed.

"This place is dead," Ben noted as they pulled further into the subdivision. Several cars blocked off the first road, turning right as they continued further into the dead house graveyard.

The next set of streets converged as the house they identified sat within eyeshot. Dan cocked his head, looking at Ben. "You hear that?"

Ben turned his head, stopping at the small intersection where kids once played. "Yeah, what is that?" Sarah and Shelly pulled up beside them, noticing the road cleared, unlike the rest of the neighborhood.

"You guys hear that?" Sarah asked as Dan raised an eyebrow, finally figuring out what the noise was.

"Selena? Someone's out here listening to Selena. What the hell?"

CHAPTER 18

The Watch

John and Nicole

Pulling up to a decaying cluster of two-story condos, John and Nicole slowly turned toward the dock. With the rain now steadily falling, the two made quick work of hiding the jet skis.

"Where do you want to set up?" Nicole asked, pulling out her pistol.

John surveyed the condos, pointing at the closest one to the waterway leading into Doctor's Inlet under a bridge they had previously driven over. "Let's see if we can clear that condo and get set up. I'm sure we're going to have company at some point, but either way, we're here and can hide if needed.

"What about the houseboats on the other side?" Nicole asked, having seen the chaotic mess of houseboats on the other side, no longer being tended to. The storm that came through the prior year had piled several of the boats in a bunch, leaving a handful of the larger ones in their respective docks.

"If we need to. It would take some time to go through

them," John said as they approached the first condo, seeing the door broken into splinters. "Well, that one's not going to work."

Nicole walked forward toward the second two-story condo as she turned back. "This one's closed up."

Nicole walked up the short set of steps, tapping on the door as she lightly checked it, finding it locked. Following the same universal logic Adam had, John lifted the obvious flower pot, finding a key to the door.

After another minute, John unlocked the door, and the two entered the house as they had practiced back at the Sanctuary. Nicole shifted to the left of the room as John entered first, covering the small hallway leading into the kitchen after doing a quick scan of the sitting room.

"Clear," he whispered, stepping in front of Nicole. "Watch the stairs as we pass."

Nodding, the pair walked into the condo. Bright colors and beach-style furniture covered the space, furthering the beachy vibes. Much to their surprise, the condo was remarkably intact, with minimal dust covering everything.

Stepping into the back room, a combo living room flowed into a kitchen area that was just as neatly organized. Glancing down, John saw a welcome notebook opened to the last page. This was a rental property and was likely the reason it had remained untouched.

"Clear," John again repeated as Nicole turned back to the hallway. "Upstairs."

Nicole moved to the right, letting John pass as he flicked on the flashlight mounted on his rifle. The stairs were sturdy, making their assent onto the second floor noiseless. Unlike the open floor plan downstairs, four doors greeted them all in a tight square landing.

Unlike their doomed companions, the pair cleared every square inch of the condo before finally realizing the space was, in fact, safe. "Let's go downstairs and get set up. That back window has a good view of the river and inlet entrance. You good?" John asked as Nicole nodded.

Sitting their gear on the kitchen bar, Nicole turned back to the front sitting room, pulling the blinds to the side. "Look," she pointed.

Next to the road beside the last of several condos was a small group of the undead lumbering around as if lost. "Let's just stay in the back of the house," John noted as they quickly retreated to the kitchen.

"Guess this place was a rental," John murmured as Nicole started thumbing through the guest book.

"A popular one by the looks of it. Check it out," she said, pointing at a drawing of a sunset clearly done by a child.

"Yup. I even bet they have a few things lying around. Notice how clean this place is?" John added as Nicole walked up to the large bay windows facing the river, fully pulling back the large vertical blinds.

"This place was built to keep the weather out, as well as the noise. It's a little musty, but I would think this place hadn't been used for months prior to everything going down. The last entry is for two months before everything went offline," she said, turning one of the barstools to face the river.

"You really think it's the leftovers from Tallahassee?" she asked, sitting down.

"Yeah. They were there before going silent. We all know Ben left Amanda alive. Who knows who else? They think we all had something to do with that mess. She's a lot of things, and vengeful is one of them. Their description of the folks they saw while on the bridge matches their security uniforms. It's them. Just not sure how many."

"Do you think it's always going to be like this?" Nicole asked, staring out the window.

"For now, yes. Don't forget I was out running around a good bit. Most folks that are left just want to be left alone and stay safe. At least around here. I can't talk much for the rest of the country. Sarah said there were groups of bandits out West, but as for the here and now, I think we have a good idea of what's around here. All I know is that every day that passes for those out there who are not situated like we are gets harder."

Nicole reflected on the statement. "We don't need to have folks out running around unless absolutely necessary."

John drew in a long breath. "Yeah. We can't stop people, but as far as I'm concerned, we are in a good place. We just need to get this over with. I agree, though. It's not getting any easier out there. Listen. I know you talked about checking on your relatives, and hell, we even talked about going out West, but the more and more I stew on it, the more I'm starting to realize just how good we have it."

"Therein lies the problem. Others will want what we have. If we keep going out, someone will find us," Nicole said as the conversation shifted.

John picked up the radio. "Ben, you copy?"

After a few seconds, the radio crackled to life. "We hear you. How's it going?"

John glanced out the large window facing the river. "All set. Things are calm for now. We have eyes on the river and bridge."

"We are in the neighborhood. There's someone or something here. We're about to check it out. Other than that, it's quiet here," Ben replied as Dan spoke up in the background.

"Except for someone blaring, Selena."

John and Nicole glanced at each other. "Selena?" Nicole asked, knowing the musician.

"Can't make the shit up if I tried. We have eyes on the

house it's coming from and are moving on it. Other than that, it's dead around here. Nothing, no deadheads. Kind of strange, but things seem in order for the most part."

John glanced back out the window, seeing the rain pick up. "It's raining here and picking up. Looks like it's heading your way."

"Good copy. It's not here yet. I'll let you know what we find," Ben stated, ending the conversation.

John took a long breath, surveying the kitchen. "Let's see if they have anything. As long as we have one of us up, I think we are good here."

Nicole smiled, standing up and walking to the cupboard.

CHAPTER 19

Selena

Rain lightly muffled the droning music as Ben and Sarah stood behind the house opposite the source of the sound. Dan and Shelly peered over the tall fence two houses down as the two started slowly moving forward.

The patter of water on wet pavement muted their movement as they switched to their earpieces to communicate. The plan was simple. Ben and Sarah would push through the fence leading to the backyard of the two-story house while the others followed.

Much to their surprise, while the yard was still overgrown, it was clear someone was keeping it up. "Someone's inside," Ben whispered over the radio as the voice-activated devices came through the coiled cables leading up to everyone's ears.

Taking the lead, Ben raised his ass-kicker, slowly leveling his rifle as Sarah slowly opened the gate. Pausing, Ben raised a hand, pointing at his eyes and then to the back door. A light lowly glowed as the music switched to another song.

"You good?" Dan whispered, following ten feet behind.

"Yeah. It looks like someone's inside. I'm moving in. Once

I hit the door, rush in," Ben instructed the group. Sarah tapped his back as the barrel of her MP5 poked out beside him.

Ben quickly turned the corner, seeing a kitchen with several dishes of food and bottles on an island. Behind that, a man taller than Ben stepped out of the front room, holding a beer. Before the man could react, Ben grabbed the sliding door, finding it open.

Within five short seconds, the entire group had followed Ben and now pointed their weapons at the man standing in the kitchen with eyes wider than the sun at noon, staring back at them.

No one spoke as the tall man let his shoulders slightly drop. Standing at roughly six-eight, the man was covered in tattoos and clearly Hispanic. On the island, a spread of tacos and fresh vegetables was sat out as if he was expecting guests.

The music continued to drone on as Ben took the first set forward, not flinching. Small drops of water dripped onto the floor. Just as Ben was about to talk, a loud woman's voice echoed from a room off to the side of the living room.

"Hey honey! You grab the extra margarita mix?"

Sarah shifted toward the room as a shorter woman walked out, holding a margarita glass froze in place. Silence again took hold of the room as the woman who had clearly had more than a few drinks smiled.

"You didn't say you invited company!" she exclaimed, continuing forward, chugging her drink before sitting it on the counter. "Well, we at least have extra tacos."

Ben didn't move as Dan glanced at Shelly. The tall, intimidating man shifted his attention to his wife, shrugging. "I didn't," he followed as Ben raised one hand flat in front of him, slowly lowering his rifle. The others knew he was about to talk to the couple in front of them.

"We're not here to take anything, just passing by," Ben

said as the two glanced at each other.

"I mean, we have some extra tacos," the woman said, motioning for her husband to hand her the bottle of tequila in front of him.

The tall man hesitated, squinting his eyes at Ben. "I know you," he finally said, reaching out for the bottle as Ben nodded.

"I get that a lot," Ben replied as the woman walked over to her husband, grabbing the bottle.

"He's that actor guy," she said, walking over to the fridge and grabbing a small glass of ice, which was clearly a commodity in the house.

Squinting eyes shifted to recognition as he leaned back. "OH shit."

"Yeah," the woman started. "He has one of your movie posters in his man room, or whatever you call it."

Ben grinned. "That's me. Look, we're not here to cause trouble. You seem like nice folks. We're just passing through. We'll be here for a couple of days." Ben didn't need to be nice, in all fairness. He and the others were the ones with the guns.

"A couple of days? Here?" the man said as Ben agreed.

"Maybe not here, but we were planning on staying in the neighborhood. What's your name?"

Ben turned, nodding at Sarah as she lowered her gun, followed by the others. The woman spoke first, still in the midst of making her drink.

"I'm Carla, and this is my husband, Andy."

Sarah spoke next. "My name's Sarah, and that is my husband, Ben."

"I'm Shelly, and this is my husband Dan," Shelly followed as Dan smiled, looking at the tacos.

"Well. You're in a Mexican house, and you eat tacos. At

least today," Carla followed as Ben walked up, shaking Andy's hand. The smile the man shared was telling of someone truly happy to meet a movie star he was a fan of.

Recentering himself, Andy walked toward the group. "Why are you guys here?"

Ben, as he often did, erred on the truth. "We have some friends who ran into a spot of trouble, and we're going to help them out."

Carla snickered as she took the first sip of her drink, handing Sarah and then Shelly one, making the extra drinks at lightning-fast speeds. "Well, by the looks of all of you, that shouldn't be a problem."

Ben grimaced. "Oh shit," she continued. "People more decked out than you?"

"Something like that," Ben replied as Sarah took a quick sip of her drink. Fresh lime and tequila tickled her tongue, putting Ben's margaritas to shame.

Sarah cut through the cordial introduction as only she could. "Why aren't there any zombies around here?"

Andy and Carla looked at each other before Andy spoke up. "The radio tower is still working. It keeps them away. We haven't seen a rotter in forever. That's why we never leave here."

"What happens when the power to the tower goes out?" Sarah followed.

"They're solar or some shit," Andy replied, not truly thinking about the question. The truth of the matter was that even though it was not sending an actual usable signal, it was broadcasting on a set frequency that had somehow cracked a very real code. A code that, in plain terms, was a potential lifesaver.

Carla whirled around, pointing her fingers in the air and talking to Shelly and Sarah. She had clearly not been around people other than her husband since everything went to shit. "Enough of that bitches, we have food and drink. Where are y'all planning to stay?"

Ben reached down, grabbing a soft tortilla shell—something the man hadn't borne witness to since the beginning of the end. "Across the street and one house down," Ben stated, looking at Andy for approval to try the food.

"Ah, the Wilson house. We checked it out a while back. It's still in good shape. We used to know the couple, but they took off to the base. Oh, and go ahead. She always cooks too much when we are celebrating," Andy replied as Shelly stepped forward.

"What's the occasion?" Shelly asked as the couple looked confused.

"It's the exact day we didn't have to ever go to work again. You know, when it all went down and the radios and power went out," Andy replied, picking up a plate and handing it to Ben.

"Oh shit, you're right," Ben said, feeling at ease with the situation enough to grab some food. "Where did you get all this and the power?" he followed.

"That house you just mentioned had a solar power system we politely borrowed. As for the food, a bunch of folks had gardens in the neighborhood. We just took care of them and transferred most of them to the adjacent houses. We even found some corn plants, and we found a shit ton of wheat in one of those FEMA trucks heading toward Fleming Island. Looks like they were picking it up off the train sitting on the tracks just up the road. The dam thing is stocked full of....,"

Carla glanced at him knowingly, as he was giving out too much information. Ben again held his hands up.

"We're not here to get you stuff. That's the least of our worries. We've been out in the mix a good bit," He said as Sarah and Dan talked to each other at the still-open sliding doors.

The two were already discussing a possible solution to all

their undead problems when the radio tower was mentioned. Turning, now that they felt the room's eyes on them, Sarah grinned before speaking up.

"We are interested in the radio tower frequency. It could be a huge deal." Just as Sarah finished her sentence, Eve chimed in on Ben's smartwatch.

"I am scanning the available and incoming frequencies. It will take several hours. Might I recommend some easy listening?" Eve chirped as Andy and Carla gawked at Ben.

"What was that?" Andy asked as Carla was already pouring herself another drink.

"It's a little complicated, but it's a fully unlocked AI for the most part. Her name is Eve," Ben replied as the two shrugged.

"Fancy," Andy stated, handing a plate to Sarah and Dan.

"I have to ask," Sarah again started, curious about the entire situation. Have any zombies come through here at all, or other people for that matter?"

Andy, being the current voice of reason, shrugged. "A few. Not many, but they mostly wander around in circles till they figure a way out. We mostly leave them alone. As for people...," Andy paused, contemplating. "This place is pretty tucked away. We had a few others here for a while, but they eventually left wanting to go looking for family."

This was a sore subject for Shelly and Dan as they had several sons who were, for the most part, unaccounted for. That was the thing with parents at the end of the world; they had a second sense about these types of things and knew their boys were safe for some reason. As with Ben and Sarah, they had communicated with all of them before everything ceased to work.

They too had a plan. If they could, they would make their way home. Shelly smiled, thinking about her own sons, and asked. "Do you have kids?"

"Yup," Carla responded with a smile. "They were in Tallahassee. Part of some group. They stopped by last year. We haven't heard from them since, but they are smart and strong. They said they would be back toward the end of this summer[JL1]."

Ben and the others, all without talking, decided to keep their mouths shut about the situation in Tallahassee. With the pleasantries out of the way, the team radioed back to the Sanctuary and John and Nicole.

Andy and Carla were surprised by the number of people they were talking to and the organization they portrayed in their actions. There was a conversation to be had once the group in their kitchen went to the Wilson house.

CHAPTER 20

Ghosts of the apocalypse past

The fading light of dusk filtered through the windows of the Wilson house as Andy opened the front door, still having the key once entrusted to him. The sound of frogs reaching out for a hopeful mate chirped in the background, unlike the rest of the world Ben and the others had been living in. Turning to leave, Ben shook the man's hand.

"Thanks for dinner and the hospitality. We have a lot to do tomorrow, but as you mentioned, if you don't mind, we would appreciate you showing us the train. If they have weapons like you showed us, it will save us a good amount of time."

Andy smiled. "No problem. Thanks for the radio. I don't know how much we can help, but," Andy hesitated. "I don't want any trouble here. You are good people. I can tell, and that story about the news and you. Crazy man." Andy breathed out. "If we can help, we will. We just don't want things to change around here."

Ben smiled. "Scouts honor. You have friends now. Hell, these folks are damn near family. I promise we'll do everything we can to keep things civil around here. Just remember, a lot is going on out there. I can't promise much outside of what we can control."

Andy beamed a smile. "Oh, one last thing. The old owner's dog is still around. A golden retriever named Max. He hangs at our place most of the time but comes over here most evenings and nights. Sad really. I think he is still waiting for his owners to come home. If you see him, watch out for his tongue. There should be some treats on the counter. He's pretty much our dog at this point. I'm not too sure where he runs off to sometimes. There is an opening in the back fence he uses."

With a casual salute, Andy headed back across the street, a hint of relief in his step. Turning, the others smiled at Ben. Dan stepped forward, already looking inside the house, smiling. "They are good people." The sounds of Selena echoed once again in the coming night.

Ben walked into the house as Sarah beamed her flashlight up the stairs. Shelly walked toward the kitchen as Dan turned left into the office, which was directly off the entrance once occupied by the homeowners. Guitars hung on the wall, with a computer sprawled on a desk once used for work.

"Look," Ben said, pointing at several family pictures on the wall. They looked like a happy family."

Dan nodded. "Yeah. This place feels like a home."

Shelly called from the kitchen. "There's a bunch of rations here. I guess Andy and Carla hadn't grabbed them yet. But there is an empty margarita glass sitting on the counter. They know this stuff is here and likely plan on using it."

"The upstairs looks in good shape," Sarah called from the small landing overlooking the entrance from the second story.

Ben breathed in. "Whelp. Looks like we will get settled. Check it out. This place even has a pool and plenty of booze."

A tall glass cabinet sat closed, displaying several bottles of fine whiskey. Glancing down, Ben noticed the dog bowl and several chew toys sitting on the back porch, now cast in shadows from the incoming night.

"What's the plan?" Sarah asked, having cleared the upstairs, finding four well-suited bedrooms, including that of two boys, full of computers and toys once used during their youth.

Dan paused before setting a radio on the kitchen island. Ben breathed out a slow, lingering lungful before speaking up. "I'm with Dan. Call the others, then get set up for tomorrow morning. Make one last check-in with Dustin and Tina for the night, then," Ben eyed the liquor cabinet. Let the house feel like it's still a home."

It was clear to the group that the other residents of the neighborhood had made an effort to keep it and a few other surrounding residences in working order. The truth was, much like the dog Andy mentioned, they too hoped some of the owners would one day return.

Dan keyed the radio call on the internal frequency they had set up outside of the regular channels. "Net call, this is Dan. You guys copy?"

John replied, followed by Ian and the others. "Go ahead," John replied as Ian stood by, knowing they were out in the wild.

"We're set for the night. The others we met are taking us to a closer supply point with weapons. Anything on your end?" Dan asked.

Nicole looked back, still sitting by the window overlooking the main bridge and river. The droning of the undead out front was present yet distant enough not to cause immediate concern. On the kitchen counter, a deck of Uno cards lay sprawled out, as did the afternoon's dinner. The two were getting comfortable in their new surroundings.

"Nothing but some lights up river near the Buckman bridge. If anything moves coming this way, we'll see it." John replied, handing Nicole a cup of instant coffee he had just brewed—the smell calming in the quite empty condo.

"Ian?" Dan asked as Sam answered.

"All good here. Ian is making dinner. Looks like a gumbo of some sort," she replied as Ian spoke up in the background.

"Jambalaya, it's jambalaya."

Ben shrugged. "I didn't know we had the stuff to make it."

Dan turned his attention back to the radio. "Any movement around the permitter or south on the river?"

"Nothing," Sam replied, staring at the security camera feed recently installed.

"Eve," Ben said as Dan still keyed the radio, sharing the conversation.

"Hello, everyone. Is anyone in the mood for some tunes?" Eve chirped.

"No. Not now," Ben instructed. Prior to leaving Andy and Carla's house, he instructed Eve to identify the signal from the local tower. "Any word on the signal?"

"Oh yes. That. One primary signal is being sent from the tower. It is not broadcasting anything. That being stated, it is a 5G signal that is on a set frequency that I have identified."

"Listen everyone. I mentioned it earlier, but there are no zombies in the immediate area. I'm not sure how far the radius is, but according to the others, that signal keeps them away from here. Eve," Ben again asked.

"Yes? Is it time for some Lionel Richie?"

"No. Send the signal information to the Sanctuary's main terminal. Also, see if you can somehow locate another tower or transmitter like the one here. It might be in some type of directory."

"Very well. I'll have some music on standby just in case," Eve replied, cutting out as she went to work on searching for information in all the databases now available.

Ben pointed back to Dan as he took back over the conversation. "We're going to call Dustin and Tina one last time to check in. Not sure what will happen from there, but we're planning on moving out as soon as the sun crests."

"Good copy," John replied as Dan switched the radio over to the main channel.

"Dustin, Tina, you copy?" Dan asked as everyone else stood by on the net, also having switched over.

Several minutes passed as Dustin finally replied. The truth was that the team on the base was getting ready to move out and had been making plans, taking them longer than usual to get back to their prisoners.

"Go ahead," Dustin replied as Amanda stood over him with the same pad of paper to relay messages to send.

At the door, Bill and Andrew stood watching the interaction. Dan's voice echoed throughout the small Conex as the rain created a rhythmic tapping on its roof. "Checking in for the night. We're heading out in the morning. No change to the schedule, ending any slowdowns. All good there?"

Dustin looked up at Amanda before responding. He was doing this on purpose, giving her time to direct him if needed. It was all part of his campaign to build trust—trust that he would throttle to death once it was no longer needed. She trusted him to respond.

"We're good. Same here. No change," Dustin replied as Amanda scribbled a note. "One thing." He started back. "Let us know when you're a day out. Looks like we are still set for two or three more days."

Amanda glared at Dustin. He said this on purpose and also to convey that he wasn't sure when they were moving out but knew it wouldn't be tomorrow morning.

"Good copy," Dan replied, glancing around the room to a nod from Ben. "We'll call once we're moving again."

"Sounds good. Talk to you tomorrow," Dustin replied as the radio went silent.

Dan turned, walking over to the liquor cabinet, grabbing a bottle of fine whiskey as Ben spoke up. "Sounds like we have at least a day."

"Agreed," Sarah added, noticing a battery-operated camping light in the living room. The night was now setting in. "Let's head to the inlet tomorrow and get set up."

"Same," Ben replied as Shelly cleaned out four glasses. "I say we all get a good night's rest. If something is going on, we'll hear it on the radio. I know John and Nicole will be up. Let's take advantage of it while we can."

With everyone in agreement, Dan poured a round of nightcaps as the group made their way upstairs for what they suspected was their last night of peaceful rest for the foreseeable future.

CHAPTER 21

Mad Max

A light beep echoed throughout the house as Lionel Richie slowly played on Ben's smartwatch. Eve had been waiting all night to play music, now finding it a suitable time.

"Morning," Ben whispered as Sarah smiled and stretched. The large four-poster bed was covered in fluffy white blankets. While the two had slept in their clothes above the covers, the night had been relatively calm as rain continued to pelt the area. According to Eve, it would likely stay the course over the next two days.

"Morning," Sarah replied as the sounds of the others waking up joined the long stretch. Ben also joined in. "You hear that?"

Ben turned his head as a scratching whimper came from downstairs. "Think it's the dog?"

"Max?" Sarah said, nodding. "He probably thinks his owners are home." Just as the words left her mouth, full-on barking started coming from downstairs.

Smiles erupted as they both turned the corner to find Shelly and Dan doing the same while barks and scratching on the back door continued to grow louder.

Turning the corner, there, in the purplish glow of the continuing rainy morning, was a light blonde golden retriever with its tongue hanging out the side of his mouth. It was indeed Max. After several more scratches at the door, including standing straight up, the team quickly realized just how large, in fact, this golden retriever was.

Massive wet paws beat a cadence on the door as Max finally saw the group now staring at him. Dropping on all fours, the dog quickly scurried in a circle, picking up one of the many toys sitting on the back porch out of the rain.

"Are we going to let him in?" Shelly asked as Ben stepped forward, unlocking the sliding glass door. Before he could get the large, heavy glass panels fully open, Max wedged his nose in it, pushing all the way in.

What happened next was the stuff of nightmares. Max circled the group several times, attacking them with his tail with violence only witnessed in the darkest of lashings. Ben took several steps back as Max plopped down on the kitchen floor, dropping his toy. To continue the nightmarish hound's actions, a full-on body shake followed, drenching the surrounding area.

As if his massive size wasn't enough to take the group off guard, the vicious tongue now hanging out his mouth, propped up by a smile reaching his now perked ears, sealed the deal. All four of the intrepid adventurers reached down, petting the dog as he winced and shook in excitement, not knowing whether to sit down or stand up.

After several minutes of ferocious petting and scratching, Max picked up his toy and dropped it at Ben's feet. It was a peace offering to conclude the vicious attack the group had just endured.

"Good boy," Ben guffawed as Max looked up, still beaming a smile.

Intelligence swam behind the dog's deep brown eyes as

he shifted to the jar of treats on the counter. This was his house, and if the dog could talk, it would tell them welcome. It wasn't the fact that it wasn't his owners, but the group made the house feel like a home again. People milling around, talking, and generally being human. Something Max had profoundly missed.

Dan reached over and grabbed the jar as Max let out a full-on guttural bark. While beautiful on the outside, it was clear this was a dog that likely had a bite to back it up. Max sat immediately, awaiting his prize. He once again looked at his toy, which happened to be a stuffed crab, which was now showing the ravages of time.

Dan chucked a treat as Max caught it on instinct, sitting back down while his tongue flopped back out of the side of his mouth. Ben grinned, not having seen a dog since everything started.

"He's amazing," Sarah spoke up, also smiling.

"He's a good boy," Ben said, scratching behind his ears as Max flopped on his back, exposing his belly. A tall tale sign of trust in animals. Max did indeed know how to read people as animals often could.

Shelly was the only one not smiling as a small tear streaked her face. She loved animals, and the sadness of Max thinking his owners had finally arrived home came crashing down on her in a flood of emotion. Dogs had a way of doing that with people. Max looked up, rolling over and walking to the woman as he sat down, licking her hand.

"Are you okay, babe?" Dan asked. She nodded, finally smiling, and reached down to petting the dog.

"I think he likes us," Ben said as the wrap of knuckles on the door broke the moment.

"Hey guys, are you in there?" Andy's voice echoed down the main hallway, followed by Carla inserting a key in the door.

"Yeah. We met Max," Ben said as the two entered the

house.

Max wagged his tail, seeing his now de facto caretakers. "He's a good boy. His food is in the pantry, but we brought him some leftover tacos."

The dog's ears perked, now understanding what the word taco truly meant as he shuffled down the hallway to greet the two. Food was sat in Max's bowl as the dog buried his face in his morning meal.

"Morning," Andy said as Dan started making coffee. Ben noted the man wearing an armored vest and carrying an AK47. He was ready for their trip to the train tracks.

After a night of talking, Carla and Andy decided to help as much as they could. The conclusion was simple. They hadn't met anyone in over a year, and the people in front of them were not there to cause any problems. In reality, they knew there was a rough, dangerous world just outside of the neighborhood.

"Morning. That's one hell of a dog," Ben said as Max took a look back, knowing they were talking about him.

"He is. I wanted to tell you guys we're going to help if we can. I'm not saying we're going to fight your fight, but we will help," Andy said as Carla cleared her throat.

"What my hubby is trying also to say is that it would be good to see what is going on out there," Carla followed. While she was also wearing protective clothing and having a pistol hanging off her hip, she was more reserved about the statement. They would help but not involve themselves in their mission.

Heads nodded as Sarah handed out cups from Dan's small gas-powered coffee maker. "Showing us this train is more than enough," Sarah followed, also handing one to Andy, who gladly accepted. "This might not be the time to get into it, but a lot is going on out there, and we have a safe place that we could show you at some point." She had made the call to speak for the group.

Andy glanced at an approving Carla, who slurped her

coffee. Max yipped, scratching the back door, needing to go out after eating. His tail was wagging so hard it was causing a light breeze in the kitchen. It reminded him of days long since passed, having a house full of people talking. The familiar smell of coffee setting the dog at ease.

"We heard you on the radio talking to the others before making your call," Andy started, sitting his rifle on the counter. "The rains set in for a few days. We can get to the train and get back in a couple of hours. It's less than a mile up the road. Are you guys planning on staying here again tonight?"

Ben breathed out his nose, taking a pull of his coffee. "Likely not. Things could change pretty fast if the people we are waiting on decide to show up early to the fish camp."

"Understood," Carla said. The couple was in synch with each other. "We'll go to the train with you, and then we'll head back here. I take it this radio will still reach you?"

Dan spoke up, letting an eager Max back in, who had his mouth stuffed with more toys to show off to the group. "Yup. That's yours. We have two extra. Like Sarah said. If this all works out, we can keep in touch or have you over for dinner."

"Sounds good," Andy replied, smiling briefly.

"What about the dog?" Ben asked as Andy shrugged.

"Max does what Max wants."

The following call to Dustin and Tina was generic, as Dustin gave no indication that Amanda had left or if they were coming along. John and Nicole were also settling in. The only issue they were dealing with was the group of zombies now camped outside the condo they were occupying. While not trying to get in, the rain had kept them in a perpetual game of ring around the rosy.

Although the rain provided good cover, keeping most noises muffled, it also set the stage for the undead to be out and about as the group pulled onto the road. Andy and Carla were now sitting in the back seat of Ben's golf cart.

Rain spattered the small convoy of golf course-faring vehicles as Ben took the turn onto a street coincidentally named Sleepy Hollow. Sarah leaned forward, seeing several downed trees and a handful of abandoned cars sitting at various angles on the road.

"It's good," Andy spoke up, seeing the hesitation. "We cleared a path a while back."

Squinting his eyes, Ben motioned for Sarah to have her weapon ready. "Just in case," He murmured, pulling around the first abandoned car.

Doors sat open as if the car was yawning. Suitcases of useless junk sat stacked on the back seats. With no signs of a struggle, they had more than likely been left out on foot for some unforeseen reason. That reason was that one of the many trains that had stopped had picked people up, according to Carla.

They had been made aware of the pickups but smartly chose to stay behind, likely saving their lives. "They were told to leave everything behind," Carla said as Andy pointed toward the treelined.

There, standing like a majestic guard dog of the ancient Gods, was Max. "Looks like we got back up," Andy said as Ben pulled up beside the dog, the end of the road now within eyeshot.

"You coming boy?" Ben asked as Max walked out in front of the golf cart, taking the lead at a slow pace. "Well, guess that answers that."

"Told you he was smart," Andy said, turning around to see the main intersection out of the neighborhood and the end of Sleepy Hollow. "Every time we come up here, he shows up."

Just as Max started making his way to the end of the road, Eve chimed to life. "Hello everyone. I thought you would like to know that I have singled out the signal from the radio tower. It appears to be a rather obscure frequency that was encrypted."

"That's great news Eve," Ben followed as Eve started back up.

"Not all good news. By my calculation, the signal has a rather short range. I would say we are approaching its limits. It also seems to be losing strength."

"Shit," Ben huffed, stopping the cart. Max, sensing this, also stopped, continuing to face toward the intersection.

"Oh, not by any major means. It's that over time, the signal may lose some of its strength, meaning its range may decrease. I only slightly noticed a variation at micro band levels."

"Eve, what can we do with this?" Ben quickly asked, also watching Max, who was laser-focused on something ahead.

"I have taken the opportunity to program a set channel on your radios. You will not be able to communicate on it. Still, it may replicate a small localized effect as the tower on the neighborhood."

"That's great news. Anything else?" Ben asked as Eve paused.

"You're the humans with human brains. I'm sure you'll figure something out."

Andy let out a snort at the dry humor coming from Eve. "She always like that?"

"Increasingly more so," Ben said, pulling forward only to have Max freeze in place.

"Is he growling?" Sarah asked as Ben nodded. "Yeah, he's not letting us get any closer."

Turning, Ben gave the universal signal to dismount as Dan and Shelly quickly joined the group, now standing behind Max.

"There," Dan pointed toward one of the open cars on the

train at the main intersection.

Sitting with its back against the train and what looked like its chest shredded to pieces was a body. Time had taken its toll on the figure as its legs and arms looked to be one with the pavement and train.

"You think it's still alive?" Sarah asked as Ben shrugged.

"Somethings got Max worked up. I'll check it out," Ben said, stepping in front of Max only to have the dog take several more steps in front of him. "Good boy. Let me get this," Ben whispered to the dog as Andy suddenly appeared by his side.

"I'll go with you," Andy said, pulling up his rifle while Ben reached for his silenced pistol.

The body was mangled from an undetermined amount of time exposed to Mother Nature. Max continued to growl as Ben raised his pistol, pointing it directly between the figure's eyes as a slight twitch tremored through the undead's face. It was indeed still alive or dead, depending on how one interpreted the entire situation.

Holding his hand up to get Max to stay, Ben snapped a round into the skull of the zombie, making Andy flinch.

"You okay?" Ben asked under his breath so the others couldn't hear.

"Yeah, it's just we haven't seen many of these dam things. How was it still moving?"

"They're like that. I bet this one's been here for maybe a month or so. The heat can get to them pretty fast. You said you hadn't been out here in a while. Looks like a mix of weather and animals. He likely got into a tangle with a zombie somewhere close by. I don't think this area is completely safe."

As the words floated out of Ben's mouth, the rattle of flesh on a fence across the street proved his statement true. They were at the very edge of the radio tower's signal power. The rain had washed the trail of mayhem the man had once dragged across the street in search of the treasure the train held.

"All clear. Weapons hot," Ben said over the radio as the rest of the team walked up to the scene. There was no way to get onto the open train car without stepping over the mess of sludge, which no longer posed a threat.

Ben glared down the tracks in both directions, seeing several more cars stretching in either direction. The rest of the train, heading north, disappeared around a corner.

"Is there any way to get into those cars stretching down the road toward your neighborhood?" Dan asked, also thinking the same thing.

We would have to move a bunch of cargo out of the way. With you guys here, we probably could. The weapons are a few cars up the tracks in the other direction," Andy replied, pointing north away from Sleepy Hollow.

Ben turned to Sarah as Max turned, now staring at a handful of the undead bouncing off a fence across the four-lane road. "What do you think?"

Sarah chewed on her bottom lip. "I'm thinking we grab as many weapons as we can and head to the fish camp. If I'm right, it's going to take some time to get there."

"I hate it when you say that," Dan huffed.

"Say what?"

"If I'm right," Ben and Dan chorused, sharing a knowing look—Sarah was always right.

"Let's get to it. Andy, do you mind going with us? You know your way through the cars as they're all connected. Shelly can stay out here with Carla?"

He was asking for help without pushing them too hard. Carla nodded at Andy, who smiled. "The boss says it's okay."

Max continued to stare into the rainy distance as Ben

pulled down the sleek tripod on his rifle, switching out his magazine for a less aggressive round to allow for the silencer to work better in order not to draw any further attention.

"What's he doing?" Carla leaned over, asking Sarah.

"Making sure we're good," Sarah said as Ben smacked several well-placed shots into the small group of zombies, now quickly falling to the ground.

"Dam," Andy breathed out. "That was awesome."

Ben turned. "Let's just hope we can get out of here without a real fight."

On those words, Dan pulled himself into the car, reaching down to help the others. Sarah scanned the interior of the rail car, seeing several stacks of corn that had been ravaged by rats or some other small animal.

"Don't worry, the other cars are all sealed off. We closed all the doors,' Andy ensured, opening the first car.

Inside this car, stacks of wheat and pallets of food made to withstand the test of time towered to the ceiling. As Andy pointed out, a large section had been cleared out.

"That's all we've taken so far, other than a pallet in the car in the opposite direction.

"There's enough food in here to last forever if it holds up," Sarah added, pointing out the FEMA stamp on the pallets.

"That's what we think. The next car has batteries, radios, and all kinds of stuff. We figured it was for a base. The car after that is where the weapons start. The rest of the cars stretching down the road are all food as well," Andy finished.

Ben didn't hesitate to walk into the next car to see the prize. Stacks of assault rifles sat in racks beside crates of ammunition. On the far end of the car was a crate labeled claymores, and beside that were several marked crates proclaiming to hold grenades.

"Sweet Jesus," Ben grinned. "Dan, you know what to get?"

Dan turned, already unstacking several crates. This was followed by him pointing at several boxes of ammunition and what looked like two grenade launchers with cylinders resembling a large revolver of eat shit and die.

"You guys know how to use all this stuff?" Andy asked as Dan put an unlit cigarette in his mouth.

"Yup," he snapped, already asking for help carrying the munitions back to the carts.

"Check those out," Ben pointed at a large crew-serve machine gun much like his own they had secured on Fleming Island. "I suggest you grab one of those and some ammo."

Andy nodded. "Yeah, I guess we could."

"We can show you how to use it before heading out. That thing will mow down an entire field of those things. Andy, "Ben paused. "This is something having this here. It will save us a lot of time and hassle. We owe you."

Andy turned and picked up one of the machine guns from the rack. "I'll be like you in one of your movies but in real life." He joked as Max started barking at the top of his lungs

CHAPTER 22

Go

Standing on top of the train, rain-spattered the pavement as the road disappeared into a grey haze. While it was still morning, the noon heat was quickly approaching like a pissed-off ex coming back for their stuff after a bad breakup.

Ben shook his head, looking down as Max finally jumped back into the golf cart, getting out of the rain. Several zombies peppering the road were heading in their general direction. Sarah stood behind him as Dan and Shelly continued to load gear into the small pull-behind trailers.

"I can't believe we didn't look under the train," Ben whispered as Sarah glanced down one more time, looking directly at the road on the opposite side of the train. Piled up like concertgoers smashed against the front rails of a popular boy band, mounds of bodies lay stacked on top of each other. Some of the disfigured corpses shifted, making the mass of meat and bones pulse.

"I guess the rain is keeping the smell down," Sarah whispered back. "How many do you think there are?"

Ben scratched his stubbled chin, wiping off the rain. "About a hundred. They're spread out thanks to the rain."

Sarah squinted her eyes, pointing at what looked like a gas

station to their right in the distance, just past a stop light. "If the images are right, we barely have a mile. What about the radios? We go slow and use that signal?"

Smiling, Ben held out a fist, only to have Sarah return the gesture. "Simply badass idea, babe. That's why you get paid the big bucks."

"We need to keep Max from barking. He probably drew them out. Either way, we need to get moving. The rain could stop, and that will cause a mess of issues," Ben whispered, turning to the ladder and climbing down.

"What's the word?" Dan asked as he sat down the final crate of claymore mines.

"About a hundred dead heads. It's a straight shot. Sarah figures we should all key up our radios on the new frequency and see if that keeps them away," Ben replied, seeing Andy and Carla looking at the newly acquired weapon.

Both Dan and Shelly nodded their approval of the genius idea. It would be genius if it truly worked.

Max huffed, seemingly also approving the idea. "We're going once we get loaded up," Ben added as everyone nodded. "What about you guys? I have to ask."

Andy turned to Carla. "We're not ready to get out there yet. Tell you what, though. If shit gets too bad out there, we'll see what we can do."

Carla nodded her approval of the statement as Shelly spoke up, having been relatively quiet since arriving. "They'll, or someone or something will eventually make its way back here. This train is a goldmine. Look at this guy." Shelly pointed at the now-covered corpse, the only thing visible under the FEMA blanket being a rotted hand.

"We understand," Carla spoke up. "If you need help. We'll help, but for now, we're staying here."

On those words, the couple turned, heading back toward their house with their newly found bounty, including several more cases of rations and ammunition. The one surprising addition to the motley crew was Max.

The dog stood resolutely on the back of the golf cart as if supervising the operation about to take place. The truth of the situation was that Max felt connected to the people he was now protecting. Proud that his house had once again hosted people, bringing back some level of normalcy. That and Ben had fed him a steady stream of treats since meeting him.

Another ten minutes passed as they made their way back down the railroad tracks to the southern butt end of the train, finally turning to make their way up the opposing side.

Ben stopped as the first signs of the undead made themselves known, keying up the radio one last time. "Switching to the sub-channel. Use Eve if we need to talk till then."

Eve was capable of near-field communication when close enough, allowing the team not to rely on their radios. Just in case they had company, Dan would keep his radio tuned in to their primary channel while scanning the secondary channel Dustin and Tina were on.

Ben looked back, seeing Max's head now poking out between him and Sarah, facing the road. "You good boy?" Ben asked as Max's tongue dropped out. After a quick round of head scratches, Ben pressed the small pedal on the cart, pushing it forward; there would be no turning back.

"You really like him," Sarah said as Ben nodded.

"I always wanted a Golden Retriever. We just never had the time. Get focused babe, and don't forget about those grenades." He pointed at the two balls of death sitting in the cup holders.

The mound of corpses started several feet before the main turn off to the road, forcing Ben to turn into the slushy muck on the side of the graveled track. With only one butt-puckering spin of the wheels, the upgraded offroad tires found purchase, finally depositing the team on the main road.

Three zombies stared blankly at the golf carts towing small trailers as if they were a lost tribe first seeing a tank pull up to their humble village. Sarah pulled up her silenced pistol as Max began to lowly growl, knowing he needed to keep the noise down.

Ben shook his head, pointing to the radio. "No time like the present to test it out." Black tape held down the transmitter button as Ben slowly pulled forward.

If the undead started moving toward them and acted unphased, Ben would floor it to the golf cart at blistering a max speed of fifteen miles per hour. A few precious seconds passed as Ben inched closer. Max lowered his head, now bearing his teeth.

Just as Ben was about to signal to fire on the two closest zombies, they seemed to slowly turn in the opposite direction.

Letting a slight grin slit, Ben pushed forward, trying not to focus on the mass of writhing bodies pressed against the train. At some point, they had been drawn in and cut down by the man they had encountered on the other side of the train.

Pressing forward, More zombies lingered in the tree line as they passed an overgrown ballfield to their right. Dozens of zombies milled around inside the outdoor sports park, stuck inside the metal fence. Someone had herded them inside, closing the main fence.

Max continued to growl as Sarah leaned over, not wanting to talk out loud. "Those are fresh."

"Yeah," was all Ben said, swerving around a parked work van on the road. Tall grass slapped the bottom of the cart as they finally made their way to the gas station.

Wooden plywood covered windows as cars jammed the pumps, as owners made a last-ditch effort to fill their gas tanks to take a trip they would never finish. Skeletons lay around the small complex, showing signs that a real-life nightmare had occurred.

More zombies shuffled in and out of the road as Ben started to see a pattern. The undead would initially be attracted to the group, only to be turned away as they approached within twenty feet. This forced Ben to slow down, allowing the radio signal to work.

"Check the battery level," Ben said as he reached down, pulling up one of the radios that now showed only two green bars.

"It's taking a good amount of power," she replied, setting the radio back down. "Look. There's the bridge."

Covered with cars and nearly impassable, the bridge connecting what was known as Orange Park to Fleming Island was a chaotic jumble of cars and luggage. Eve chirped to life as Dan's voice came over the smartwatch.

"We can take a left. There's a row of houses facing the fish camp. We can get set up and head over on foot," Dan suggested. Ben started slowly turning left.

The choice was easy. The third house down had a chest-high fence surrounding his front yard leading into the back. On the ground, signs of flooding from the storm last year left debris as well as random long-since deceased fish in the middle of the road. Sprawled across the road, stopping any chance of them going further.

Ben supposed this might be a good thing, keeping zombies contained or preventing them from coming at them from the general direction. On the other hand, it could also cause a traffic jam of unwanted guests.

"That house is going to have to do," Ben stated as Max

leaned his head further between the pair.

The crackle of gravel and loose debris under the tires of the cart came to a silent halt, replaced by the light patter of rain still present and still giving them sufficient cover to move. Max, without warning, sprang from the back seat, jumping in front of the small convoy.

"Guess that settles that," Sarah grinned as Dan pulled up beside him.

Max sniffed the air as Sarah also stepped out, holding her weapon at the ready, scanning not only the house but the fence on the opposite side of the road containing another small neighborhood. A boat sat in the front yard next to them, covered in green moss.

"Everyone turn off the radios. Let's just leave one on, echoing the signal as we scan the house. I'll open the front gate. Everyone else, pull the golf carts in," Ben instructed, seeing the padlock securing the gate.

With a quick, muffled shot from his pistol, Ben made quick work of the mechanism, only able to pull one side open. More debris from fallen tree branches lay strewn across the front yard as an old minivan sat in front of a closed garage. Once upon a time, the house was occupied by a family that had the property passed down to them by their parents.

The one-story brick home looked untouched beside Mother Nature's embrace in the gray afternoon as Ben started noticing the rain easing up. Closed shutters, a glass door, and the front of the main entrance door meant the house was likely empty.

Before Ben and the others parked both vehicles inside, Max made his way to the front door and sniffed the area, only to turn and wag his tail.

"I guess that means it's safe?" Ben asked no one in particular.

"The dog hasn't been wrong yet," Dan supposed, also noticing the lack of rain. "We need to get inside in case the rain is starting to clear up and get on the radio."

With a quick nod, Ben made his way to the front door, pulling out his crowbar. It was time to get the party started.

Max walked in circles as Ben lightly pressed into the door while prying the lock open. As usual, Ben lightly tapped the door frame, stepped back, and pulled up his pistol. Before anything alive or dead inside the structure could react, Max let out a light yip, pushing his nose into the cracked door and running inside.

Ben turned while the others shrugged. "I think it's safe," Shelly said, focusing on the supplies.

Sarah and Ben entered as Max stood in the hallway. The light from the window facing the fish camp and inlet beaming light inside the gloomy one-story house, visible from the sitting room.

Chaos and scattered furniture lay in confusion from what looked to be a fight. Not moving, Ben noted the water line several inches off the floor, staining the molded wall.

"This is more than the water," Sarah breathed out, not liking the stale air she was now breathing. Smelling like a sauna full of people who hadn't showered for months, Ben agreed, wrinkling his nose. It would take a few minutes to get acclimated.

Max interrupted the thought, scratching one of the bedroom doors down the main hallway. Like most older Florida homes on the water built in the nineteen seventies, the main area in the front of the house was used as a sitting room with a hallway tracing the length of the house, having bedrooms and bathrooms on either side.

"What is it boy?" Ben asked, walking over a mangled couch.

Max turned his back to the door, sitting down before

barking. "I think he's saying not to go into that room," Sarah called, opening the door as Shelly and Dan walked in, also experiencing the wretched stench.

Testing the theory, Ben reached for the door handle only to have Max stand up and nudge his hand. "Okay. Got it."

Max stood running off to the back of the house. Dan, now lighting up a cigarette to cover the odor, let out a sigh.

"What's up?" Ben asked, pulling out the marksmanship rifle they acquired on the train.

While similar to the one Tina carried, it was also supplied with all the fixings. A thermal scope, silencer, and even night optics used to tag targets at night all sat in neat holding areas protected by grey padding.

"Not gonna lie. That trip here had the hairs on the back of my neck standing on end."

"And your back," Shelly joked, sitting two claymore mines on the now cleared-off kitchen counter.

A large glass window overlooked the inlet, surrounded by two smaller windows. To the left, a large living room, still having some form of normality, opened into the backyard via a set of double doors.

"No," Dan started with a thoughtful look on his face. "That radio deal could be a game changer. I just don't know if it's going to work on the crazies. They're too fast if they get that close."

Ben took his helmet off and sat it on the half-smashed wooden dining room table. "We need to focus on the here and now. My battery is about gone. We'll have to talk to Eve about that." Remembering this, Ben quickly plugged his radio into a small portable charger he carried with him. "Not to change the subject, but what do you think happened here?"

Dan glanced around the room. Ben was trying to keep the focus on the current situation. "Don't know. The water for sure, but it looks like something went crazy in here."

"That's what I'm thinking," Sarah followed. "Max here doesn't want us going into the far left bedroom down the main hall. If I were to bet, since the house was locked. Someone turned in here and went crazy. This looks like damage from a close struggle. Maybe they got lucky and took who or whatever down and then locked them in their room and left."

Dan chewed on the statement, unpacking the claymore detonators. Unlike the ones he learned to use in the military, these were remote.

"Sounds about right. So," Dan paused, overlooking the weapons to be set up in the house on the counter. "What's the plan?"

"Doesn't look like we can get the carts across the bridge without moving some things around. It would take too much time. I'm thinking Sarah and I walk over and get ready. We either set up an ambush…or…, wire the entire place to go boom," Ben flared his fingers. "It all depends on what's coming. Either way, I think we are going to have to split up here."

"We can take the bikes," Sarah suggested, making a good point.

"Fair enough," Ben replied as Dan lit another cigarette. Even though he had significantly slowed down his puffing habit, he was nervous. "You okay?"

"I just don't like splitting up," Dan grumbled.

"Me neither. You know it will give us more coverage. Tell you what," Ben paused to gather his thoughts. "If we get done in time and John calls us with good news, meaning a small group, we can head back. Sound good?"

"All right," Dan replied as the others nodded. Over the past year, the team had formed an odd form of communal governance. While Ben was the clear leader of the pack, everyone had a voice.

As if the dog Gods themselves were part of the plan, Max let out a full-bellied woof, agreeing with the vibe the humans were giving off.

CHAPTER 23

A three-hour tour

The droning of rain had stopped peppering the metal shipping container, making the heavy footsteps walking up the wooden stairs to the door echo in the small space. Dustin stood as Tina stayed on the hard couch, ready to make another radio call.

Hinges creaked as the sound of the lock being clicked open gave way to Bill, Andrew, and Amanda. Standing outside, several more guards loomed in the background. This was different than their prior visits.

Amanda set the radio on the small table. "It's time to call and find out the others' status."

Dustin took a steadying breath, knowing they were leaving soon. "Very well. Sounds like the rain is slowing down."

Amanda looked as if the words floated through her body, not stopping to be processed. Bill cleared his throat. "Is there a problem? She said to get on the radio."

Dustin, seeing that the time for winning friends and influencing people was now over, picked up the radio. "Just saying the rain makes good cover to travel."

"Point taken," Amanda finally responded.

"Ben, you copy?" Dustin asked as Dan replied while watching Ben and Sarah finally cross the bridge.

"Dan here. What's up?"

"Not much. Just checking in. About to pack up and make the final push into town. Rain has been slowing us down. Wanted to see if the weather is bad there as well," Dustin casually said as Amanda scribbled on the notepad still sitting on the table.

"Same here. Rains still falling," Dan started. "Still about two days out. We're going to bunk down the last night and make the final push by noon."

Dustin looked down at the note. He knew it was to forward but to the chance to follow orders. "You guys around Palatka?" Amanda was trying to gauge their location.

A pause followed as Dan was gauging the question. "Yup. They're thick down here, but we're making it."

"Sounds good. We're on the backroads. Loads of them on the main highway. Talk soon." Dustin clicked off the radio. "Good?"

"Yes," Amanda snapped back. She was wound tight. "If things work out. We will consider your future. Till then…, you stay here."

Amanda turned on her heels, walking straight out of the shipping container. Dustin noticed Bill not moving. "Andrew," the gruff man instructed. "Close the door. I'll be out in a few minutes."

Dustin rolled his shoulders back, knowing this wasn't going to be a pleasant conversation. In reality, he could snap the man's neck before he could blink.

"I'm not going to be as civil as Amanda. "If either of you try anything. We will kill you."

The sounds of someone flushing the toilet caught Dustin

off guard. He had been too busy on the radio to notice one of the guards slip inside. "Ah, Bill continued. This is Jacob. He will be keeping an eye on you."

The man looked like a greaser straight out of the 1950s. His hair was slicked back, not by oil but rather by grease from not being washed. A toothpick hung out of the man's mouth, sealing the deal for Dustin. The man in front of him was a tool.

"Hey. No funny business," Jacob sneered, pulling out a pistol and waving it at them. "Andrew's getting your dinner. Enjoy it. I don't plan on opening the kitchen up for you while this little situation gets handled."

Dustin simply nodded. In reality, he was thinking how fun it would be to snap the man's neck then and there for waving a pistol at them. He already had a plan for Bill. Bill had a special place in hell waiting for him after waving the shotgun in Tina's face.

Bill motioned Jacob out. "One last thing. Jacob is one call away. I suggest you let us know now if there's something we need to know."

Dustin knew the look on Bill's face. He couldn't care less if they lived or died. "Not that I can think of."

Bill turned, leaving the trailer as Andrew walked up with two trays of food. "Don't stay long. We need those two locked up."

Andrew walked in as another guard reached out, closing the door. "The last supper," the young man grinned.

"Seems like it. Sound like you and grease head out there are staying behind," Dustin said under his breath.

"Yeah, that guy's a real dick. I thought about shutting him up a few times," Andrew said, standing up. "You know I was a national karate champion?"

"No shit," Tina said, leaning forward, seeing another pile

of sandwiches. As she reached out for one, Andrew tapped his foot, shaking his head. Tina hesitated.

"You guys get a full belly and get some deep sleep," Andrew said, winking. Dustin nodded. He was telling them the food was laced with something. "Yup. The real deal. Any who, get some rest."

The door once again clicked shut as Dustin sat beside his wife, leaning in to talk. "We're getting out of here."

"When?" Tina asked, actually wanting one of the sandwiches as she pushed the tray away.

"Next time someone walks through that door," Dustin assured, putting his arm around his one and only love.

While their relationship was a game of patience, as is usual with military families, they never grew apart or became unhappy with their time apart. Like Ben and Sarah finding themselves against insurmountable odds, the universe told both Dustin and Tina the other was alive.

While Tina was a one-person wrecking crew all unto herself, the two together were unstoppable.

CHAPTER 24

Cradle to the Grave

L arge moss-covered trees gave the gloomy, desolate fish camp a hellish yet almost peaceful vibe. Cars sat in the graveled parking lot as if waiting for their owner to step out and head home. A home that likely hadn't ever been returned to.

"You ever hear about this place?" Ben asked. Sarah nodded, having spent many a night in the eclectic restaurant and fish camp.

"I used to hang here with my girlfriends. This spot has been here forever. Look," Sarah whispered, changing her tone.

A lone truck, looking out of place, sat in front of the restaurant attached to the property, stretching along the water. The two ducked behind an abandoned truck that declared that if you rode too close to their bumper, you could kiss their ass.

"You think someone's in there?" Sarah asked.

"Yup," Ben replied, pulling up his rifle and zooming in on the front of the building.

"Dan, Shelly, just a heads up, there's someone in the fish camp," Ben followed.

Dan glanced at Shelly as the two took a step back from the

windows. "Turn the thermals on," Dan instructed, pointing to the second thermal scope attached to the massive death-dealing belt-fed machine gun.

Laying on their bellies, Shelly and Dan pushed into the scopes, flipping the thermal scopes on. Three heat signatures appeared in the scopes.

"I see three figures," Dan whispered.

The two pulled back as she confirmed what he had seen. "They're on the back dock bar just sitting there."

"I don't have a clear shot," Dan followed, using the sniper rifle.

"Ben, you copy?" Dan asked, knowing this could throw a wrench into things.

"Go ahead," Ben quickly responded.

"Three people by the docks in the outdoor bar area. I can't get a good line of sight on them, but they're in there."

Ben turned to Sarah, breathing out. "I say we go introduce ourselves."

Sarah looked skeptically at her husband. "Why don't you go introduce yourself? I'll be within eyeshot in case things go south. These folks are likely not part of Amanda's group."

"Agreed," Ben whispered, pointing at another row of abandoned vehicles facing the outdoor bar. "Stay here. If something happens, make your way back to the bridge."

Sarah nodded, knowing Ben could handle himself as he keyed the radio. "Dan, you copy?"

"Go ahead."

"I'm going to make contact and see what's going on. Keep your eyes on. You think they saw us cross the bridge?"

"Nah. The cars are piled up on the left side of the bridge. We lost sight of you as soon as you stepped off."

"Got it. Cover me."

"Good copy," Dan replied, glancing at Shelly, who was feverishly staring through the scope. "Hey, babe?" Dan asked, looking around. "Have you seen the dog?"

"No," Shelly replied, not looking up. "He probably went home or something."

Sweat dripped off Ben's brow as humidity from the wet ground smacked the land across the face after the rain stopped. Stepping out from behind the truck, the once silent gravel was now a full-on concert of noise.

Thinking of the possible hornet's nest inside, Ben stopped at the final car before walking to the outside bar entrance where the truck was parked, turning Eve on silent.

"What are you doing?" Sarah asked as Ben whispered into the mic.

"Back up." Leaning down, Ben placed his rifle under the front wheel of the truck. The once vibrant red paint was now a faded, dull rust color.

Quickly pulling out his pistol, Ben continued his short walk to the front doors. Leaning forward, all the man could see was fuzzy light cutting through the building.

Ben wrapped the kevlar knuckles of his gloves on the side of the truck as the light clank of a glass echoed from inside. Time didn't wait for the clock as a gravelly voice barked from Ben's right.

"Drop it. Hands up."

Ben slowly turned, holding up both hands. "Not here looking for trouble," Ben replied, slowly lowering his pistol to the ground.

"Jesus, H, Christ. Hey Tanner, get out here and look at the size of this fella." The man barked.

Ben took in the man's features, as sunken eyes and pale

skin sat on a chubby frame. Blue jeans that hadn't been washed since the start of time melted into a flannel shirt soaked in sweat, all topped off with a camouflaged ball cap. The more he observed the man, the more Ben figured he was likely drunk.

Another taller man walked out. This time, the man was thin and sporting a matted beard down to the middle of his chest. Slicked-back hair and a large knife hanging off his hip made the man look like something out of a slasher film. It didn't take Ben long to compute that these were not good people.

"Holy shit. You know who that is?" The new addition to the party gasped.

"No dumbass. Who?"

"That's that movie star guy. Ben something or other. He's a big fella," Tanner observed.

Ben often forgot just how big and intimidating he was in person. The year of working out and chemical enhancements had built the man a solid frame of muscle.

"Looks like we have a guest, Billy," Tanner said, whistling toward the third man Ben knew was there.

The clear leader of the group walked out holding a shotgun, looking more put together. Washed clothes and a clean face were accompanied by a lean, muscular figure. This was the brains of the group.

"Afternoon," Derick said as Billy and Tanner kept their guns trained on Ben, their fingers twitching with unease. "Easy gents. We have a movie star in our presence."

Derick squinted his eyes, seeing Ben's fatigues and other pieces of well-used gear. Ben was no longer an actor but rather a survivor.

"Afternoon," Ben replied. "Just passing through and saw the truck. I was knocking to see if anyone was inside."

"Is that so?" Derick asked, motioning the others to give

the man some space. "Billy, Tanner, show some decency and put your weapons down. One can't be too careful these days."

"No, you can't," Ben replied, putting his hands down. "I'm heading East. You guys from around here?"

"Now, we need to get to know each other a little better before we start talking beans and bullets," Derick replied, smiling. "Where are your people?"

"People?" Ben asked rhetorically. I'm heading back to them. I'm out on my own. I had someone with me, but they didn't make it."

"Is that so?" Derick also asked, not really meaning it. "Why don't we get inside and have a drink? Maybe some food. Not like you've missed any meals by the look of you."

"Fair enough," Ben replied as the three men backed up, letting him walk forward. Ben took his time watching their mannerisms. Billy and Tanner were wound tight as if about to strike, while Derick stayed cool, calm, and collected.

"After you," Billy motioned as the four walked under the outdoor bar entrance.

Sarah glanced under the truck, seeing them disappear into the dark building that had been built as an open-air bar. On the side facing the river, large windows were closed, preventing Dan and Shelly from seeing inside.

Shuffling to her feet, Sarah knew the building. To the far left was a back entrance into the kitchen, separated enough to keep her entrance quiet. It wasn't up for debate as she called over the radio. By then, Ben had swiftly switched off his radio.

"Ben went inside with the three men. They're trouble. I'm going in on the far left side of the building. You're right," Sarah said, already in motion.

"Good copy," Dan replied, not taking his focus off his scope.

Within the gaggle of cars, Sarah continued to move, staying low through smoldering, mildewed cars lightly steaming from the now-absent rain. Unless someone were on the roof, they wouldn't see her. While the others saw three heat sources inside the building, it didn't mean there weren't others.

Not thirty seconds later, Sarah reported back that she was in position. It wasn't time to rush in, so Sarah gave herself a moment to pause and gather her thoughts. Crouching down and checking the door, she immediately froze with what felt like the nudge of a gun against her back.

"I'm not here to cause any trouble," Sarah started, standing up with her hands held tightly to her submachine gun tucked close to her chest. If needed, when she turned around, she would unleash a spray of hell on whoever was behind her after seeing the trio Ben walked inside with.

"Gruff," Max chuffed as the tension flowed out of her body, the adrenaline slowly fading as she turned.

There, standing in the steamy small area by the back of the garage, was Max in all his glory. Blond flowing hair swayed as the dog's hair was slowly drying out. On the books, Max was considered a British Cream Golden Retriever. His square head and alert ears now pushed forward as Sarah leaned down to give him a quick pat on the back.

Chuffing, Max stepped forward, sniffing the door, only to back up with a low growl.

"What is it boy?" Sarah asked, knowing there would be no answer.

Turning to the door, Sarah lightly turned the handle, only to find it unlocked. With teeth clinched, She slowly pushed the door to find it give way without protest. The entrance had been used.

A light squeak abruptly ended as she took several steps back after the smell of absolute death wafted from the opening.

Max also moved back from the door, lowering his head with his teeth bared.

The smell was a mix of decay and rot. Not the usual scent found in the now decaying world, but one of fresh rot. Whatever was in the kitchen was something Sarah had no interest in confronting on a full stomach.

By now, she, like the others, was used to the smell of the undead. After the past several days, they had once again been reacclimated to the smells of a dying world full of zombies. This was something different and raw.

Max stepped forward again, curling his lips back and joining her in repressing the disgusting smell wafting from the kitchen. In her mind, Sarah couldn't imagine what would create such a foul odor.

Sarah, not wanting to draw any attention to herself, pulled up her face covering and walked slowly into the kitchen with her gun raised. Max, knowing she was going inside, pressed against her leg, moving in tandem after a light whimper.

What lay before Sarah was a thing of not only nightmares but a scene of sheer terror. Laying on the prepping tables once used to prepare meals for the iconic fish camp were two flayed open corpses.

The light from the open door was all she needed to see the hellish landscape inside the room. Pans covered in blood held what appeared to be organs, only to be topped off by slabs of muscle and flesh sitting on the counter, ready to cook.

Cannibals, Sarah thought, seeing Max continue to bare his teeth. Not wanting to draw further attention, she quickly retreated.

"Anyone copy," Sarah asked, dazed by the vision she was trying to compute.

"Yeah, go ahead. Are you okay?" Shelly asked. Dan was laser-focused on his weapon and thermal scope, now seeing four heat traces.

"Their cannibals. Ben's inside. I'm going in," Sarah breathed out, not wanting to raise her voice over a whisper.

"Wait," Shelly said as Dan raised a finger, letting her know he was listening. "We don't have a clear line of site unless they're outside."

Sarah didn't respond, hearing the message loud and clear and shifting her focus to the docks. She knew the layout of the place. Once through the kitchen, she could go through the actual restaurant portion and be on the far side of the outside dining area with cover. Sarah was about to go native and knew her husband Ben would follow her all the way to the hell she was about to unleash.

Glancing down, Max looked up with curiosity in his eyes. "It's okay boy," she whispered. "I need you to stay."

As the words skimmed her lips, Max sat on his hind legs, looking alert yet understanding.

CHAPTER 25

You Reap what you Sow

The scents of a rotting building slapped Ben's nose while Billy, Derick, and Tanner seemed unfazed. A wooden bar rotting from a mix of flood water and mold lay covered in liquor bottles, giving him a good idea of what the men had been up to. Sitting on a high-top table, a plate of what appeared to be beef projected a pungent odor, making Ben hold back a gag.

"Where's our manners? Care for a drink?" Derick asked as his two sidekicks leaned against the bar, still holding their weapons at the ready.

"You sure there's no zombies around here?" Ben asked as the three chuckled in unison.

"Zombies? Hell, you got it all wrong. Those things are demon ghouls," Billy declared as Derick held back an eye roll.

Derick stepped forward, reaching for a half-drunk bottle of whiskey. "The old brown it is," he said, pouring two glasses and handing one to Ben.

"We took care of those things when we got here. That's why it stinks in here," Derick downed his drink in one pull, pulling out Ben's pistol while Ben held his glass steady.

"I see. So what's the plan for you guys?" Ben asked. The thing was, Ben knew the only reason he was likely still alive was his status as a movie star and the gear he wore. At the same time, Ben was feverishly scanning the bar for anything out of the ordinary.

Quickly glancing at the floor behind Derick, traces of fresh blood streaked off toward the main dining area. Derick noticed Ben's gaze and cocked his head.

"Now that the pleasantries are out of the way, I'm going to ask you the same question. Why are you out here all geared up like you've been fighting a war?"

Ben took a steadying breath, getting another whiff of the rotting meat. "Surviving out there is tough. I found the gear at an abandoned military outpost. The folks traveling with me got taken out in a house about ten miles west of here."

"Ten miles West, you say," Derick was chewing on the statement. "Where's home? You're heading somewhere. Hell, everyone is."

By this point, Ben quickly realized that the man in front of him wasn't going to answer his questions, letting him know who was in charge. "East toward the beach. We have a small island. It keeps us safe."

Derick poured himself another glass. "There's my real question. Why leave it and be this far out? There's plenty of shit lying around before you cross the river."

As Ben was an Actor, it was time for him to act. "We received a signal on our radio that there was a group of people out West, toward Tallahassee. It sounded promising. We didn't make it. I turned back."

"Tallahassee, huh," Derick chuckled. "Guess you got that call a while ago. That place burned to the ground. You sure you waited that long to go?"

Ben nodded, acting as if he was taking a sip of the whiskey. "Yeah. It took some time to get everything together. We lost contact a while back, but I figured it was something else going on. The radios have been spotty at best."

"You got that right. We went to Tallahassee. It looked like the devil himself paid it a visit. Well, Ben. I gotta admit, I used to watch your movies. I also remember you getting in some trouble. You still trouble?"

Ben shook his head as Dean pulled his pistol up, pointing it at Ben. Before Ben could move, a woman's voice barked from the shadows behind Derick. "Drop it or die!" Max's low growl followed.

Bill and Tanner scrambled to their feet as their inexperience started to show in their clumsy drunkenness. Rule ten of the zombie apocalypse. Don't get drunk when in the wild.

"Now, let's not get all hasty," Derick said with his back still exposed to the dark innards of the fish camp. "You shoot me.... Well, we shoot him. I take it you know each other."

Ben stilled, knowing the three men were utterly psychotic. Sarah's voice again echoed from the shadows. "Drop the weapon, or you will be the first. If you think I'm the only one here, you're dead wrong."

"See las, that's the issue. I don't see them," Derick scoffed just as he pulled the trigger. Ben crashed to the floor as Sarah ripped several rounds into Derick, making the man appear to be dancing before he turned to fire one last shot, forcing Sarah to jump out of hiding.

Ben lay on the floor as Sarah shifted her focus to the smack of shotgun rounds shattering the wall she had once been standing behind.

"Get her. She's behind the tables!" Billy yelled as she ripped a handful of rounds into the air, forcing the two men to scramble behind the bar.

Ben huffed as the stars behind his eyes started to fade into visions of the rusty roof. Reaching up, Ben pulled himself behind a table, patting his soar chest. Even as smooth as the three goons thought they were, they forgot to have Ben take off his body armor. Lodged neatly, in the dead corner of his chest plate was the ass end of a bullet.

Tanner stood first, blasting a chunk out of the table. Sarah was behind as several pellets ripped into her arm, with a handful reaching her face. While it wasn't enough to truly hurt her, it stung enough to drop her to her hands and knees.

Ben scanned the floor, looking for his pistol, only to find several rounds being pumped in the general direction from the drunk driver behind the bar.

Just as Billy stood to finish ripping through the table Sarah was huddled behind, the howl of a hundred angry wolves, all mustering from one fierce animal, roared as Max's crash into the man boomed. Ben, seeing his chance, whirled to his feet, lightly unsteady as he dashed to the front of the building through the open entrance, quickly grabbing his rifle only a few dozen feet away.

The thing worrying the man was the lack of gunfire coming from his wife. In Ben's eyes, neither of the two goons would make it out from behind the bar alive.

A shriek came from inside as Bn cocked his rifle, charging the entrance. Tanner stood, rearing the butt of his shotgun down on Max as Ben ripped more rounds than he could count into and through the man, instantly turning his upper body into a twirling red ballerina.

On the other side of the river, two stray rounds zipped through the air, pounding into the back of the house Dan and Shelly were occupying. As luck would have it, the two were already moving to the front door after hearing the gunfire, heading across the bridge.

Ben made it to the bar before what was left of Tanner hit the floor. Looking down, Max had Billy on the floor, holding onto a rail, trying to get on his feet, and the other locked in Max's jaws.

Knowing what he was going to do next, Ben called out, also motioning Max to back up. "Sarah!"

"I'm good. You good?"

"Yup," Ben replied, locking eyes with Billy.

Snot oozed from his face while the man reached down for his bloodied arm. Max zipped off toward Sarah as the sounds of her pushing chairs out of the way clacked. Finally making her way to the bar, Sarah glanced at the two, not seeing Ben flinch. He knew she was there.

"Call the others. Let them know we're fine," Ben huffed, not taking his eyes off the cowering man.

Sarah turned only to find Dan and Shelly already on the bridge after a quick radio call. "We're good. Just have some cleanup to do," Sarah said loud enough for Billy to hear.

"You had us worried," Shelly replied as Ian's voice chimed in. "What's going on!"

"Had a run-in with some cannibals. Nothing major," Sarah replied sarcastically. Dan and Shelly gawked at each other, mouthing the word. No one responded for a few seconds. Ben turned to refocus on the man now curled in a ball. Max stood at the entrance of the bar area with his head down, ready to finish what he had started, the light red heugh of blood peppering his chin.

"Okay, you need us over there?" Dan asked.

"No. There are a few RVs at the far end of the parking lot. We're going to get this place wired up, then head over and clear one," Sarah said, finally turning to Ben.

This time, Ben got a solid look at her. The man's resolve hardened. "Your face and shoulder," Ben grumbled.

The adrenaline started trickling out of Sarah's body as she reached up, wiping blood from her face. Her cheek and neck, all the way to her shoulder, were dotted with several small red pits from the shotgun. If it weren't for the lightly loaded bird shot, she would likely be bleeding out.

"It's not that bad. Stings a little. I think we need to get this wrapped up," Sarah urged, not wanting the man in front of them to take in another expanding huff of their lungs.

"Cannibals? How do you know?" Ben asked. While he trusted his wife, the words were not fully computing. Things weren't that bad, the man thought. Are they? He asked himself, finally seeing his pistol.

"Kitchen 's full of hacked-up bodies." Sarah, also seeing his pistol, picked it up, handing it to Ben over the bar before walking into the open area, seeing Dan and Shelly in the backyard of a house across the creek.

"Could just be injured."

"They had them cut in chunks beside the bodies in a pan, including a pile of seasoning next to the saw."

"Jesus," Ben whispered under his breath before nudging Billy with his foot. "You. Where did you all come from?"

"You ki..., ki.... Killed them," Billy stammered.

"Yeah. We did. Answer me."

"You're going to ki...ki...kill me."

Ben didn't speak as Billy finally got the message. "South. We came from Orlando." Billy paused again. "It's not like things up here. It's safe up here."

"Safe?" Ben asked the room as if he had an audience. "Are you saying the people or the zombies?"

Billy nodded. "There's s...s...so many more ghouls. And the people. In the city, it's bad. We left after hearing things were good up here. It seems to be fine down south, also. It's just Orlando." In his mind, he, like Dustn and Tina, was trying to win favor with the man who had killed his companions.

"That it?" Ben asked, lifting his chin lightly. The truth of the matter was they didn't have time to go over this with Billy. Ben glanced at the small dots on his wife's face.

Billy, finally calming down, nodded while shuffling back. "Yes. Nothing else. Hey..., you think I can get some water?"

Seeing what he was about to do, Sarah turned and walked toward the parking lot to get the Claymore mines and set them up around the fish camp.

Glancing around the bar, Ben spotted several dusty water bottles. Handing one to the man, Billy grimaced as he took it with his good hand. Several violent chugs later, Billy let out a sigh.

The muffled thud of Ben's silenced pistol reached Sarah's ears, making her pause at the entrance. It was done. Max walked up, wagging his tail, getting a fresh breath of human air.

Ben walked out, holstering his pistol. He didn't like that type of violence, however necessary. "We need to get this good boy cleaned up," Sarah said, seeing her husband's face, handing Ben the bag of claymores. "And extra treats. He saved my life."

Sarah paused at the statement, realizing the truth of it. "That's one hell of a dog," Ben added, smiling, taking deep breaths, his adrenaline also wearing off. Leaning down, he patted Max on the head. "Sorry about that in there Max. I hope you stick around. I'll give you your own house even."

The two grinned just as the reality of the horror show inside hit them both in the guts.

CHAPTER 26

A Call to Arms

Nicole yawned, feeling as if she hadn't slept in an eternity. Morning fog hazed the entrance to Doctor's Inlet, obscuring the bridge until it was barely visible. John shuffled over to the window, scratching his head and handing her a cup of coffee after his long shift.

"Hey babe," Nicole said, yawning as she sipped her coffee. "Anything going on?"

"Just talked to the others. Sounds like they're all set. Ben and Sarah gave a few more details on that shitstorm in the fish house. Some sadistic pukes were staying there."

"Were?" Nicole asked, turning back to the foggy water.

"Said they tried to act all nice, then they noticed a bunch of flayed open bodies in the kitchen. Ben said they had been staying there for about a week, scouting the area. They had even been out West."

"Tallahassee?" The coffee hadn't fully kicked in, leaving Nicole with one-word responses.

"Yeah, they saw what was left of the mess. It sounds like they have been doing this kind of stuff for a while. Said there were three of them. All brothers."

Nicole took in the coffee's aroma. "That's the problem with things these days. Like you said, they're only going to get worse...."

Nicole trailed off, squinting her eyes toward the inlet. "What is it babe?" John asked, stepping to the window.

Two dark shapes emerged from the fog, slowly growing larger. Within another five seconds, the silhouettes of two boats appeared on the river, turning toward the inlet. Within another five, they can make out the type of boats now heading toward the others.

"Shit," John huffed, grabbing the radio off the counter.

"Anyone on this net, we have incoming. Two boats."

Dan answered immediately, having been on night watch. "How fast are they moving? Any read on how many people are on board?"

With still frayed nerves, little sleep was had at the fish camp. Ben and Sarah hunkered down in one of the RVs, knowing any moment could bring chaos.

Nicole was already holding the binoculars up to her face, crouching down just in case whoever was on the boats could see in. John moved quickly around the kitchen, gathering his gear with a sense of urgency.

"No clue yet. They look like small military boats. The kind with inflatable tubes around a center console that looks to be enclosed.."

"Skiff boats. They can hold about four people inside. You can generally have about six other people on the deck," Dan rapidly fired back, knowing the vessel type.

"There's people on board. It looks like there are about five people on each boat. Wait, there's a third smaller boat that just popped out of the fog. It looks like it's carrying supplies," Nicole whispered, not moving the binoculars from her eyes.

"They're not moving fast at all. It looks like they might be using trolling motors," John said, his observations being heard in the background. Dan keyed up the radio.

"Ben and Sarah are still on the other side of the inlet. We have eyes on them," Dan stated as Ben cut in.

"We hear you loud and clear. We just stepped outside for a few minutes to get cleaned up," Ben said tightly.

"That's good copy," Dan replied. Shelley's voice could be heard in the background. She, too, was preparing her gear and ensuring the ammunition boxes were open and the detonators to the Claymore mines were ready to go.

"Shit," Nicole mumbled, slowly handing the binoculars to John. "They're stopping at the base of the bridge. Look who's on that lead boat."

It took several seconds for the figure materializing in front of his eyes to make sense. It was somebody he knew, someone he not only despised but someone he steered clear of while in Tallahassee.

"It's Bill." Was all the man said.

Knowing what this meant, a shocked expression swept across Sarah, Dan, and Shelley's faces while listening to the radio. This was a new name for Ben and someone he had likely never met or heard of. After all, there was a veritable cornucopia of shitheads in Tallahassee to hear stories about.

Sarah spoke up first. "This isn't good. That man is ruthless and smart. They're pulling in here ready for a fight."

Sarah turned to Ben. "Remember that guy I told you about? Even Chris didn't like being around."

"I think so. There seemed to be a lot of those in the city."

Sarah started heading for the RV after one more check of the fish camp's main entrance area for zombies as Ben grabbed his rifle. "They called him Billy the Kid. He usually stayed outside the city. If I were to bet, they didn't let him into the bunkers. He's just that batshit crazy."

"Yeah, isn't he the guy that got caught hunting the people that you all released?" Ben recalled, reaching for the details of the conversation.

"The one and only. Amanda and Chris used him for what they called special missions. I'll let you fill in the blanks," Sarah followed. Looking back at the fish camp, they both realized they had done the world a favor, killing the trio of psychos. Not only were the killers, but they were also cannibals.

"Let us know when you're set," Dan chimed in as John and Nicole realized what the three boats were now doing.

A truck pulled up to the Doctors' Inlet bridge as Bill gave the driver a thumbs-up. They were not only coming via water but also sending a secondary group on the roads.

"Guys, another thing to pay attention to," John spoke up while Nicole also started putting on her vest and gear. "It looks like they also have a small truck traveling south. You guys need to keep an eye on your asses. It only looks like two people are on the road. Bills making sure everything is in order by the looks of it."

"Great," Ben exclaimed over the radio as everyone's nerves started to scream like an out-of-control freight train. Sweat beaded and trickled off Dan's forehead as he once again checked the positioning of the sniper rifle, nestling it into his armpit and looking into the scope toward the opening of the small Creek leading off into the inlet.

Inside the small RV overlooking the fish camp, Ben drew the blinds and cracked open a window. They had stayed the night in the small once-upon-a-time home. Overnight, dozens of the undead made their way through the parking lot, only to scurry back into the surrounding shadows as the early morning sun made itself known.

The RV felt cozy, with a small pull-out bed and minimal decorations. Max had claimed one of the sitting chairs, keeping a vigilant watch over the RV. After a quick wash, the dog was back to his glorious golden self.

Focusing on the window, a dark screen kept the two concealed as Ben again closed it to ensure it would open. "We're all set," Ben reported. "We have two ways out of here. We'll also see them pulling in from the road. If I'm right, it will take them significantly longer to get here by road than the water."

"That's a good copy," Dan spoke up, finally relaxing after the initial jolt of excitement. "John, what are you guys doing?"

"Once they clear the bridge and the truck is gone, we're hitting the water. The fog is still pretty thick, as I'm sure you can see. If we hug the bank of the inlet all the way up to one of the docks before we hit the turnoff to the fish camp, we should be able to stay out of sight." John relayed over the radio

Of course, this was all part of the plan if needed. Nicole and John would utilize one of the docks in the neighborhood a quarter mile away from the fish camp. From there, they would make the rest of the journey on foot if needed. After seeing Bill, John concluded they would indeed be needed.

"They're moving," John radioed the group, turning to Nicole. "Get ready to move."

"What about the zombies outside?"

"We're leaving out the back door. We can hug the dock. Let's just not take our time," John noted, pointing at the small walkway leading down to their ride. Just off the docks, a spattering of zombies was milling around as if they had not been picked on the dodgeball team during PE class while the rest stood in front of the condos.

CHAPTER 27

Open the gates

Dustin and Tina

The chain rattled on the container door Dustin and Tina occupied as the two stretched after a long night. Sleep had been forced as Dustin insisted the two rest, knowing Amanda and the others were leaving any minute.

"Game faces," Dustin whispered. Tina nodded, already knowing this might be their last chance to escape. She knew the door would not close again without them closing it.

"Morning," Andrew's voice boomed as the young man walked in. This time, he was wearing a chest plate and carrying a pistol as well as a katana strapped to his back. I have some coffee brewing, but thought I would come by and say good morning before Jacob wakes up. He doesn't think I should be in here, and giving you coffee would be a no from that guy."

Dustin sat up straight as Andrew continued to walk toward them, finally plopping down in the chair across from the two. "Did they leave yet?"

"The others?" Andrews smiled, only to let it slip. "Yeah. About an hour ago. Jacob got wasted last night and was up long enough to see them off."

In an unexpected move, Andrews pulled his pistol out, putting Dustin's reflexes on overdrive. Before Dustin had to react, Andrew placed the gun on the table between them.

Dustin and Tina remained laser-focused on Andrew, unsure of what was happening.

"How about that coffee?" Dustin asked as Andrew leaned further back.

"Sure," Andrew smiled again, standing up. "Oh, and you can get it yourselves. You guys think I'm sticking around with these A-holes?"

Dustin slowly started reaching for the pistol as Andrew turned and walked toward the door. "You might want to get a move on," Andrew said, facing the door.

Slowly picking up the pistol, Dustin immediately did a quick check on the weapon to find it indeed fully loaded and ready to dispense violence. Standing up, Dustin lightly whistled.

"Yeah?" Andrew turned.

"Why didn't you just take care of Jacob, then come get us? I don't understand." Dustin was being genuine in his statement.

"I could have handled that guy a long time ago. I'm like you two," Andrew paused, his youthful intelligence showing through. "I know you could have got out of here at any time. Hell, I knew it the second I laid eyes on you. Thing is. So did the others, for the most part. They mostly bought your bullshit, but I didn't. I saw right through that. Trying to make friends and all that. I know those folks you mentioned. They're good people like I said before. That means you are as well. What happens next?" Andrews simply shrugged. He had made his choice, and that was to join Dustin and Tina in saving their friends.

"Hey," Tina said, standing up. "Thank you."

Walking out of the shipping container, the two finally took in their surroundings. Stacks of shipping containers and trailers full of supplies sat in an organized manner, only scene on a military base. Andrew gestured toward a nearby trailer. "Jacobs in there."

The young man turned to Tina. "Coffee's over there," he pointed at another trailer closer to the water. Ten feet away, a boat Andrew had prepped sat ready to go.

Dustin turned, not wasting time, taking off at a trot toward the trailer. Tina breathed in the morning air. "You sure about this?"

"Me. Yup. Just promise me one thing."

"What's that?" Tina replied as the sounds of a struggle echoed from the trailer. Andrew was surprised by her lack of concern.

"Is he okay?"

"He'll be fine."

Andrew glanced over, watching as Dustin walked out, holding Jacob's rifle and wiping his bloody hand on the trailer. The young man didn't want to know what violence had just unfolded, even understanding how much pain and suffering Jacob had caused.

Refocusing, Andrew opened the door to the small kitchen. "Promise me you aren't like these a-holes."

Tina took the request in. She knew what she had done to Tallahassee, making her much like the people Andrew hated for their violent actions. "Only when needed. We don't go looking for trouble. But if it comes looking for us. We'll take care of it."

Satisfied with the response, Andrew grabbed three coffee mugs and filled them to the brim. Steam wafted from the hot brown liquid as Dustin walked in, handing Andrew his pistol back.

"I'm good. You guys keep it. I got this," he pointed at the sword slung over his back.

"They didn't know you could truly fight, did they?" Dustin asked, taking half the hot coffee down in one gulp.

"Nope. I didn't want to be part of the goon squad. But yes, I can fight. Look, we don't have much time. They have a truck heading south as well. Oh..., and one more thing," Andrew handed Dustin one of their radios, along with a backup from his own vest.

"Keep one on the main channel we've been using. I suggest you call your friends if you can. Your other radio is with the others."

Tina walked out, looking at the boat. "What about our gear?"

"You mean the bikes and all your weapons? I loaded your weapons up on the boat before coming to get you guys. I didn't know how things would turn out." Andrew replied.

Dustin was starting to think the young man in front of them could have handled himself in a straight-up fight with him and knew it. Tina grinned as she ran down to the boat, finding her rifle, vest, and biker helmet.

"The rest of your stuff is in the large blue trailer. We can come back and get it later."

The two liked the man's optimistic outlook on current and ongoing events. "You're pretty confident," Dustin stated, now heading toward the boat.

Andrew smiled. "Why not?" The young man's smile then faltered. "I just want to get away from these people, and if Sarah and Nicole are with you guys, I'm sold. These people are crazy. Don't even get me started on what happened on our way here. You know..., when you all were drugged."

"I have to ask," Dustin started, getting into military mode. "Do you have a plan?"

"Go and help?" Andrew asked in the form of a statement.

"Here's the deal. We need to stay on the radio and call Amanda and the others to see what's happening. I'm guessing you have a radio for that," Dustin started.

"Yeah, here," Andrew pulled a tac-comm radio from his vest.

"Turn it on and turn it up. I have a feeling that by the time we get close, things will already be in motion, so subtlety is not a concern. Do you have anything that does not take being sneaky into consideration?" Dustin grinned lightly, picking up his rifle and vest. The familiar fit and feel of the gear warmed the man.

"Sure. I think we have some rockets in the trailer."

"Rockets?" Tina chuffed.

"Yeah, sure. I'll go get them."

"You have more than one?" Dustin asked as Andrew trotted off.

Tina turned to Dustin as she also finished putting on her vest and gear. "What do you think?" she asked.

"He's a good kid. His heart is in the right place," Dustin paused, looking out into the foggy river. "Do you have the feeling that kid can handle himself?"

"I was thinking the same thing. He could have likely left at any time. It's almost like he was using them to get to Jacksonville. We might need to dig into that. But, to answer your question, I like him."

Those were all the words Dustin needed to hear. He would not only get them and the others back to the Sanctuary safely, but now that also meant Andrew. In reality, Tina herself was a force to be reckoned with, and together, they were an army all unto themselves.

"Hey, guys. Can I get a hand?" Andrew asked, carrying two large cases toward the boat.

Upon further inspection, Dustin was shocked to find two

RPGs with six rockets each. "This will do," Dustin said as Andrew picked up the radio.

"Rock one, this is rock two over," Andrew called.

Billy quickly replied. "This is rock one. Go ahead."

"Checking in. Need us to talk with our guests?"

"Good copy. Not at this time. Let me talk to Jacob," Billy asked as Dustin's nerves started to tingle.

"He's still asleep," Andrew was on point, not missing a beat."

"Yeah, he had a long night. Make sure he's on the next check-in. We're entering the inlet."

Dustin gave a thumbs-up as Andrew snapped a response. "Good copy. Everything's good here."

The radio went silent as Andrew shifted into motion. "We have to go now. They'll be there shortly."

Pushing off the shore, they looked back at the bland stack of shipping containers. While not as robust as the larger boats, the small four-crew vessel floated away at a quick pace.

Dustin cut the short-lived silence as the Buckman Bridge came into view. "We're going right up the middle. I'll get the rockets prepped. We can stay close to the coast, but we're going to be in open water either way. We'll likely hear them before we see them. The fog will be mostly cleared soon. Tina, you good taking point with your rifle?"

"No problem. Maybe Andrew can drive while you take care of the rockets?"

As was usual, the two were in synch with each other. Andrew cleared his throat. "You want me to drive?"

"If you're good with it," Dustin followed as Andrew grabbed the throttle handle. "One question. How do you know your way there?"

Andrew snickered. It wasn't that he was trying to be deceptive, but rather, in the limited time they had, they hadn't asked. "I used to live here, man. It's actually not far from the fish camp. I know this area like the back of my hand. Trust me, I got your back. If things don't go right, I'm in the same boat. Literally."

"Babe," Dustin said, shifting focus. "Weapons hot. We're going all in."

Tina nodded, still adjusting the scope of her rifle.

"What does that mean?" Andrew asked, passing under the Buckman bridge.

Tina smiled, seeing the man she not only loved but respected. "That means we are going to fight no matter what. We see anyone, we fight. This isn't a game of hide and seek. I'm pretty sure the fact that we have rockets helps that."

Dustin looked up from the RPG cases. "That's a good point. What did they take with them?"

"Probably a few of these rockets and some heavy machine guns. I can tell you one thing, besides Bill, the rest of those scrubs suck at all that fancy stuff. Don't get me wrong, they're good with guns and stuff, but I don't think I ever saw them fire one of those. Amanda was always insistent that we don't waste ammo. That is until she found out about some FEMA camp here in Jacksonville. I believe you said that was what you were looking for, one of those?" Andrew waved his hands, remembering that little detail before refocusing on his initial thought. "Hell, they think I'm a dud and know how to use all that stuff more than they do."

"We mentioned it, but not where," Dustin replied, focusing on this bit of information. "Where is the camp?"

"She said something about a train and the Fleming Island area. Then, she started talking about a bunker in Green Cove Springs."

"Yeah, I ran through the FEMA Camp on Fleming," Dustin slowly recalled. "The place had been overran early on. When I was there, only a few holdovers remained. The important people that knew what was going on didn't make it. They had a bunch of weapons, but nothing I didn't already have besides more ammo."

"You make it to the train?"

"No. I knew where it was, but the zombies were thicker than fat kids in a candy store. I never found out what was on it. Hell, every train I ran into was being used to haul people, so I mostly stay clear of them."

Tina leaned into the conversation. "Did she happen to mention where it is? Or leave behind any information at your camp?"

"Ain't my camp anymore," Andrew smiled, slightly running the small boat toward the inlet. "If you can find it, she keeps a tablet with all that stuff on her. I don't think she left it behind, but who knows? They trust…, well, trusted Jacob for some reason. I'm not too sure what is in the bunker, but I overheard something about it being crazy big."

"Yeah, they trusted him because he was a controllable psycho," Tina chimed in. "Hey, I had a thought. I know they modulated the radio channels we used to use. I'm sure the Sanctuary changed all the channels they were using. They know something's off. They're not dumb. Either way, Dan always had a backup channel programmed on GMRS. I don't think the radios you guys have will scan for it."

Dustin looked impressed. "You seem to know a lot about radios, babe."

"While I was out, I don't know. Looking for you," Tina enunciated. "I found a rebel radio guide for dummies and actually read the dam thing. Pure gold. If you told me how useful that stupid book would be in the future, I would have paid every penny I had for one."

Dustin motioned for Andrew to cut the small electric motor. "Go ahead," Dustin urged as Tina quickly flipped a few settings on her radio.

"Sanctuary, you copy?" They would know her voice.

The still eerie calm of the morning river allowed the sounds of birds chirping to travel over the water. This was a recent addition Mother Nature had given back. For the first year, no one heard anything from the birds—not in the sky, not in the trees, nothing. The birds, for some reason, had all either migrated, died, or stayed on the ground from some unknown cause.

The following minute felt like an eternity as Ian's voice came over the radio. "Is that you guys?"

"Yes," Tina quickly replied.

"Sorry it took so long; I heard you, but I had to look at Dan's notes on how to switch it over. Where are you? All kinds of things are going on!" Ian spit out in a slurry of run-on sentences.

"Safe. Heading toward the Fish Camp. You guys on another radio frequency?" Tina asked as Dustin nodded.

"Yeah, I don't know how to push it to your radio. I'll look through Dan's notes or see if Eve can help. Listen, I'll get with everyone, but all hell's about to break loose."

CHAPTER 28

Ripples

Light grey clouds shielded the still-wet ground from the drying embrace of the late morning sun. Ben scanned the RV before resting his eyes on the small sink and faucet.

"Funny thing," Ben said, reaching over and turning the handle, only to find no water coming out. "

"What's that?" Sarah asked, still glaring out the window.

"How useless a sink is when there's no water. I mean, we have a well and everything, but we really don't need a faucet. Toilets, I get that."

"Why so reflective? I get nervous when you get like this."

"We're about to get into a fight no matter what. I just worry about you."

"You're worrying about everyone. And now the dog. It's just who you are," Sarah smiled. "Stay focused, and we'll be just fine."

"I don't want to hurt anyone," Ben sadly replied. Memories of the prior day burned through his thoughts. This was new to Sarah. "I just feel like I've been sinking this entire time. It was like I was floating on water, and then, over time, I just kept sinking deeper and deeper into the water. I think if it wasn't for you, I just don't know."

"You did the world a favor yesterday. You saw it....," Just as Sarah was about to change the subject, Ian's excited voice boomed over the radio.

"Listen up. Tina and Dustin reached out to me on the GMRS. It's really them. Like really."

Ben reached for his radio, but Dan interrupted before he could respond. "What's going on? Were we right, and someone's coming?"

"Oh yeah. Big time. Everything. Amanda, you name it. They're also heading this way. Dustin said it's too risky to talk over the old channels, and they didn't have the new radio fills. I told them that as soon as they get closer to you guys, Eve should be able to handle it. They also have company, a guy from Tallahassee named Andrew. They said he's a tall, red-headed kid.

Sarah nodded. "Yeah, he used to hang out at in-processing. He was one of the good ones."

John, overhearing this, chimed in. "Yeah, he was one of the good ones. What else did they say? We can't see anyone in front of us, but we're moving slowly and along the shoreline, up and down the docks, about to make the rest of the trip on foot. We're about a mile away from our stopping point."

"They're heading to the Inlet. I'm not sure what they're going to do, but it sounds like they are going to get there as fast as they can. It sounds like they have a small, slow boat."

"We'll chat with Eve about loading their channels when they get in range. It sounds like you'll just have to relay information until then. Just tell them to keep off the roads. That truck John and Nicole mentioned is out there somewhere."

"Good copy. Sounds like whatever is going down is about to happen." Ian said as Ben looked back out the RV window.

Motion flickered out the corner of his left eye as two

figures sporting black tactical gear from Tallahassee walked between the very set of vehicles they had hidden behind earlier.

"Someone's here. Looks like they have some people coming up from behind. They must have split up." Ben quickly called out. Dan and Shelly shifted uneasily. Both Ben and Sarah slowly grabbed their weapons, not daring to breathe.

John cut off the small boat, knowing the inference. "We're pulling up on a dock now and moving the rest of the way on foot. We'll keep to the river banks. If they pulled up to a dock, we'll see it. Just plan on us being a little longer."

"Shit," Dan huffed to himself, focusing on the entrance to the waterway leading to the fish camp. In the distance, a tiny dot appeared.

"I have eyes on," Dan called over the radio as he pointed toward the water. Shelly shifted away from the fish camp also seeing the small, growing dot.

"I see it," Shelly whispered, turning. After cleaning up the prior day's mess, Ben and Sarah took the time to open the large bay windows surrounding the outside bar area, giving Dan and Shelly a clear view of the inside guts of the building if needed.

Ben shifted closer to Sarah. "They see the truck out front looking out of place. Look, they're radioing it in."

"What do you think we should do?" Sarah wondered aloud as Ben scrunched his face.

"I say we wait. The more people in and around the building, the better. Those aren't the folks driving on the road. It takes time to get through Fleming Island." Ben correctly suggested.

Looking at her husband, Sarah noticed a slight tremor in his hand. He was nervous, and the more they didn't act, the more the tension grew like a massive spring about to break.

"How long do you think it will take for Dustin and Tina

to get here?" Sarah asked, shifting his focus to the one piece of recent good news.

"Sounded like they were moving slowly. Maybe forty-five minutes. It's one hell of an insurance policy. I doubt Amanda and that Bill guy knows," Ben replied as Max slowly jumped up beside Sarah, pinning his ears back. For a brief second, the two froze, worrying he was about to bark, only to find the dog fully understood the assignment.

"If what John and Nicole saw was right, each boat had about six people on each. Now that we know the others aren't onboard, we can fully address the situation," Sarah whispered even lower as a third person appeared.

This time, the man standing was more like he was out for a leisurely stroll. The two other armed goons were now inspecting the truck, pointing at the opening to the outside bar area.

"You know who that is?" Ben asked as Sarah shook her head.

Dan's voice cut in, barely audible. They knew sound traveled over the calm early morning water like a megaphone. "There's a boat just hanging out in the water. It's not doing much. Likely waiting to hear back. Also, it sounds like a damn herd of zombies are moving on the bridge."

"We might not need to make the first move, but if it gets loud, I say we take advantage of it," Ben said, starting to form an idea.

"What?" Sarah asked, clicking off the radio.

"Maybe a little nose couldn't hurt. Get the natives restless and use that for cover."

Sarah nodded just as the third goon also noticed the slow charge of the undead heading directly toward them after cresting the bridge.

"Dan, they see zombies on the bridge," Ben called, realizing there were only three-foot soldiers in front of them. Shifting, Ben called John, "There are three people from the other boat. Keep an eye out for three or four others."

"Good copy," John replied, sounding winded. The two were moving as fast as the overgrown neighborhoods would let them and also keep from drawing unwanted attention from the undead.

The third man, clearly in charge of the group, whistled as the other two men turned and walked away from the truck. They also knew that if they let things get out of hand with the zombies, it could present an entirely new set of problems.

Ben leaned forward as far as he dared, only to see one of the men pull out a small bell. Fingers were pointed as instructions were given. They were going to divert the group into the river as they exited the bridge.

"Think we should wait?" Sarah asked as Ben turned.

"Yeah, I'm not sure what they're going to do, but all it takes is one crazy in that group, and they'll have to start fighting." Ben was hoping to see one of the more violent, fast-moving zombies in the mix for once.

"They know what they're doing," Sarah whispered, seeing the flow of the undead start to drop off the edge of the walkway leading to the bridge. "I bet there's more coming. We've been making a good bit of noise. Let's check in with Dan and Shelly. This can't go on much longer."

After a brief radio interaction, Dan leaned back from his rifle, only to find cold metal stopping him from fully leaning back.

A rumbling dark voice lowly gave out several instructions in rapid succession. "Hands off the weapons, Lean back, and if you fucking do as much as reach for those radios, it will be the last thing you two ever do," Bill growled.

Shelly briefly glanced back, seeing Bill standing over Dan. Instead of a sleek silenced pistol, he held a gleaming .357 Magnum directly to the back of Dan's skull. Somehow, someway, they had also come in from the West while the fog was still thick, something none of them had expected.

Dan slowly raised his hands as Bill smirked. "That's a good boy." Seeing his face, Bill recognized the man. "I've seen you before. Amanda will know. You sure as shit set this up. That's all right. We will ensure your friends back on the base are made well aware."

Shelly also slowly raised her hands, but not before lightly tapping the red voice-to-talk button on her radio. The movement was slight, but as Bill was turning to get the other guards to take charge, she had made the swift maneuver.

"Tie them up," Bill instructed as two of the goons, as they were now lovingly known by the others, quickly jumped on the task at hand.

Seeing Dan was not having any of it, Bill leveled his pistol on his head. "Stop struggling."

Immediately on the other side of the small inlet, Ben and Sarah froze upon hearing the interaction. Not wanting to talk over the radio, Ben switched to another channel, queuing up Ian and Samantha.

"You guys hear that? Who is it?" Ben asked as Ian stood up as if he could do something.

"Eve, who has the most elevated heart rate?" Ian asked, learning that it was Eve's favorite pastime to monitor heart rates and suggesting cheesy old Jazz tunes from the seventies.

"Everyone that I am tracking has an elevated heart rate. Shelly and Dan, however, are exceedingly stressed," Eve announced.

"It's Shelly and Dan. I checked with Eve. That's all I got," Ian replied as Ben started feeling an uneasy pull in his guts.

"Shit. The others likely heard that also. We have to stay off this net. I'll have Eve switch us over to the backup for all those in range. That means Dustin and Tina will be blind," Ben whispered, still holding on to every last word.

"No worries," Eve typed out on his watch. "They are now in range, and I can upload the backup channel. I am also switching off the other radios. And...done."

Some days, Eve was like having a superpower. On others, she was like having a cheesy jukebox. "Be advised," Eve typed out on Ben's watch while talking with Ian and Samantha. "Their watches just went offline. I no longer have control of their radios."

"Shit," Ben growled. This was quickly becoming his favorite word. "Everyone listen up. They have Dan and Shelly."

John was the first to reply. "We heard but didn't know who. We can see their boat. It's about four docks down from us. We were about to call it in."

Tina's voice came over the radio next. "We heard it. They are already calling the base to take us out. Andrew is going to reply so they don't think anything's wrong."

"Good copy. We're about to get this party started with or without everyone," Ben stated flatly.

Just as the words left his mouth, a loud, ringing gunshot echoed from Dan and Shelly's general direction. There was no longer any need to hide.

CHAPTER 29

Stuck

Sarah's face dropped even further than she thought possible as Ben started to move toward the door. By now, Max felt the tension and stood on all fours, ready to go. Just as Ben was about to move, a rumbling yet feminine voice boomed over a megaphone.

"Good afternoon, Ben. We know you're here. Might I suggest coming out and making this easier on everyone?"

While she was asking, she was, in reality, telling. Ben let the air grow thick as Amanda again came over the megaphone. "Your friend Dan had seen better days and likely needs medical attention, not to mention the group of zombies we just woke up. You have two minutes."

Ben looked back at Sarah. "What are we going to do?" she asked, seeing him hold up the detonator for the claymores in the fish camp.

Without hesitation, Ben pressed the button as ever living hell broke loose. They had not only underestimated the violence of the explosives placed in the building and surrounding area but may have also just hurt their friends. Dan had the other detonator for the house.

A blinding white flash boomed as the RV rocked back on

its two side wheels. Chunks of wood and other random objects flew into the small hiding place just as several of the cars exploded, also joining the symphony of destruction.

The three men's truck was the first to go. Ben and Sarah didn't hear that, as their ears rang. A chunk of the thin metal and plastic roof was shredded off the top of the RV as Max let out a full-on bark, not liking the situation and also losing all relevant thought for a few brief yet angry seconds.

Ben lay on the floor, slowly pulling himself together as he looked over to see Sarah holding her leg. She had been hit by something.

"Babe?" Ben called out, not sure how loud he was being. "Babe?"

Sarah slowly turned, pointing at her ears and finally nodding. If they were having trouble hearing, so were the others. After another few seconds, she gave her husband a thumbs up and pulled a small shard of glass from her calf. She would be okay.

Ben was already in motion, picking up his rifle and seeing the door to the RV in tatters. Red flames and dark smoke from the burning of tires in the parking lot, not to mention the raging inferno, shielded the two from anyone seeing them.

"Babe," Ben called again. This time, his words found purchase.

"Yeah, I'm good." Ben looked at her bloody leg and lightly scared face from the prior day.

"We have to move now. They'll be here soon."

Sarah got to her feet, steadying herself. "Where?"

"The bridge. Take out those other goons if they didn't get blown to pieces. We're swimming across if we have to."

Scooping up his radio, Ben hit the talk button, his ears still sounding as if he was underwater. "We're good."

"What the hell was that?" John quickly asked. His voice was low.

"We blew the camp. It's a mess over here, but we got to move. They know we're here."

John knew this meant that being sneaky was no longer on the menu. They would engage the boat from a distance. To his and Nicole's right, in the distance, a small speck of a boat materialized.

"Gotta go, and we see Dustin and Tina. We have to get to this boat before they see them."

Ben sat his radio down, knowing things were now in motion. Looking down, Ben noticed Max tucked closely to his head.

"You good boy?" he asked, petting the dog on the head. A light trickle of blood came from Max's left ear from the blast.

Max shook as if he were walking out of the river. A light dusting of hair and a simple chuff signaled that their new K9 partner was ready. Holding up his fingers, Ben counted down to three as he lightly opened the door, letting the barrel of his rifle seek any attention that may be present.

Nothing happened as smoke from the burning building and vehicle filled the RV. They had cover. Sarah tapped him on the shoulder, letting him know she was there.

With no more words needed, Ben stalked out of the small RV as if a lioness were tracking their prey. The entire time he moved, he could feel Max against his legs moving in tandem.

Another crackle of something exploding forced the three to drop to one knee. The explosion and subsequent fire had reached several propane tanks next to the kitchen.

Two more popping bangs echoed as Ben began to move again, seeing them out of harm's way. The explosions rocked the far end of the building toward the bridge. If the dead hadn't already been awakened, they were now.

Ben started moving again, feeling his sore ribs press against his chest armor. Even though he was wearing a plate, the shot to his chest had still bruised his ribs. Upon further inspection, Ben also noticed a trickle of blood coming from his side. There wasn't time to stop and look. He would address the situation later. All he knew was that he was still moving, and his friends were in danger.

A waft of smoke cleared in front of the bridge as several burning zombies staggered in various directions, clearly disoriented by the explosion. Max launched forward just as one of the goons appeared from the opposite end of the road leading to the other side.

The man was clearly disoriented. Max didn't hesitate as he rammed into him as if it was the last thing the dog would do. Somehow, some way, he knew they meant trouble.

"Gahhh!" The man exclaimed, turning and working to punch the dog. He had dropped his weapon at some point and was down to his fists.

Seeing this, Ben dropped the man in one single shot. Moving forward, Sarah shifted to a tree still intact with a clear field of fire on anything or one coming out from the ravine.

Max ran up next to Ben as a flaming zombie slipped and fell in front of them as he looked into the ravine. The two other goons were covered in a mass of zombies. The crack of a pistol forced Ben to flinch, only to realize it was the last dying attempt at an already fading life.

There wasn't time to address the twenty or so zombies distracted by the fresh meal, so Ben turned and pointed at the house sitting off the side of the road a few feet away from the ravine. Sarah ran to Ben, getting the message.

Together, the three trotted to the front side of the house, seeing no more zombies. Two more houses sat still, covered in moss and weeds. Overgrown ground palms and cracked driveways gave them a clear shot to the far end of the small grouping of houses.

Ben glanced down at Max, seeing him wag his tail. It was a clear shot to the riverbank on the far end of the last two-story home. When the group finally stopped, the continued sounds of chaos still sounded muffled.

"We swim across from here," Ben stated, only to have Sarah point at a small canoe.

"The bridge will cover our movement. Plus, with all this gear, I'm not sure I won't sink," Sarah said.

Nodding, Ben inspected the small boat, seeing a set of short paddles. "Alright. We go now."

Max jumped into the canoe before they started sliding it to the small water crossing. Rising water had pushed it up into the yard. To their left, they had a clear view of the zombies, slowly realizing they had finished their meal.

The rattle of machine gun fire put their asses in motion with a slosh of the water on Ben's boots. Sarah jumped in the canoe, grabbing a paddle as Ben pushed off the shore, finally jumping in the boat.

More gunfire echoed. "Zombies. That's not the sound of a gunfight."

Reassured by the sentiment, the two pushed hard, finally reaching the other side of the small tributary. After getting resituated, Sarah turned to a thinking Ben. Max had jumped into the water as they pulled in, now covered in a layer of mud up to his stomach.

"What's the plan?" Sarah asked as Ben pulled up his rifle, walking into the fenced backyard out of sight of the bridge.

"Not get killed," Ben huffed as they started moving.

CHAPTER 30

The Charge of Big John and Nicole

Shouts came from the dock as two of the goons shuffled as if confused about their next move. They glanced back at the water to see another small boat turning toward a dock. The explosion had created enough of a diversion to keep everyone occupied in the opposite direction.

Black smoke flowed into the air as if the Devil himself was paying the Earth a visit. John pulled up his rifle and sighted in on the man near the boat's cockpit holding a radio mounted on the center console. The radio's curly cable was stretched almost straight as the goon stood outside, also staring at the billowing smoke.

Standing behind a fence, John gestured for Nicole to aim at one of the other men. "Get the other one closest to the boat."

"You have a lot of faith in my aim," Nicole replied as he shrugged.

Nicole steadied herself and gave a thumbs up. The crack of muffled bullets whipped as the man dropped out of John's line of site. This was followed by not one but two rounds from Nicole.

John shifted his aim to the farthest goon, scrambling for cover inside the boat's small enclosed cockpit. Just as he was about to squeeze the trigger, Nicole again fired off two shots, finally landing her target. The distraction was enough to throw John off as the proverbial last man standing dove into the assumed safety of the boat's enclosure.

"Dammit," John muttered, already moving. No longer worried about keeping things calm, John charged toward the boat faster than Nicole thought possible.

Within thirty seconds, John was on the same dock as the boat, finally slowing down. Sweat poured from John's brow as he slowly stepped onto the creaking wood. The goon inside the boat could not only hear the steps but was also able to see through the tinted front windshield.

As the boat rocked lightly and the radio chirped, John started smacking rounds into the windshield. The crackle of glass spidered as heavy rounds punched into their target.

Now, only feet away, John heard Nicole finally make her way onto the dock. Letting his rifle drop to be caught by its sling, John quickly pulled his pistol out, popping off two more rounds before finally stepping onto the boat.

"Please," a whiney high-pitched voice came from inside the boat's cockpit.

Not trusting the plea for mercy, John stopped. "Come on out with your hands up. You twitch. Well, you know the deal."

"All... all right, man, just chill."

Nicole stood on the dock, now pointing her rifle at the metal door half open. Neither was fazed by the two bodies now floating away from the dock. The sounds of the door slowly pushing open raised the damp hairs on John's arms.

A thinner young man with his hair in a ponytail stepped out with his hands up, a light streak of blood from glass slicing his face from John's shots peppered his cheek. "I'm unarmed."

John stepped closer, seeing the youth behind the man's eyes. He was no older than twenty at most.

"On your knees," John commanded as the young man dropped to the deck. "Did you radio into your friends?"

"No...n...no. I couldn't get my dam hands on the radio."

John could see his hands trembling. He was shaking all the way down to his bones as if about to fall apart. Nicole turned to see the boat now turning toward them. "Call them and let them know to pull up here."

Nicole walked down the dock, pulling out her radio. John again focused on the man in front of them. "What's your name?"

"Jake. My name's Jake."

"All right, Jake from State Farm. What's the deal with your group? Specifically, what's the plan?"

Jake hesitated, looking down at the deck. "To hell with it. They dropped people off all around the fish camp. There's another boat in the inlet just waiting for the word to come in with four more people with heavy weapons. They knew you would be here. They're going to kill you..., well, most of you. Amanda is obsessed with that Ben guy."

"I see. And where do you fit into the equation?"

"We're here to ensure no one comes up the river. Until that explosion, we thought we could see a boat coming. I guess that was you, and them." Jake pointed at Andrew, Dustin, and Tina, who were jumping on a dock. With no more need to be quiet, they had pushed the little boat's trolling motor to its limits.

"Shit," Jake huffed. "That's Andrew. He's with you guys?"

"Looks like it. Listen Jake. I don't think things are going to work out how you think they are."

"You sure about that? Bill is ruthless. He had a backup plan. He didn't even tell the rest of us about it."

"You mean the truck?"

Jake's face slacked. "You know about that?"

"No. I just saw it. Sounds like you are in the same boat as us." John shrugged at the light-hearted, ill-timed joke.

"Man," Jake drawled out. "They left us out here because we aren't considered part of the main fighting group. We usually do stuff with supplies. We left a supply boat anchored in the middle of the inlet. You know, cook and stuff. I don't know how I can help you."

Jake's eyes shifted as the others walked up. "John," Dustin said as Andrew stepped forward.

"Jake, you look rough, buddy," Andrew stated as the young man again lowered his eyes.

Dustin and Tina hadn't seen the man before. Dustin lightly patted John on the back. "Good to see you brother."

Nodding, John, with a brief smile, refocused on Andrew. "Tell us about this guy." He wanted to confirm what he had been told, knowing Jake was in front of him listening.

"Ah. He's okay," John was taken off by Andrew's casual attitude. "He usually did all the dirt work like me. Surprised he made it through this mess." Andrew pointed at the bodies floating off.

"All right, Jake from State Farm," John again started as Tina snickered. "Today's your lucky day. We're going to tie you up in one of these houses, and if we feel so inclined, we will give you a way out."

Dustin stepped forward. "I got him."

Everyone glanced around the group, not arguing the point. With the reunion short-lived, it was time to get to the others. "I won't hurt anyone, promise," Jake looked up at John, finally recognizing the man. "You're John. That's right. Listen, I'll just leave. I want to head North anyways."

"It's worse up North until you get into the country. Better off somewhere around the water. It's safer," Dustin stated, picking the man up by the arm. "Relax. You're still breathing."

After five minutes, Dustin walked out of the closest house. As with all higher-end neighborhoods, tall fences and houses sat like mini fortresses.

"How did everything go?" Tina asked while the others prepared the boat to leave.

"It's handled. He has a way out. It's up to him," was all Dustin said without meeting eyes with his wife. In reality, it all came down to Jake's ability to un-hogtie himself and then survive the fall after being strung up in the garage from an exposed beam.

"It's good to see you guys," John said, finally starting the boat.

"Yeah, it's been a long couple of weeks. We need to let the others know what's going on. Do you have any news from Ben or Dan?"

"Just a call from Sarah. They blew the place up. Sounds like all hell is breaking loose," Nicole followed.

The radio crackled to life with a request for an update. The voice at the other end sounded stressed. "Blue one, status report."

Dustin turned to Andrew. "You have the youngest voice. Make yourself sound like Jake and call back." The others were surprised by the flatness in Dustin's tone.

"Yeah. I can do that. Sounds like the other boat. He doesn't seem too happy." Picking up the radio, Andrew's voice morphed into a slightly deeper version of Jake's.

"We're good. What's going on?" Andrew replied.

"We need you to head this way. We're going in."

Dustin let a slight smile slip. Andrew keyed the radio. "Good copy. Enroute."

"Looks like we may still have some element of surprise," Dustin stated, pointing at the dock. We need to load the weapons up."

Ben's voice cut over the secondary radio channel, not hearing the other conversation. "We're moving. There are zombies everywhere. You guys good?" Ben was smartly not being overly open on the radio.

Dustin took the time to chime in. "We're just fine."

Ben and Sarah both took a brief second to smile at each other. "Great to hear your voice."

"Same," Dustin followed. "Heading your way with some fireworks."

Ben looked on the other side of the weed-covered chain link fence separating a small house from the main road leading to the home Dan and Shelly were still presumably in.

"We don't have time to stay put. We're heading to the house. John and Nicole know where it is," Ben said as Dustin glanced back at the pair, getting a head nod.

"Five minutes out," Dustin said in a tone of finality as Tina pushed the boat's throttle forward at full speed.

CHAPTER 31

A View to Die for

Droves of the undead faced the smoking rubble left burning on the opposite side of the bridge. Old, abandoned neighborhoods were calling their inhabitants out to watch the fireworks. Even though time had passed, death and its leftovers hadn't.

Time was the one factor for the remaining inhabitants of the small, unremarkable third pale blue dot from the sun. While the ravages of time had absolutely slowed the older zombies down, Ben and the others were still shocked by their longevity.

Ben swallowed a life full of spit, creeping to the small gate leading to the road. Max lowered his head, copying Ben's movements. Sarah, knowing it was time to go, leaned down, crouching on her knees on the opposite side of the small gate.

"We're going to have to move. No time to stop or deal with anything else," Ben whispered. There was a group of zombies slowly heading their way, not to mention the cluster now on the bridge.

Sarah took a clearing breath. "You think we just go straight to the house? Then what?"

"I was thinking we could go to the house next door, and I can check it out," Ben replied, slowly lifting the clasp on the gate.

"You think they're still shaken up?"

Ben bobbled his head. "No. They are... " The sound of gunfire cut him off.

"You think that's the others?" Sarah asked as Ben shook his head, slowly pushing the squeaking gate open.

"No. Zombies." Ben stood up, taking off at a full-on sprint, not giving Sarah a chance to move. Max joined the sprint, keeping at Ben's heels. He was ensuring the open air between them and the other side of the road was safe.

Much to their surprise, it was indeed safe. Ben pressed his back against the garage, facing the road as the wave of dozens of zombies started turning. Max lowered his head, not happy with the current situation. But the dog stayed. Hell or high water, Max had chosen his hill to die on. It also might have had something to do with Ben's promise of endless treats for being such a good boy.

Sarah joined Ben, noticing the wall of problems approaching. "No. Ben whispered. "This is good. It will keep them occupied."

The sounds of gunfire again rattled, confirming that the other group of Amanda's goons were indeed in the same house Dan and Shelly were in. Ben was starting to think it would be better to keep them occupied while they regrouped.

Sarah turned, walking to the corner of the garage, seeing a clear path to a side door leading into the house. "It's clear."

Moving first, Sarah ran forward, reaching the door as Ben finally rounded the corner. Checking the door, the owners clearly thought they would be coming back home to a secured house.

Ben lifted a finger, tapping it as it counted off. Ten seconds later, the rattle of more gunfire was the signal he was waiting for, and he backed up, using his massive frame to kick the door open.

Wood chipped from the lock area, flying into the yard. The three quickly ran inside, closing the door behind them. With no lock, the two promptly grabbed the refrigerator, slowly sliding it behind the door, as well as a large wooden table. Max stood guard, facing the living room of the one-story ranch home.

Ben slung his rifle quickly, pulling up his pistol. Before moving, Sarah grabbed him by the collar, planting a quick kiss on his cheek. "I love you."

"Love you too, babe. We get through this, I'll do the laundry."

Sarah smiled, leaning the rim of her ball cap against his helmet. "No. I'd rather my clothes not get shredded. How about dinner?"

"And drinks? Margaritas?"

"It's a date," Sarah replied as the spatter of gunfire stopped.

Knowing the moment had passed, Ben walked into the living room, checking every corner and shadow. Max slowly sniffed the hallway leading into the far bedrooms, not showing any sign of concern. The house was empty, much to Ben's surprise. He was, in reality, expecting a fight.

The house felt more lived-in than the other. Older furniture was heavily used, while pictures were plastered on the walls. An ashtray sat on the three end tables, and piles of crossword magazines lay in a stack on a coffee table in front of the TV. Beside the magazines, dozens of empty, dusty beer cans sat, remembering better times.

"Far room," Ben motioned down the long hallway.

The doors to the rooms were all open, giving them a lived-in feel. Mismatched blankets sat on messy beds while even more mismatched paint covered the walls. The small bedroom at the end of the hall was no different.

Toys sat on the floor as if played with until the last minute. Posters of football players and video game characters had been thrown up in the room without any organization.

Sarah slowly pulled back the curtains, enough to see the brick fence surrounding the house next door. The house they occupied was slightly more elevated, giving her a slight view of the front yard next door. While the fence obscured half the yard, what she could see shocked her. Quickly leaning back, Sarah's face went blank.

"What is it?" Ben asked as Max cocked his head.

"You need to look."

Ben stepped over several Hot Wheel cars and saw the nightmare taking place in the small front yard. There, sitting in the middle of the yard, was a blood-soaked Dan tied to one of two trees. While he was clearly alive, he had seen better days.

Two guards stood in the yard looking at the other side of the fence. These were the goons shooting. Ben holstered his pistol, pulling up his rifle. "Hey, who's that?" Ben asked as a man walked out of the front door.

"That's Bill," Sarah replied, shaking her head. The man was bad news. "How do you want to play this? Dan doesn't look good?"

"Shelly's likely inside. We can take a few shots from here, but they will likely have the upper hand from the house. Shit," Ben chuffed. "Maybe... he trailed off, pulling out his radio.

"What are you doing?"

Ben switched the radio back to the original channel they used with Dustin and Tina. "Hello."

Bill froze in place as the two watched. Pulling out a radio, Bill signaled back to the house out of their view.

"Yes," Bill's gravelly voice replied as the man, in one fluid motion, lit a cigarette.

"I'm sure by now you know, we know, you know."

Bill nodded to no one, agreeing. "Yup. I'm going to need you to surrender yourself and whoever is left of your group."

"Yeah, not going to be able to do that today. I think you may want to check in on your other goons. I have a feeling you're down a few."

Bill's face hardened as he pulled out his .357 magnum and walked up to Dan. Sarah flexed her hands, her nerves flaring.

"If you don't surrender to us in five minutes. I'll put a bullet in your friend Dan. Well, another one. And trust me. It will be the last," Bill replied with no show of emotion.

"If that cigarette doesn't kill you first," Ben snapped back. He was letting the man know he had eyes on him.

Before Ben's synapses could reach from his brain to his feet, Bill whirled around, firing into the side of the very house they occupied. The slap of the heavy bullet cracked like a whip overhead on the eves of the house. This was followed by another round being fired into the house across the street.

Shouts barked orders as Ben leaned forward, keeping his eye on the front yard. The two goons were dragging Dan toward the house as Bill stood in the middle of the yard with his pistol hanging slack in his hand. At the same time, he took several rapid puffs before getting back on the radio. He wanted Ben to focus on him while the others moved.

"Ben," Bill started. "Five minutes." This was followed by him glancing at his watch before turning back to the house.

Sarah pulled out her radio, calling the others on the water. "How far out are you? We have to move."

"We heard," Nicole replied, still having her radio set to the primary channel. "We can see the other boat. It's about to get loud." Nicole's eyes shifted to the rocket launcher John was holding as Dustin finished loading one of the belt-fed machine guns.

Sarah turned to Ben. "We use the distraction and move. I don't know what else we can do," He replied as Max started lowly growling.

"What's up boy?" Ben trailed off as Amanda pointed a small submachine directly at Sarah. She knew the man wouldn't react. Somehow, someway, Amanda had even fooled Max.

The reality of the situation was she had been in the house in a game room, off the living room, and down another hall they hadn't explored. Two more men entered the room on either side of her.

"We have them," Amanda called over the radio.

Bill's rumbling voice replied. "How many?"

"Two and a dog."

"The backyard gate is open and clear," Bill replied. They had fooled Ben and Sarah into walking right into a trap.

The two men, shouldering Amanda, stepped forward as Ben flexed.

"Easy," Amanda hissed out. Her hand was still as calm as the early morning water on the inlet.

Ben eased his stance, seeing the weapon still fixed on his wife. By his count, there were four goons, including Bill and Amanda, to deal with. By this point, he wanted to be in the other house to ensure his count.

Knowing the abilities of the others heading their way, all Ben and Sarah had to do was buy time. Max, by the time the goons reached Ben, was gone. The dog had run out of the room. Not wanting to take her weapon off Sarah, Amanda hadn't even twitched as he flashed by her.

"What about the dog?" One of the goons spoke up.

"What about it? Let the undead take care of it," Amanda

scoffed as zip ties were pulled out while being motioned to put their hands behind their back.

Ben gave a slight nod to Sarah, letting her know he was focused. "Why?" Ben asked as bags were plunged over their heads.

Amanda didn't move as she tapped her covered ear. "We can talk shortly."

CHAPTER 32

Two if by Sea

The droning sounds of the undead filled Ben's ears as they were finally pushed through the door after a short walk through the backyard. With no signs of Max nor any distractions coming from the water, the clock was ticking. The others should have engaged the boat by now.

"Put them over there," Bill's familiar, rumbling voice ordered as Ben and Sarah were shoved to the floor. After a moment of shuffling, the bags were pulled from both of their heads.

In the room, Bill, several goons, and Amanda stood in front of Ben, Sarah, Dan, and Shelly. While Shelly was alert, Dan looked drunk as his head bobbled slightly.

"Now that we have the team all together," Amanda started as Bill glanced down at his radio again as if missing a check-in with someone. "Where is the rest of your group?"

Ben looked up, knowing the hatred the woman held for him. "This is it. You have our other friends."

"Hmphh," Amanda scoffed, motioning for one of the goons to correct Ben's attitude.

With a quick crack from a rifle butt, Ben slumped against the wall behind him. While the blow didn't really faze the man, he wanted to appear as weak as possible. Being an actor, Ben realized it was time to act.

Amanda cleared her throat. "You come to our home, you destroy it, and then think everything's fine? Well, they were fine. We were building the future, and you destroyed it. I'm not here to do the talking. Where are the others?"

The truth was that Ben, in a roundabout manner, was responsible for destroying an entire city. He and the others had taken out two groups of bandits, including Jim. They had blood on their hands. Even though justified, they had left a trail of destruction behind them.

"We travel around. You know Dustin and Tina. We lost two of our other people heading back. I don't know what else to tell you. We didn't do anything to your city. If anything, we barely got out ourselves."

Bill stepped forward. "Times up. Answer her question."

Ben shook his head. He needed to buy what little time he figured they still had left. The others in the room intended to kill them.

"What do you want?" Ben asked as Amanda smiled slightly.

"You and your friends dead. But, before that, what do you know about the FEMA bunker? It's location and where your home base is. If we get that, we may be able to work something out," Amanda stated. She was lying, and everyone from the Sanctuary knew it.

"The bunker? You mean the train?" Ben asked, perking her attention. She didn't speak, giving him more time to explain.

"The supply train to stock the bunker and the camp on Fleming Island is right down the road from here. I don't know where the bunker is."

This confirmed one fact Amanda knew. There was indeed

a supply train in the area they had reports on. In reality, they had sent a scout to investigate, only to have that person be the very body Ben and the others had encountered.

"Is that so?" Amanda said, having a good idea that he was telling the truth. "Bill, how far out are the boats?"

Bill gave her a telling glance. "I'll see."

Ben glanced at Dan as an odd blanket of clarity covered his body. "Hold on," Ben said, even stopping Bill from leaving the room. "We're staying on the other side of the river. We figured out something was off about Dustin and Tina calling us from Jacksonville."

Bill raised an eyebrow. "How did you know that?"

Ben nodded his head toward Dan. "Dan was in the Navy. He has a signal finder. I'm not sure what its name is, but we knew they were in the area."

"See," Amanda said, her ego taking over. "You can be cooperative. Continue."

Ben noticed One of the goons had turned and was scanning through the channels on their radio. "Channel 202.56. Hit the scan lock button and punch in one two, one two."

Even Sarah glanced at him, not sure what he was doing. Noticing his calm demeanor, she refocused on the goon pointing a shotgun directly at her. Ben knew with every fiber of his being that the people standing in that room would find the house their grave.

The goon keyed the radio as Ian's voice chirped to life. "What's going on? John, Nicole? You copy?" The others were also not on the radio, being preoccupied.

That raised eyebrows as Amanda glanced at Bill. This simple gesture told Ben everything he needed to know. Their time was up, and this revelation was the nail in the coffin.

Amanda smirked. "Sounds like you're not being

completely honest with us. How unfortunate. I don't have to explain myself, but I would like to tell you why I'm here." Amanda paused. "To watch everything you love burn."

"It doesn't have to be like this," Ben followed. "We can help each other. Look around. What's left of this world? Just us here and now."

Bill took the time to chime in. "Sounds crowded to me. Do you think you're the only one out running around burning things to the ground? You'd be naïve to think that. Your wife knows what's out there. I bet you all have no clue what's North of here. Naive." He repeated.

Bill pulled out his pistol as Amanda stared in thought before speaking. "Enough. Keep them tied up. Remove any other tool or weapon they have and throw them in the middle of the road. Ben is coming with us."

This is what it had come to. Instead of wasting a bullet, she wanted to throw them to the undead. The woman was clearly fulfilling some type of an eye-for-an-eye ending.

Amanda, as well as the others in the room, had watched several of their friends die at the hands of the zombies. If they were lucky enough, they had made it to the bunkers to live a relatively comfortable life for the next ten years.

Motioning for the radio, Bill also pulled up his pistol, slamming a round into Ben's left shoulder, shredding it to pieces. No acting could prevent the grunt that came from Ben as he gritted his teeth. While the shot was to keep Ben under control, it was also a show of just how inhumane the man was.

Sarah fell over, trying to reach her husband, as the sounds of two boats echoed from the small tributary.

"Good," Amanda said, genuinely smiling for the first time in hours. "Move them once the others get up here."

Two boats, instead of one, pulled up, causing Ben and the other's hearts to sink. Something was wrong. Something was horribly wrong.

Ben pushed himself against the wall, breathing heavily. "I'm okay, babe," he gasped before everything broke out into chaos.

A whooshing whap and streak of fire launched from the rear boat as the first boat erupted in an explosion. Under the pressure of the rocket, any glass left in the back of the house flew inward.

Before the others could react, machine gun fire erupted from the rear boat. While it wasn't meant to hit the house due to the others likely being inside, it was a distraction as Dustin, John, and Nicole ran from the boat. Tina was laying down suppressive fire. There would be no response from the lead boat.

"Dammit!" Bill yelled, being the first to squeeze off several rounds from his pistol before grabbing Ben's rifle. While Bill was distracted, he also quickly realized that none of the bullets were hitting the back of the house. "Fight, damn it!" Bill shouted as the goons opened fire.

CHAPTER 33

Surprise

Smoke bellowed from the burning boat, choking out the scene inside the house. A chorus of bullets rang from the small room as Ben and the others' ears rang like the bells of Notre Dame.

Amanda ducked behind the table Dan was once sitting behind, aiming into the growing smoke. Something thumped the side of the house as a loud bang smacked the backyard. Dustin had thrown a flashbang in the yard.

Under the cover of the constructed confusion, Tina continued to rain down hell on the house, shifting her aim to the backyard, still avoiding the large open windows. The door swung open as Ben glanced up, seeing Bill running out. The sting of his numb shoulder started to set in as the shuffle of Sarah backing up to him came into focus.

Shuffling her hands at lightning-fast speed, Sarah started pulling on the bindings around Ben's wrists. Blood pooled in his hands, making them slippery. "Hurry," Ben whispered just as Amanda noticed the interaction.

"No," She barked, swinging around.

There are moments in space and time when things happen as if the gods above had always ordained them. A light blonde flurry of motion blurred through the door as Max leaped through the air, catching Amanda's hand as several shots slapped into the roof.

"No!!!" Amanda barked again as Max bore down on her forearm, forcing her to drop her gun.

With the snap of something unseen, Ben's wrists came free, allowing the man to grab Sarah's, snapping the zip ties in a matter of seconds. Max continued to wrestle with Amanda as several shots rang out from the backyard, smacking into the goons and causing another layer of violence to an already chaotic scene. Dustin was in the fight and showing just what he was capable of as an operator.

Sarah, seeing Ben was not in fighting condition, pulled the gag off Shelly as Max continued his dance. Letting out a gasp, Shelly quickly shifted to Dan after having her hands freed.

Between the explosion and the gunfire, everyone's ears were ringing beyond the ability to hold a conversation. Two of the goons continued to fight as another spatter of gunfire smacked into them.

With a brief lull in the punishing noise, Shelly lightly tapped Dan's face as his eyes came into focus. Not only had Bill shot the man in the arm, he had beaten the man into a pulp, knowing how to put the man on the edge of life.

Closer, more focused, now silent gunfire came from John's pistol as he lept through the furthest window, seeing the still moving goons. Turning, John focused on Max on top of Amanda as Nicole and Dustin turned the corner coming through the window.

Max, as if knowing the cavalry had arrived, let go of Amanda. Blood covered her forearm as she sneered. John drew down on Amanda at the same time Andrew and Tina made it to the window, now looking in.

"Don't move," John huffed.

"Dan," Shelly repeated several times as the man smiled. Two of his front teeth had found themselves on vacation as he smiled into the face of his lifelong love. He was alive, and more importantly, she was alive.

Sarah was torn between the two men, kneeling over Ben as she pulled the lower half of his shirt sleeve off, wrapping it around his shoulder.

"I'll be fine. Check on Dan, babe," Ben smiled. The pain was still visible in his eyes.

Dustin walked over to Ben. "You okay man?"

"I am now. I was starting to get worried," Ben yelled, his ears still ringing.

Amanda groaned, slowly pulling herself off the ground, finally sitting on her rear end. Max stood within arm's reach as blood covered his photo-perfect blonde hair.

"A dog?" Nicole asked as Ben grimaced while smiling.

"He's a good boy." Max, hearing this, let his tale wag for a few seconds. "All the treats. He gets all the fucking treats."

Shelly was crying as Dan slowly started holding his good arm up. Bill likes to shoot people in the arm, making them unable to protect themselves. "I...I'm sorta gonna be fine." Dan got out as Shelly finally lost it. She started crying, putting her hands over her face to hide her tears.

"Babe...," Dan huffed out. Time stopped as even Amanda watched the interaction.

"Yeah."

"Can I get a smoke?"

Shelly found herself crying while smiling. She shuffled around, finally seeing his pack on an end table. Before another word was spoken, Shelly lit the smoke in her mouth before gently placing it between Dan's lips.

"He's good enough to smoke; he'll be fine," Dustin said, turning to Amanda.

Sarah, remembering Bill leaving the house, stood up. "Bill, he left out the door."

Andrew, a new face to the group, ran to the door and quickly closed it. As the young redheaded man turned, his face told the group everything. Bill had not only left his companions to die. He had opened the front gate to the property.

"Yeah. I wouldn't go out there. It's a creeper party, if you know what I mean," Andrew said as Dustin simply nodded. While the others were focused, Dustin truly understood the shitstorm they were now in.

"It wasn't supposed to happen like this," Amanda gargled as she talked, revealing her true injury. A large chunk of glass was lodged in her neck. Her talking had shown it was, in fact, lodged in her jugular vein. No matter what they did or how they did it. She would die in this house.

Knowing the other goons were no longer a threat, Sarah's instinct kicked in as she walked over to the women kneeling. "Shhh," Sarah whispered, inspecting the wound.

Amanda didn't care to take orders from anyone else speaking up again. "Why would you help me?"

"We aren't monsters. We didn't mean any of this to happen. We are just trying to help our friends," Sarah replied as Tina shuffled lightly, knowing she had caused all of this. Dustin picking up on this, tucked it away for later.

Ben felt the statement in his guts. Once again, he felt like a sinking man in the water as he looked around reflectively before talking.

"We aren't like this. This isn't us. I'd rather be home having a drink," Ben focused on Amanda. "I left you alive after trying to kill me because I care…, we care. But now, after this? I don't know. Just look outside; we are all better than this."

The room was still listening to Ben talk. Life flowed from Amanda as Sarah started to work on keeping her alive.

"No," Amanda gargled. "No. I earned this. Do you know I used to be a teacher? I was good at it." She paused, gathering her dying thoughts. The others let her talk as John lowered his gun. "I was in love before this all happened. I was happy. But, things change, people change."

Sarah turned to Ben, shaking her head. There would be no saving her.

"You did what you thought was right," Ben said. This was clearly a conversation between the two.

Amanda chuckled lightly. "You know, I just...huuuuh...," she gasped for air as more life drained from her. The sounds of the undead growing in front of the house. "I just wanted to......" These were the final words she ever spoke as her eyes glazed over. Sarah leaned forward, slowly lowering her to the ground.

No one spoke as Dan took a final drag from his smoke. Andrew, in only a way he could, spoke first. "She wasn't that nice to me, but she was a person." Looking around, the young man shook his head. "You guys sure know how to make a mess."

Ben finally stood up, wobbling slightly under the stress of his injury. "We can talk in another room." Ben was referring to the bodies on the floor, no longer surviving the end of times.

Max walked up, sniffing Ben's leg, licking his good hand as it hung by his side. Not seeing a viable option away from the front of the house, Andrew, Dustin, and John helped move Dan to the house next door through the backyard.

"What about Bill?" Ben asked the group as Shelly and Sarah continued to clean Dan up as best they could.

"The truck," John remembered. "They had a truck heading this way. I'd say they should be here soon, if not already."

"He had an exit plan," Nicole said as Andrew shook his head.

"That turd," Andrew huffed. "Maybe, but I bet he has something else up his sleeve. He couldn't have made it that far. Hell. I bet he's across the street."

Making a good point, Ben winced, forming a thought as Nicole started putting Ben's arm in a sling. "He's right. There's no way West down Highway 220. It's packed with zombies. He's close by. I might not have been paying attention, but I haven't heard any gunfire. Bill's waiting on his ride."

John ran back into the house after picking up everyone's weapons and what he could salvage from the boat. Ben and Sarah's gear had been left in the home they now occupied, minus his rifle that Bill had dropped before leaving the house. "The boats dead in the water. It looks like one of those goons smoked the engine," John relayed before turning to grab the rocket launcher.

"We have to make it back to Black Creek. Has anyone called Andy and Carla?" Sarah asked, looking up from Dan, who no longer resembled a zombie.

"Not yet," Ben replied, picking up his radio. In all the confusion, they had been through at least three channel sets as Ben changed to the main channel they had been on with the others.

"Andy, Carla, you there?" Ben called over the radio, wincing as he shifted in his new sling.

"We hear you. What the hell is going on over there?" Andy answered as Carla could be heard in the background.

"Long story, but it's over. Well, mostly over. What are you guys up to?" Ben followed.

"Well, when the explosion hit, we....," Carla could be heard yelling in the background. "We're coming."

Ben glanced around the room. Dan was actually smiling as Shelly rubbed his back. "Uh, it's a nightmare outside."

"Yeah. We know. There was a school bus on the other side of the train next to the ballfields. We got it started, but...," Andy paused. "Will a bus make it through that many zombies?"

Angry, hungry hands slapped the outside of the bus as Carla adjusted the metal pan she had fashioned as a helmet. In all fairness, it fit perfectly. Topping it off was her leather jacket and gloves.

Andy was wearing fatigues and a thick blue jean jacket and pants. He had been lucky enough to find an old camouflaged bulletproof vest in the house Max once called home. Besides the butt-drenching sweat their outfits provided, they were, in fact, more prepared than they knew.

John took in a heaving breath, looking out the front window. "It will make it. We used to use them on the outskirts of Tallahassee. Just tell them not to stop. That means we have to be ready to go."

"So we're just leaving Bill out here?" Nicole asked as John turned to her.

"If we keep going East. We'll run into the truck," John said.

"They'll want to go back home," Sarah spoke up.

"So we get them home," Ben started. "They're good people."

On those words, Ben keyed the radio. "Yeah. One of our people has done it before. Just don't let off the gas. Once you get to the bridge, we'll be ready to go. Just be ready for a little time away from home."

Max whimpered, looking out the window. Even the ever-fearless and surprising K9 knew the situation was getting worse by the minute.

"Heading your way bitches!" Carla shouted over the radio

in a battle call worthy of any army, taking the device from her husband to let him drive.

Dustin chuckled. "Bitches?"

"She's hard-charging," Ben replied. "When we met her, they were having taco night and gave two shits about us. Those two are survivors."

CHAPTER 34

Charge of the yellow bus brigade

T he loud roar of the once-living diesel engine screamed back to life as Andy mashed the accelerator to the floor, lurching the yellow noble steed into motion. Surprised by the power, Carla grabbed the driver's seat, doing her best to stay standing.

Undead speed bumps popped like watermelons under the massive tires as Andy's face became a concentrated brick. He was focused on one thing and one thing only: making it to the bridge.

"Slow down!" Carla barked as Andy didn't let off the accelerator.

"We slow down, we die," Andy said as dozens of the undead rolled off the front of the bus. At this rate, they would be at the bridge in minutes.

Carla leaned back, looking at Andy in a way she hadn't before. The man was changing before her eyes. It wasn't that the world around them was transforming. It had already died in a sense, but like Ben, it was their time to face the truth.

Back steady on her feet, Carla again let out a bark. "Car!"

Andy, not seeing the vehicle, swerved the bus seconds before slamming into the car, covered in the undead. The smack of flesh on the thin yet sturdy metal sides of the bus reminded

Andy just how dangerous the road indeed was. He floored the bus only to find the wheels spinning in the fresh mud separating the road.

To their right, the gas station sat like a beacon of salvation as he pressed the accelerator to the floor. Mud spun from under the wheels, spraying not only the growing crowd but also the sides of the bus.

"Go," Carla said, stepping up beside her husband.

"I'm trying. This things like a tank," Andy replied, letting off the gas only to press it back down, slinging more mud.

More of the undead reached the back of the bus as the sounds of crunching bone echoed from the rear end of the yellow freight train of death.

Carla paused, scanning the area in front of the bus. "If too many pile up in front of us, we won't make it." Andy nodded as Carla placed her hand on his shoulder. "You got this."

Andy solidified his resolve. This time, he slammed the bus in reverse, putting it in a gear that it had long since forgotten. With a violent lurch, the bus slammed into the pack of zombies behind it.

After another round of teeth-rattling and cracking, Andy slammed the bus back in gear, again pushing it to its limits. Unlike last time, the bus found traction with crumbling bones under its wheels.

With a jolt of power, the bus lurched forward in an explosion of raw power. With a quick swerve of the wheel, Andy righted the yellow demon as it screamed back onto the road, turning the chaotic scene into a blurring afterthought.

Andy cracked his neck while Carla's hand again rested on his shoulder. "We got this," Andy said as Carla squeezed harder.

"We have to," Carla replied, smiling. "Who else is going to make you tacos?"

With the moment over, Andy quickly noticed a light break in the not-so-living speedbumps. "And margaritas. I'm going to need a margarita after this. All the margaritas."

"All the margaritas it is," Carla promised.

Sarah's voice crackled over the radio, asking for an update. "Where are you guys?"

"Getting there," Carla replied. "You should hear us any second."

Dustin quickly cracked a window and was met with the drone of shuffling zombies doing their darndest to locate their next meal. As promised, the rumbling sound of the bus pierced the veil of uncertainty, catching everyone's attention.

"We have to move," Dustin ordered, pulling out a smoke grenade. "Sarah, tell them to pull next to the green smoke. Dan, you good to move?"

Dan shrugged. "Babe, light me another smoke. It's time to get out of here."

Shelly quickly sparked another cigarette, placing it in his mouth. "Andrew, help me get him up," John said as Dan chuckled while John put his arms around him.

"You going to buy a guy dinner first?" Dan joked, spitting out the cigarette directly at the curtains. He knew what he was doing as a light flicker of flames took hold of the old dusty fabric. "Yup, I didn't like this house anyway." He concluded as Dustin nodded.

Max let out a light chuff, seeing the fire take hold.

"We might need the distraction to cover our movement," John concluded as everyone stood by the door.

Dustin chucked the smoke grenade out the door just as the yellow bus, caked in mud, turned the final corner. "We see you!" Carla yelled over the radio, her voice as loud as ever.

"Move," Dustin grunted, taking the lead, only to be

followed by Ben, now holding his pistol in his good hand. Max followed closely behind, making it to the door first.

John and Andrew moved with Dan while Shelly, Nicole, Tina, and Sarah covered the now curious zombies turning their way while carrying various additional weapons. The brakes squealed as Andy finally let off the gas, bringing the bus to a stop in the road.

After popping several zombies, Ben slammed against the bus, pointing his pistol toward the bridge. Dustin began eliminating the undead, now walking toward the bus. Ben glanced back, motioning for them to hurry up as the door swung open.

"Move, they're coming," Ben huffed, surprisingly out of energy. The loss of blood slowing him down.

After a round of pulling and pushing, Dan flopped down on the front seat. Andrew pulled one of the rifles off his back and handed it to the man.

John glanced at Andy and Carla, "Thanks for the ride."

"Any time," Andy replied as Ben ran onboard, followed by Dustin.

"Let me drive," Dustin quickly requested.

"I got this," Andy replied, seeing that the man had clearly been a soldier in his past life.

Dustin paused before Carla spoke up. "He used to race cars when he was younger. My man got this."

Taken back by the confident sass he was now receiving, Dustin grinned. "I see why you like these guys."

Ben turned to Andy. "The right side of the bridge is mostly clear. There's two cars on the eastbound lane. Just push through them."

"What about Bill?" Tina asked, wanting nothing more than to put an end to the man's ability to breathe.

"He's on the other side of the bridge by now, waiting for his ride," John spoke up. "He's running."

Not waiting for permission, Andy punched the yellow demon back into motion just as angry hands started slapping the rear of the bus. Everyone grabbed whatever was close as Ben instinctively used his injured arm to grab the step-up pole, wincing in pain.

"Hold on!" Andy yelled once again, focusing on nothing but the road in front of him.

Green bushes blurred as the bus swerved onto the road, pushing its way to the opposite lane. Andy again lay on the gas. "Grab something!" Andy followed as he slammed head-on into two cars sitting on their sides to block the zombies from crossing.

One car flipped up, launching into the tributary, while the other crunched the front end of the bus, warping the hood before allowing the bus to pass. In front of them, a clear section of road lay like an open invitation.

"There!" Carla again yelled louder than needed.

The red truck John and Nicole had watched Bill stop on the Doctor's inlet bridge was just coming into view as a man ran out from a small drive-through liquor store. Dustin, without hesitation, butted the safety glass on the opposite side of the windshield, immediately opening fire with Ben's rifle. "Go," Dustin ordered as if on a mission to save the world. Andy obliged, accelerating more smoothly this time.

Empty shell casings tinkled while chunks of the road erupted around Bill. In all the excitement, he had failed to hear the bus, only moving after hearing the crashing rush of something coming on the bridge. They had taken him by surprise.

"Everyone get down!" Dustin yelled as whoever was in the bed of the oncoming truck opened fire with a machine gun.

Glass crackled and exploded into the bus cab, forcing Andy to look out the window of the door, keeping the vehicle lined up with the road. "Keep going?" Andy asked, not taking his eyes off the road.

"Yup," Dustin replied, turning to Tina. "Rocket."

Tina quickly moved, snapping open the case to the rocket and pulling it out as she worked the weapon, loading a round. An RPG in the right hands was a show-stopper.

Carla was amazed at the organized chaos their new friends were capable of. "You go, girl," she huffed, to be greeted with a smile from Tina—something she rarely did.

Without looking back, Tina carefully positioned the RPG on Dustin's shoulder. A brief lull in the gunfire was a tall tell sign that whatever they were shooting was being reloaded.

Andy, seeing Dustin move, sat up and saw the truck much closer than before. Bill was about to jump in the truck bed as Dustin let the rocket rip. Smoke filled the cab as Andy brought the bus to a stop.

A bright bloom of yellow and red fire burst into life as the rocket slammed directly into the grill of the truck, blowing it to literal hell. Chunks of truck debris bounced off the yellow demon's hood. Dustin had nailed his target.

The first person to speak was Carla. "That was the craziest shit I've ever seen."

Dustin dropped the now empty rocket, picked up Ben's rifle, and moved to the door, which Andy quickly opened. The man was not going to let Bill escape.

Ben followed behind, shifting his pistol to his good hand. Sarah stood up. "I'm going with them."

"No, hold back at the bus. Let them go. There may be a few goons running around," John was right, not wanting to spread the group too thin. "Plus, it looks like Max is joining them as the dog jumped off the bus, not happy with the ride.

Nodding, Sarah motioned for Nicole and Tina to join her. "Tina and I will step out and secure the area around the front of the bus. Nicole, Shelly, you guys good keeping an eye out the back?"

Shelly and Nicole nodded as Carla picked up her rifle. "I'll go too."

Andy looked back at John and Dan while he lit a smoke. "Let the girls handle this one. They got it."

Smiling, Andy winked at Carla as she got off the bus with their newfound friends. John leveled his rifle beside Andy, looking through the now-gone windshield and over the burning mess as the two men finally reached the truck.

Flames bellowed from whoever was once sitting in the front seat driving the truck. There would be no doubt that Dustin had hit his target. The tail end of the vehicle lay several feet behind the truck, which had been blown off by the gas tank exploding.

Dustin motioned Ben to go around the left side while he split off to the right. Max stayed in front of the truck, not wanting to get close to the flames bellowing from under the wrecked hood. Before they could fully reach the rear of what was left of the vehicle, a moan came from Dustin's side of the road. Quickly turning, it was apparent Bill was in mid-leap into the truck bed when the rocket hit.

"Ben," Dustin called as he quickly ran over, seeing that the remaining threat was likely trying to negotiate with Saint Peter about his future home.

"Christ," Ben shouted under his breath, seeing the condition Bill was in.

The man's hands had both been heavily burnt and were mangled in clenched fists. His right leg was in an unnatural position. Blood ran from his ears and nose as he gritted his teeth, finally focused, seeing Dustin.

"Bill, can you hear me?" Dustin asked, not lowering his rifle.

Bill sneered out of both defiance and pain. "You....." His voice rumbled.

"Yeah. Me. I figured you would run away from this," Dustin said, taking a jab at the man's ego, knowing it would hurt more than bullets at this point.

"You are supposed to be...," Bill stopped to wheeze. "Dead."

"Nope."

Bill's eyes shifted to Ben as Max stayed back with the hair on the back of his neck standing up. "And you. You caused all this mess."

"No, I didn't. You did. I was just trying to get out of the city when I ran into Amanda. You think I wanted any of this to happen?" Ben spoke up, justifying himself for a reason he didn't truly understand.

"Yeah. You keep telling yourself that," Bill got out before coughing again. "None of you will make it. Only the strong survive."

Dustin leaned down, turning dark in a way Ben had not yet seen. "These people aren't animals. I, on the other hand, am."

Ben pulled his pistol up as Dustin stood back up, putting his hand on the silenced barrel. "No. You've done enough. Just as Ben was about to talk, he snapped his jaw shut.

Unknown to the two men, Tina had split from Sarah and Carla, walking up to them and realizing the current situation.

"Guys," Tina said, looking down and seeing Bill. 'Oh. He's still alive." She followed flatly.

Dustin looked into Ben's very soul. "We got this. Check on

everyone else. We need to move out." He motioned around as several zombies were quickly approaching.

Tina and Dustin now both stood over the man who had once pointed a shotgun directly in both of their faces and subsequently gave the order to kill them.

"Bill seems to think we burnt the city down," Dustin said as Bill let out another round of coughs.

"We did. No. I did," Tina finally confessed as even Dustin turned to her surprise.

"What?" Dustin asked as she stared at the dying man. Just like Amanda, he was also not going to make it off the ground he now lay on.

Leaning down, Tina picked up Bill's pistol, which was sitting on the ground beside her. "I came to your city after not being welcomed, and at night, when your guards were all high-fiving each other while eating real food, I firebombed one of your side gates after spending two days collecting a herd of meat bags. I soaked them in gas. Hundreds of them. Then I let them in your city."

This even took Dustin aback as she continued. "I thought everything I loved was either dead or dying. And I was right. You know it, and I know it. You turned so many good people away to their inevitable death. People who are here now are surviving and helping others. I want my face to be the last thing you see." A tear streaked Tina's face. She wasn't ashamed of what she had done, but that she had saved her friends.

She also knew the pain she had also caused to good people, but in the end, she would live with that.

"You don't deserve this world," Bill spit out.

"No one does anymore," Dustin said in finality. "We're not going to kill you. We'll let the world decide."

Tina and Dustin turned away from Bill, walking back

toward the bus just as several zombies started walking through the smoke. This was an old dead zone, as it was called. No crazies or fresh-turned zombies were rushing the scene.

"What's up?" Ben asked as they finally reached the bus, holding hands. He was lightly petting Max.

Dustin glanced at Tina before speaking up. "Let fate figure it out. There's been enough death today. Hell, there's been enough, period. He's not going anywhere."

"Where are we going?" Carla asked, also seeing the zombies slowly moving toward them.

"There's a neighborhood about a mile up with several gated houses on the water. We can't go back the way we came. We left someone there. Chances are they need some help. It will be easy to secure for the night. We stay there and then move out in the morning. If the sun is out, it should be safe to travel. Maybe get Ian to pick us up in a boat," Dustin said. No one argued the point as they loaded the bus.

CHAPTER 35

Reflections

J ake appreciated the help as the early morning turned into a sunrise worthy of a Bob Ross canvas. After a couple of hours of attending to wounds, only Dustin stayed awake as the snores of exhaustion echoed through the house, with the group all huddled in the living room of the house on the inlet.

Dustin was used to late nights and trained to stay awake for days at a time if needed. He was right in resting while they could. Ben was the first to join Dustin on the back deck, overlooking the water.

"You okay?" Ben asked as Dustin chuckled.

"You're the one that was shot, and you're asking me?" Dustin replied.

"What's on your mind?" Ben asked, seeing the enjoyment in the man's eyes watching the sun take its rightful place in the sky.

Reflecting on what he had learned about Tina and the lengths she had gone to save, not only him but the others had put things into perspective. These were more than friends. They were family.

"I think things are going to be okay for a while."

"A while?" Ben asked.

"I'm just thinking about everything, and everywhere I've been since this all started. We got lucky yesterday. But at what cost? I see it in your eyes. You aren't a killer. You've been forced to be. I respect that in a man. You didn't have to do what you did for us."

"Why wouldn't I? You would do the same for us if it came down to it."

Dustin licked his lips, knowing Tina, in fact, had. That secret would go to their graves. "Yeah. I guess you're right. I was thinking, instead of being out running around, we are going to stay."

"Here?"

"No," Dustin smiled. "At the Sanctuary. There will be a time when we will have to go back out in this mess. No, we need to focus on the long haul, and that includes you and the others."

Ben smiled, this time with a hint of relief. "That reminds me. We need to get Carla and Andy back home. I think we should take them to the Sanctuary first. I didn't think of mentioning it last night in the afterglow, but I think we may have found a way to keep the zombies away."

This caught Dustin's attention as Ben finally turned Eve back on. "Good morning. You have thirty-two blood pressure alerts..." Eve paused. Are you injured?"

"Morning Eve. Sorry to turn you off so long. Yeah, I got shot but am fine now."

"Well, how about some music?" Eve asked. "I also recommend turning on the other's devices."

"Yeah, some music would be great."

Sitting by the dock of the Bay by Otis, reading started lowly humming out of the small speaker on Ben's watch as Andrew and Jake walked onto the back porch. After an hour of debating and talking with Andrew, the group agreed to let the man stay with them overnight. While still bound, Andrew finally untied him once he was awake.

"Morning, dudes," Andrew said, pointing at Jake. "My boy here has something he'd like to say."

Ben and Dustin nodded. "Hey. Sorry about all that. I wasn't one of their ground soldiers. I'm not asking to go with you guys, but I want to head to Orlando. My family is there." Jake paused, knowing the likely truth. He was young, like both Andrew and Ian.

"Andrew, are you going with him?" Dustin asked, knowing the young red-headed man better.

"No. I was thinking about taking you up on your offer."

Ben cocked his head. "Offer?"

Dustin cleared his throat, no longer focusing on the early morning water. "Andrew is coming with us. He saved us and brought us to you. I trust him fully."

To Dustin, he had made a promise he would not go back on. "Jake, as for you." He continued. We can find a vehicle in the neighborhood and get it running. There are several on Fleming Island. Even a few armored trucks. I'll get you loaded with ammo, food, and a radio. I trust Andrew. I'm not saying you aren't cut from the same cloth, but the offer was made to Andrew for saving us."

"I wasn't asking. I want to go home. I don't care if it is destroyed or a mess, but I want to go home," Jake said in a low voice. Tears welled up in his eyes. "I just want to see. I need to see. You know, I don't even have a picture of my family or fiancé? My phone was smashed, and I was in Tallahassee at a baseball tournament when they shut down the roads."

Ben spoke up this time. "I'm not saying you won't be welcome one day, but I stand by Dustin. We will help you get on the road. There are plenty of supplies close by."

"You found the train I take it," Dustin said as several of the others started walking around the kitchen, stretching.

"Yeah, we did. What about the bunker?" Ben interjected.

"Yeah," Dustin echoed. "I know where that is also. We can talk later about it. Ian said to call him when we all got moving. I'm thinking we can get what Jake needs from the FEMA camp on Fleming Island."

Jake smiled. "Thanks. You know something. You guys aren't anything like the others said. They blamed you all on the fire and everything."

Ben patted the man on the back. "Don't believe everything you hear. Not all the people in Tallahassee were bad. Just a few. Sorry about any of your other friends."

Jake's shoulders dropped. "They would have killed you. I'm a grown man these days." He turned to Andrew. "This guy is solid. The nicest out of the group. That's why they kept him back. Sounds like I will be able to keep in touch."

"As long as the radio reaches. We'll set up a channel to use," Ben added as Sarah snuck up, wrapping her arms around Ben.

"Morning, rockstar. I see Eve wanted to play you some tunes this morning," Sarah said as Ben leaned back into her.

"I think she didn't know what to do when I told her I was shot, which reminds me. I could use a drink." Ben wanted nothing more than to be by the pool sipping a cold beverage.

"We can make that happen. There's still a good amount to do." Sarah was making a good point. The day ahead would be just as long, yet less violent than yesterday.

Andy and Carla joined the group. "What's up?" Andy asked.

"Just working out how to get you guys back home," Ben breathed out. "We got to get Jake set up to hit the road, and then we want to take you two with us for a few days if that works."

Carla grinned, shrugging. "I hear you guys have a pool?"

"Yup," Sarah drawled out.

"I could use a vacation. Andy?" Carl turned to her husband.

"Beats waiting in line at Disney World. Sure," he smiled as Max slowly made his way out the back door.

Yawning, Max stretched as if he had sat still for weeks. Sore muscles and also feeling the stress of the day, the dog plopped down on his hind legs, seeing the calming water before letting his tongue slip out of his mouth.

"Well. We can't forget this good boy," Ben beamed as Max's tail lightly wagged. "He's one hell of a dog."

"You have a dog?" Eve chirped to life. "Are you replacing me?"

The odd question caught Ben off guard. "No one can replace you, Eve. How about checking in with Ian."

"Of course," Eve replied, sounding more confident. The odd, now unlocked AI system gave Eve her personality.

"We might need to get him some water. It looks like he went through it, also. We put some provisions on the boat we came in before taking theirs." Dustin pointed several docks down.

With the conversation over and plans quickly forming, the icing on the cake was seeing Dan walking out on his own two feet and joining the party.

CHAPTER 36

Where we go one, we go all

Afternoon heat from days of rain, now partnering with blue skies and beaming sun, created humidity worthy of the densest jungles of South America. With all the noise and still burning fires, the undead had decided to inspect the commotion, leaving most of Fleming Island proper void of zombies.

Before leaving, they had identified the location as a new safe house. After exploring the sprawling residence, it was clear the owner had kept a tidy home. Several jugs of water and a pantry full of canned food gave the team further confirmation that every house very well may contain treasure and safety.

Between the high-end construction and sturdy fence, they would be back. The water had clearly reached the back of the house but had never flooded. It was odd to Ben and the others how Mother Nature picked and chose which structures to take back.

Knowing it was time to get moving, Ben recalled the stash of military vehicles on Fleming Island, which were likely still in workable condition. This would be their next stop.

The two MRAPs they found were identical to Adam and Alison's but needed new batteries. Much to their surprise, they were able to get one of the smaller yet just as sturdy trucks up and running.

After loading the vehicle with food, water, and weapons from the FEMA camp, Jake was still determined to go south. After reviewing his route again, the young man finally departed.

Ben watched as the vehicle turned south on Highway 17. "Everyone good to go?"

Dustin looked over the rest of the now-empty camp. The ever-ominous Home Depot, still standing, was likely full of the undead, stuck behind a mass of fallen shelves and their own kind.

"Grab some more ammo. We can come back," Dustin saw Ben's face. "Maybe when we bring Andy and Carla back home."

"Yeah," Ben huffed. "What about any radio equipment? That thing with the radio tower is something we need to look into."

Dan, now back on his feet, pointed at a trailer attached to one of the trucks. "That's a portable version of a radio tower. Does internet and radio. Dam thing complicated, but it is fry your brain powerful."

"Fair enough," Ben followed. "Let's pull it to the river. We can get it later without much hassle."

Dan nodded, pointing to the hitch. "Shelly and I will figure out a way to get it attached to the bus."

While the yellow demon was still working, several bullets had lodged into the engine block. It was a testament to how well-made school buses actually were. Sam's voice crackled over the radio.

"Ian just left. Everything's good here. It should be about forty minutes or so," Sam said. Her voice was warm and excited, knowing everyone was coming back. The truth of it, however, was she was more interested in meeting Max, who was now eating a can Ben had opened of beef stew.

Within thirty minutes, the trailer had been attached to the bus, and the group had loaded most of the yellow demons with ammo and other weapons. With the blazing sun beating down, the zombies close to the river had retreated to the shadows.

Remnants of their prior adventures lay as a reminder of just how lucky they had been while retrieving the solar equipment from the old AT&T building. Now, in eyeshot of the blue house they had grown all too familiar with, sitting on the shore of the mighty Saint Johns River, Ian ran up the boat ramp that sat neatly beside the house, providing direct access from the small road.

Smiles spread across everyone's faces as they brought the yellow demon to a stop. Seeing the muck-covered, bullet-riddled bus, Ian finally grasped just how rough the previous day had been.

"I got the pontoon." Was the first thing Ian said as Dustin jumped off the bus first, followed by Tina.

Smiling, with a heavy burden finally shared, Tina reached out and hugged Ian. Not used to the woman's show of emotion, he stood still as Dustin patted him on the back. "Good job, kid," Dustin complimented as the others piled off the bus.

"It's good to see you guys," Ian said as Andy and Carla walked up to the young man. "Ah. You must be Andy and Carla."

"And you must be Ian," Andy smiled, shaking his hand.

Andrew stepped forward next. "Sup man."

"Sup," Ian replied, surprised by the young man with red hair.

"I heard what you did for Dustin and Tina. Thanks."

Andrew grinned. "No problem. I hear I might get a hot shower today?"

"For sure. We cranked up the power to the water heaters and laid out some steaks."

"Steaks?" Ian asked.

"Yeah, for special occasions. I didn't think Ben would mind," Ian turned, getting his approval.

"Hell. I must have either hit the lottery or am dead," Andrew joked. Ian immediately liked Andrew, motioning him to check out their pontoon boat.

Before he could turn around, Max trotted off the bus, running up to Ian and requesting a pat on the head after a quick sniff. "Holy shit. You weren't kidding! Sam is going to freak out."

"He's a good boy," Ben beamed with pride.

The following hour was spent telling stories and loading the now-packed pontoon, which had been modified to carry golf carts and gear. With the ripple of water behind them, the group unknowingly turned to look at the now shrinking shoreline. They had made it.

It didn't take long for Andy and Carla to be amazed by the sanctuary's safety and lifestyle. After being set up in Ben's house in a spare bedroom, they took showers and put on clean clothes, knowing how lucky they had, in fact, been.

Sarah washed Ben as he came to grips with his new scars and the reality that his left arm would be unusable for months. The two held each other in the shower while hot water poured over their bodies. It wasn't an intimate embrace but rather one of calming frayed nerves.

With one final kiss, Ben and Sarah walked into a kitchen full of noise and friends. Eve had chosen some Bob Marley to play in the background, setting a chill vibe.

"Looks like the party started without us," Ben gushed. John handed him a drink.

Andrew and Ian were standing in front of the main screen

in the kitchen as he showed off Eve and everything she was capable of. Sam stood beside Ian with her arm around his waist.

Dan sat in a high chair by the kitchen island while Nicole cleaned two heads of lettuce in the sink. Shelly sat by Dan, pouring another round of drinks as Carla and Andy leaned over the island, already having cocktails in their hands.

"Andy, Carla, you guys good?" Sarah asked as Carla stood straight.

"You know how long it's been since we been to a party? Hell, since we have spent time around people? You just need to make sure I don't have too many of these, or I'll be in that pool later."

Everyone laughed as Ben cut in. "That can be arranged," Ben paused, feeling as if he was missing something. "Hey, have we heard from Adam and Alison?"

Knowing voices stopped talking as Ian shook his head, turning around. "No. They never checked in now that you mention it. I figured they made it back and were doing something."

"They don't miss check-in. Plus, they had to be listening to the radio at some point," Dan interjected as the mood shifted.

Standing up, Dan spent the next five minutes calling over the radio on every channel they had assigned, including a few older ones, to no avail. Finally, seeing things were likely not good, Dustin cut in, knowing the team needed a rest of the prior day's violence.

"We can worry about that tomorrow. I'm sure they're fine. I can take the truck out tomorrow and see," Dustin offered as even Tina sighed.

"Fair enough," Ben replied as conversations and the sipping of drinks continued. "Where are the steaks? I got the grill." He added.

"They're in the fridge, ready to go," Sam said as Ben grabbed the packet of rehydrated steaks and headed toward the outdoor kitchen.

Ben stood outside looking into the kitchen through the window, smiling. It had been too much for the man to handle, and he found himself lightly tearing up. In many ways, he didn't like having to hurt others, but he knew he had saved his friends. Flashes of the prior day zipped through his mind as a wet tongue slurped his lowered hand.

Max's cold nose nudged Ben, requesting a pat on the head. "I almost forgot about you boy," Ben joked as Max cocked his head.

Looking at the grill, Ben sliced off a small piece of steak, chucking to the well-deserving dog. "You going to stick around?" Ben asked as if he was talking to a person. For some reason, he felt like Max understood him.

After munching down the steak, Max's tail went into overdrive before he jumped on the outdoor couch, keeping guard over Ben and the grill. Max rested his head on his front paws.

"Well, you have a home here boy," Ben said before turning back to the grill.

Now happy with the grill's state, he turned again to find Max fast asleep. Taking another look through the window, Ben felt the weight of everything he had done over the past year. The sinking feeling again took hold of him just as Sarah walked out with a tray to carry the steaks back inside.

"I know that look," Sarah said, setting the tray down, once again putting her arms around Ben. "We did what we had to do."

"I know. I just..., I don't have to like it."

Sarah squeezed him one more time before letting him go. "You see those people in there? They're all here and smiling because of you. I'm here because of you, and everyone knows it. You know I figured something out about you."

"What's that? I can cook a mean rehydrated steak?"

"You weren't born to be an actor," Sarah said, as Ben looked confused. You were born to be a leader—a good leader."

Ben took her words without a response. It was the kind of thing a person tells you that you can't reply to. Sarah cleared her throat, holding up the tray.

"Yeah," Ben smiled. Even after a year, he hadn't fully digested everything.

As the kitchen door opened and the smell of steaks hit everyone, while cheers erupted. Dinner was served.

EPILOGUE

Dustin stared at the back of the MRAP, sitting on the stretch of road between the Sanctuary and the Lot. With another surprising change in weather, a cool breeze had marched in as if taking over.

Grey skies muted the tree-covered road. This was one of the few stretches of road that rarely saw any issues when traveling to and from the Sanctuary.

Andrew scanned the trees not seeing any abnormal movement. "Why'd they stop here?" Andrew asked, frowning as Dustin shook his head.

"Look at the road. I'm guessing they hit that big ass pothole back there. They must have taken off on foot," Dustin suggested as he tried opening the driver's door to no avail.

Leaning forward, Dustin wiped dust and grime off the window, revealing the minigun sitting in the passenger seat. "That's not good. They left the minigun."

"They had a minigun?" Andrew asked as Dustin crouched, scanning the side of the road for tracks.

"Yeah. That thing is a beast. Remember that story Ian was telling about Costco at dinner last night?"

"The one where they found you, yeah. It sounded too crazy to be true," Andrew replied as Dustin honed in on a set of tracks leading to a gravel drive.

"All true. Every last bit of it, down to Ben and Tina being drunk off Crown Royal tearing the place up."

Andrew chuckled lightly. "You mean before they tried to kill you."

"Yup. Look," Dustin pointed at the tracks as the rustle of wind through the trees started putting both men on edge.

Four boot prints were visible in the sand, though nearly washed away by the recent rain. "You think they went up that road?" Andrew asked as Dustin turned.

"Radio in and let the others know where we are and what's going on. We're going to check it out either way. Something's not right."

"You feel that too?" Andrew started. "It's like someone's watching us."

"Or something. We need to get moving. There's houses up these drives. If they went to one, they may be injured. Or...," Dustin stopped himself from saying anything else as Andrew keyed the radio.

———

BOOKS BY THIS AUTHOR

Sheltered

Part 1 of The Sinking Man Series

Awakened

Part 2 of The Sinking Man Series

Released

Part 3 of The Sinking Man Series

Fractured

Part 4 of The Sinking Man Series

Swarmed

Part 5 of The Sinking Man Series

Max Abaddon And The Will

Book 1 of 8 of The Max Abaddon Series. Urban Fantasy

Asher's Fall

Book 1 of 3 of the Descending Worlds Series. SCI-FI